The Other Wife

By

Wanda Arrington Akorede

The Other Wife

Wanda Arrington Akorede

The Other Wife

Published by

For Information, please contact

This novel is a work of fiction. Any resemblance to real people living or dead, actual events, establishments, organizations, cities or countries is given to make the work appear authentic. All other persons, events, places, are from the author's imagination and used fictitiously.

DEDICATION

I thank God for allowing me to complete this book and have it published for others to read. To my late father, John Dandridge Arrington Sr., and my late brother John Dandridge Arrington Jr., you did not get to read the truth, but you heard about it from me. To my mother Dorothy Arrington Ceralde, mother you are my inspiration you gave me all the prayers and support to get me to this level. To my husband Shehu who believed in my ability to tell stories and supported me through publication. To my friend Kim Alvarado I thank you for giving me the courage to put my story on paper. Kim if not for you I would never have tried. To Clyde El-Amin, your first edit gave me insight into how much work I had to do. To Gwendolyn Sides-St. Julian, thank you for assisting me with finding the information needed to get published. To my children Derrick, Surajudeen, and Aisha, this is only the beginning. To Kafilat, Mutiat and Muyinat, there are always two sides to any story. To the grandchildren, Ryu, Be'lanna, Hassan & Hussein, Salaam, and Aminat, I love you all. To my dear friend Renee Gray you saw the value the words that I wrote and believed in me. My dear friend Chrisita Alagbala I will always remember your smile and your friendship. This book is also dedicated to all women who have been in love with a man who is married to someone else. To them I say persevere, for in the end God will be the one who makes the final decision.

Foreword

The Other Wife is a fictional story about one aspect of Nigerian culture. It invites the reader into the institution of multiple marriage (polygamy) told from an American woman's perspective. Most of the story takes place in Nigeria the largest populated nation in Africa. I am married to a Nigerian and had the opportunity to live and work there for ten years. This experience and the fact that several family members were polygamists gave me a deep personal understanding of this part of the culture. Through my marriage, I was able to see firsthand how polygamy affects women. Though all the characters are fictional, they represent many people who may have had a negative experience with a relationship. What makes this story unique is the main female character is American. I have completed the sequel to The Other Wife called Difficult Choices. It continues with the relationship between Janice, Femi, and Lola and how they finally resolve their conflicts. I hope you enjoy reading this novel as much as I had writing it.

Acknowledgements

I would like to salute Nigerian women who are able to survive whatever adversity comes their way and still have a smile on their face: from the sometimes harsh conditions of their country, to the uncertainty of their places in their husband's household. We women can learn a lot from them. Their strength is to be admired. My late Mother-in-law, Alhaja Aduke Agboola Akorede who was the fifth wife of my late Father –in-law Alhaji Rufai Ahmed Akorede who had twenty-one wives and twenty-eight children. She was an independent businesswoman who left a legacy behind for her children to follow. In her I saw the beauty and irony of the Nigerian marriage.

Lagos and Kaduna my adopted homes in Nigeria, I am blessed that I had the opportunity to live there and come full circle. Thank you Nigeria for your rich and vibrant culture, your music, your fashion, and most of all your food, I will forever be a part of you.

Chapter 1

This morning started off like any other weekday for me. I got up, showered, dressed, and headed to my job at the University of Chicago. It's a good job that provides me with a paycheck every two weeks. It was also better than the job prospects that I had at home in New Orleans, and this job allowed me to move away from home and live in Chicago, where I shared an apartment in Hyde Park with my cousin Melinda. Melinda and I were close, almost like sisters. Our mothers made sure that we saw each other every summer when school closed. I grew to look forward to the trips up north. She was a year older than I was, and my mom trusted her to look after me. Sometimes she took that option too seriously.

Like I said, it was a predictable day until Aduke Bakare came floating into my office and plopped herself down on my desk. Little did I know that her visit would change the very direction of my life.

"Hey, girl, what are you doing tonight?" Aduke asked, her lilting accent making her sound as if she were singing rather than talking.

"I was just going home to wash my hair."

"Oh, Janice, that's so boring," she replied, wrinkling up her nose distastefully at the prospect.

"We're having a party in the International Hall for the African students at the university. I was asked to bring an American guest to the affair. I would like you to come with me."

I put my head on my propped up, interlaced hands and looked smiling into her face.

"Oh, Aduke, you know how I feel about parties, especially those on campus. It's enough for me to come here every day. When I finish work, I'm ready to get out of here for my peace of mind."

"Please, please, please, Janice," Aduke begged. "I won't ask you for anything again."

"Oh, yeah, right," I said, "like the time..." I thought for a moment, looking at my African friend.

"Okay, okay, you win," Aduke, said laughing, her fine white teeth showing as she did.

Aduke Bakare was, in my opinion, the perfect example of the beauty of African women. She was tall, with cocoa-brown skin and a flawless complexion. She had a smile that could light the room and was built like a ballet dancer. Aduke always wore her African attire proudly. We were opposites. I was medium height, with long, light brown hair, and tan skin. I wasn't one to fuss in the mirror. My smile was warm, friendly, and welcoming. It would make my eyes glow with a promise of friendship when I laughed, that is, when I didn't have an attitude.

I was twenty-seven years old, and I had no prospects for marriage. I didn't even have a steady boyfriend. I dated about twice a month, and lately, the men I went out with were either married or looking for a one-night stand. After I graduated from Dillard University with my B.A., I thought I would settle down and get married like all my other friends.

With no prospects in New Orleans, I found a job in Chicago and hoped I would find a suitable husband there as well. Since that did not happen, I settled down into the continuous cycle of going to work, going home, and watching television.

"Okay, Aduke, I'll go."

"Great!" she said, excited, jumping off my desk and headed for the door.

"Wait!" I shouted, stopping her. "What should I wear?"

"Wear something African!" she shouted back to me from the doorway.

"But I don't have anything," I yelled back.

"Then borrow something from Melinda. You know that she has some; in fact, why don't you invite her to come with you? After all, it's a celebration and the more, the merrier."

I gave her suggestion some thought and agreed with her. Then, with a wink, she adjusted her head tie and left.

My boss, Mr. Dotson, the head of Student Affairs, buzzed me on the intercom:

"Janice."

"Yes, Mr. Dotson," I answered.

"Do I have any appointments?"

"No sir, not on the afternoon calendar."

"Good, then you can have the rest of the day off, if you wish."

"Thank you, sir," I replied thinking, *great! That will give me more time to get ready for tonight.*

I picked up the phone to call my cousin Melinda. She worked at a law firm downtown as a legal secretary. The receptionist answered.

"Hello, may I speak to Melinda Anderson?"

"May I ask who is calling?" the receptionist asked politely.

"My name is Janice Bordeaux."

"One moment, please."

I waited for my cousin to pick up the line, listening to elevator music.

"Hi Mindy!"

"Hey girl, what's up?" she replied.

"Nothing much," I answered, "... except, Aduke invited me to a party at the university tonight. Are you busy? Would you like to come?"

"Umm, don't know, Jan. You know I haven't been around Africans since I broke up with Dele."

"I know, Mindy," I started, disappointed, "but this is a party at the university, and you know Dele doesn't run with that crowd anymore."

Melinda had a bad relationship with a Nigerian named Dele Onibanjo. Dele was the type of man who was not satisfied with just one woman, so he had many girlfriends. It ruined their relationship. Melinda got tired of his infidelity and vowed she would never date a Nigerian again.

"Oh, Mindy, that was ages ago, and besides, you're seeing Bill now."

10

"I know, Jan, but it still hurts. What time is the party going to be?"

"Its 8:00 tonight," I said anxiously, hoping that she would not refuse to go with me.

"Bill might call, Jan."

"Girl, you've been waiting for him to call since last week."

"I know, Jan, but he was out of town on business. Anyway, I expect him to pop the question at any time," she said happily.

"Mindy, don't bet on it," I said angrily. "Hell will freeze over before he does."

"Oh, don't be so negative, Jan," she said sadly. "I know ... I know he loves me..."

"Yeah, right," I exclaimed sarcastically. "So, Mindy, how about tonight? Come on girl, Aduke says it'll be fun."

"No, thanks. I'm not going into the African scene again."

Well, I can't say that I blame her, I thought.

"Okay, Mindy, and then I'll see you later. Oh, by the way, can I borrow one of your African outfits?"

"You can have them all, girl. I won't be using them anymore."

I turned off my computer and walked through the parking lot to my car. The traffic was light so I got home quickly. Walking into the flat, I went straight into Melinda's bedroom and began searching her closet until I found the African garments. They were all enclosed in plastic and appeared new. I chose a purple and gold two-piece dress. It had a long skirt and matching hat. Then I went into the bathroom to shower. I

11

wrapped myself with the towel and returned to the bedroom, almost dry. I was finishing drying myself off when Melinda walked in.

"Hey, girl," I said.

She returned the greeting and asked, "Did you find a suitable outfit, Jan?"

"Yes, I choose the purple and gold two-piece."

"That'll compliment your color, Janice; you'll look like a queen. At least someone will get some use out of it. I swore never to wear it again after Dele and I broke up, but it's such a beautiful outfit."

I brushed my hair into a ball and put the cap on, stepping back to look into the mirror. I looked great, completely different from the conservative picture I presented at work.

"Janice, you look exquisite," Melinda exclaimed, admiring me. "That dress never looked that good on me."

I looked into the mirror, thinking *I hope I have fun tonight.*

"Wait, I have a pair of gold earrings that will go great with the outfit."

She ran to the dresser and searched through her jewelry box until she found what she wanted, then she handed me the most beautiful pair of earrings I had ever seen.

"Melinda, where did you get these?" I asked, admiring the delicate engraving on the gold earrings.

"Dele gave them to me. It was the only good thing that I got from the relationship." Melinda said unable to stop complimenting me. "Girl, you do look like a

Queen from the Mother Land. You do our ancestors proud, Jan."

"Do you really think so?"

"You look great. Wear it with confidence, Janice."

Just as I was getting ready to leave, the phone rang. I answered and a man's soft, mellow voice asked to speak to Melinda.

"Who may I tell her is calling?"

"Tell her, Bill," he said politely. I put the phone down on the table calling,

"Mindy! Mindy! Telephone, its Bill!"

She ran to the phone, her face beaming with excitement.

"See, I told you he would call," she whispered, holding the receiver to her body so he could not hear what she was saying.

"Okay," I said. "So, I was wrong."

I left, closing the door behind me, listening to the sound of Melinda's voice filled with excitement. I ran downstairs to my car. Once inside, I turned on the radio and one of my favorite songs came on. I listened to it as I drove towards the university hall.

It was a clear, early-spring night. The weather had been unusually mild for Chicago. The moon was out, and you could see the stars, for a change, through the city haze. I reached the university and parked my car in the lot. Walking towards the hall, I met a crowd of people standing at the entrance, dressed in an array of African fashions. I could see that there appeared to be a very large turnout as people lined the walkway in front, waiting to go inside.

I was in good spirits because Bill called Mindy. *I hope Bill has good news for her,* I thought as I finally reached the front of the line. Walking inside, I searched the room for Aduke and was relieved when I saw her standing in a corner, surrounded by a group of people.

"Janice, Janice, over here," Aduke called out to me as I made my way over to where she stood. I felt nervous when I could see people watching me as I made my way to the group. When I reached her, I complemented her on the outfit she was wearing. She proudly told me it was made of *Ashoke*, hand-woven cloth from Nigeria.

"Everyone, this is my good friend, Miss Janice Bordeaux. She is the administrative assistant for the Student Affairs Department."

I nodded to the group and shook hands with a few people that Aduke personally introduced me to. The group consisted of Kofi Amponsah, from Ghana, Lata Ewe, from Cameroon, Donald Payne, Andrea Nelson, plus Ouchi Nwachukuwu and Olufemi Adegoke, from Nigeria. When I reached to shake Olufemi's hand, our eyes met; I saw his twinkle as he let his hand linger on mine before Aduke abruptly grabbed me to join in with the group now complementing each other on their traditional African attire, showing me to the table along with the others as the music began to play.

"Oh!" cried Aduke, "that's Sunny Ade — he's one of my favorite musicians!"

I began to feel the night's excitement transferring itself to me from Aduke as she began to perform a solo dance to the music of her favorite musician. She was not alone for long because she was soon joined by a number of men, each vying for her attention. I went to a table and sat down alone, watching her having a good time, dancing and flirting with the men.

Dinner was buffet style, with featured dishes from all over Africa. As Aduke was occupied on the dance floor, I decided to go ahead and eat. The food looked so luscious. I fixed a plate for myself from the platters containing food with unpronounceable names.

After sampling a few of the dishes, I was ready to have some fun when I felt a hand tapping me gently on my shoulder.

"Would you like to dance?"

I turned my head around to see who spoke and saw Olufemi Adegoke. I smiled and replied. "No, thank you. I don't know how dance to African music."

Aduke, returning to the table, heard my refusal.

"Go on, Janice. It's easy ... just dance like everyone else."

I was about to refuse again when Olufemi took hold of my hand and said, "Please, please don't disappoint me. I want to be the first man in the room to dance with the most beautiful woman at the party."

I was flattered and unable to refuse anyone who complemented me like that. As I stood up, I found myself unable to stop looking at him. His eyes were so sexy and when he smiled, I saw the most perfect set of white teeth. He put his hand around my waist, leading me to the dance floor. I watched the other dancers on the floor and attempted to imitate their sensual moves. At first I was a bit shy to move my waist and hips in a way that imitated moves that belonged in the bedroom, but soon I was able to keep up with my partner. Olufemi complimented me on my dancing.

Olufemi was a tall man, about 6'2", with a medium-brown complexion. What attracted me to him was he had the most beautiful eyes I'd ever seen on a man. They were oval-shaped and ringed with long lashes. The dance floor was crowded, and we bumped each other several times. The last time we touched, he gave me a look that left me feeling weak inside. We looked at each other, shyly laughing at each other. Olufemi was impeccably dressed for the party; wearing African attire that he later told me was called an *Agbada*, traditionally worn in northern Nigeria, made from material called guinea brocade. It was all white, with an intricate design embroidered down the front. Through his robes, I could feel his body heat, and as he moved, I could see the strength in his arms. A small patch of dark hair stuck out of the back of his cap. His eyes caught me looking at him, and I blushed.

As the dance progressed, he began moving in time to the drumbeats. I attempted to keep up with him, but I was beginning to tire. He explained to me that African records are long. I told him that I was not used to dancing for so long. We danced the rest of the song in silence, but I could see him looking at me with a great deal of admiration. As we whirled to the music, I could smell his cologne. *Umm,* I thought to myself. *The smell is very appealing.* When he spoke, I expected he would have a strong accent like Aduke, but instead, his was barely noticeable and sounded so sexy, that when the music stopped, I was kind of disappointed.

"All this dancing has made me thirsty. Can I get you a drink, Janice?"

I said yes as he escorted me back to the table.

"Janice, he said, pulling back a chair for me, you can call me *Femi* — most people do. It's the shorter version of my name," then he walked to the bar to get us a drink.

While he was gone, two men came and asked me to dance. Femi returned as I was getting up. I shrugged my shoulders and went to dance to another long African record.

I was having a great time. The guy I was dancing with told me he was from Sierra Leon. He said he watched me dancing with the Nigerian and was now going to monopolize me. He was also handsome, wearing his native attire. I guess I was feeling fickle due to all the attention I was getting from all the men.

I was not my usual self at all. Suddenly I was not tired anymore. When my last partner escorted me back to the table, my face was flushed with excitement. Fanning, I excused myself to the ladies' room. On the way there, I searched for Aduke, but couldn't find her anywhere. There were a few ladies in the restroom, and they were admiring my outfit when Aduke rushed in.

"Janice, Janice, what did you say to Femi?" I looked at her anxious face.

"What do you mean? I didn't say anything particular; I just danced with him one time."

"Well, girl, he asked me a lot questions about you, like what you do, are you married, where you live, and your phone number."

"My phone number?" I asked perturbed. "If he wants that, he can ask me himself!" I said with an angry attitude.

"Maybe he's shy, Janice," Aduke said, defending her friend.

"He doesn't look shy," I replied, remembering the handsome man I danced with.

"Well, Janice, it appears that Femi likes you."

17

"I will have to hear that from him, Aduke."

"Believe me, girl, you will before the night is over. He is crazy about you!" she said, her voice tinged with excitement.

"Okay, Aduke, I believe you."

After freshening up, we went back to the party. It felt as if everyone was watching us as we walked back into the hall. Before I could sit down, a warm hand grabbed mine and I turned around to face Femi.

"Where are you going?" he said huskily, looking into my eyes, searching deeply.

I blushed and began to stammer, pulling away from him. "I ... I ... I ... was going to sit down."

"Yes," he said, "but not before you dance with me."

The lights were dimmed for this dance, a slow one by Luther Vandross, "Anyone Who Had a Heart." We walked to the floor. It was as if we were the only ones there. I looked at him, and he at me, then he put his arm around my shoulders and we began to glide on the floor, my face on his shoulder. I would not look at him, afraid he would see me blush, for I felt his body was warm and saw fine sweat beaded on his brow. Even through his heavy robes, I could feel his heart beating fast. His mouth was close to my ear, and he whispered,

"I like you, Janice. I'd like to see you again."

My cheek tingled at the touch of his breath. His hand slid up and down my back. It felt good to be in the strong arms of a man. It had been such a long time ... too long since I'd felt so comfortable with someone, especially someone whom I'd just met. When

I pulled back to look at him, his eyes were gazing deep into mine, alight with a soft glow as if he read my thoughts. Then the song came to an end, but we stayed on the dance floor for a few seconds. It was as if time stood still there, he holding my hand, comfortable just being.

"We'd better sit down; everyone is staring at us," I said through my teeth, as if with difficulty. We pulled apart. Holding my arm, Femi escorted me to my seat. Aduke came over to sit by me, and he excused himself from the table to get more drinks. I watched him walk away before I gave Aduke my attention.

"Janice, do I see something going on, girl?" Aduke asked, her accent tingling with excitement. "What did he say?"

I began to tell her about the magic that had just occurred on the dance floor. We were still talking when Femi came back to the table and sat next to me. His closeness felt good. While we sipped our drinks, I asked him how long had he been in this country? He told me two years and that he came to earn his doctorate in engineering and would graduate this summer. He also told me he was an associate professor at the university. Then he turned his attention to Aduke, and they began to converse in their language. Even though I did not understand what they were saying, every fourth word or so, he would look at me.

The crowd began to thin. As the people in charge blinked the lights to let everyone know that the party was over, we began to walk outside with the crowd. Femi was holding my hand possessively as we passed the other African gentlemen that I had the pleasure to dance with. They all stared with envy at the man who appeared to win the honor of my company. Outside the hall, Aduke, surrounded by a crowd of friends, came

19

over to thank me for coming. I walked away from Femi when he called...

"Wait, Janice. Let me walk you to your car. Where are you parked?"

I told him, and then he reclaimed my hand as we walked to the car, making small talk. When we got there, he asked me for my key and opened the door.

"When can I see you again, Janice? Can I see you tomorrow?" he asked, without waiting for my answer.

We stood outside in the moonlight looking at each other.

"Okay, Femi," I said shyly.

"Great, I'll pick you up tomorrow evening at seven."

I wrote my address and phone number on a piece of paper. He held it as if it were made of gold. I entered my car and he closed the door. Waving good-bye, I drove off, feeling tired, but happy that the evening had gone well. Arriving home, I walked in to find Melinda out, so I showered and went to bed, dreaming about Femi Adegoke...

Chapter 2

The next morning I heard Melinda puttering in the kitchen. The smell of sausage frying and coffee brewing was overpowering. I walked in and to my surprise; I saw that we had company. Bill sat at the head of the table. Melinda was pouring him a cup of coffee.

"Well, good morning," I said, surprised to see the two of them there.

"Good morning to you too!" they said in unison, beaming...

"You want some breakfast, Janice?" Melinda asked, smiling.

She was still smiling at me as she walked to the stove to get the sausage and eggs. Her eyes were twinkling. I really felt like I was intruding, but my hunger overcame my feelings, and I decided to stay and have breakfast with them. Melinda sat down at the table and I glanced at her hand as she poured a cup of coffee and passed it to me. I took and held her hand, looking with amazement at the ring. A marquis diamond with at least two carats glowed on her finger.

"Oh, Mindy, it's lovely. Bill, you and my cousin are so funny," I said laughing.

"We are?" she asked, teasing. "Bill asked me to marry him last night, Janice, and I said yes."

She continued talking to me, gazing at him with love. I congratulated the two of them asking,

"When is the Big Day going to be?"

"We haven't decided," Mindy answered. "But as soon as we set a date, you will be the first one to know."

"How was the party last night, Jan?"

"It was great!"

I paused, sipping the steaming coffee.

"I met someone ..." then seeing that she was not listening to me, I said, "I'll tell you about it later."

I went back into my room after finishing breakfast and lay down on my bed. Closing my eyes, I began to daydream about Femi when the phone rang. It was Aduke.

"Hi, Janice. I just called to say thanks for coming to the party last night."

"No, I should be the one to thank you, Aduke. I had such a nice time. Aduke, how well do you know Femi?"

"I know him pretty well, Janice, I guess, and I also know that he is one of the most handsome men on campus."

I laughed and she continued...

"And that he is alone. Femi stays pretty much to himself. He is a friend of my brother Tunde, and I went to school with his sister Bisola. I also know that a lot of women want him. In fact, I know of three that were furious last night because he gave you all the attention. They would do anything if he would just talk to them."

"Really?" I said. *Umm* I thought to myself, *he is very good-looking and has a sexy way about him.*

"Do you know anything else?" I was anxious to know all I could about this man I met last night. I was very attracted to him.

"Well, I never see him with other women. I always see him either alone or with the other professors."

"How old do you think he is?" I cut in.

"I guess around 32 or 33."

"That's young to have a doctorate in engineering," I remarked, impressed.

"Well, maybe he's smart, Janice."

"Aduke, before I forget to tell you, Melinda is engaged to be married."

"Really, when? Where and who??!!!"

"Slow down, girl," I said, laughing at her excitement.

"His name is Bill, and they haven't set the date; he asked her just last night."

"Oh, how romantic," she crooned. "I remember when she was with that fool, Dele Onibanjo. Boy was he a jerk."

"Yes," I replied, "he really hurt her, but now she is really happy. It took her a long time to begin to trust men again."

"Sounds like someone else I know," Aduke said softly. "Janice, what do you think of Femi?"

"He asked me out tonight, and I'm really looking forward to seeing him again."

"Go, girlfriend. See? — I knew he liked you."

"Okay, Aduke. I've got to go now. Talk to you later."

I hung up the phone and lay down again, thinking about the party and Femi. Chills went through my body as I began to fantasize. *I wonder what kind of lover he is. Umm, he looks like he can take care of a woman. He's built for it.* I shook it off, jumped up, and went to wash my hair.

It was seven in the evening when the doorbell rang. It appeared that my date was prompt.

"Mindy!" I shouted from my room, "can you get it?"

I heard voices in the hall as I continued to get ready to go on my date with Femi. I chose a black and red dress that showed off my figure to perfection. I selected perfectly matching black pumps with a red bow and carried a small black clutch bag. I also grabbed my leather coat in case it was cool, since spring weather in Chicago can be unpredictable. Then I walked into the living room and there was Mindy, talking to the man who looked so different from the one I met last night. He looked splendid in his gray suit as he turned and met my eyes, holding a bouquet of roses in his hand.

"Janice, how are you?" he asked, handing me the roses.

"I'm fine. Thank you for the flowers, Femi. I'll put these in water."

"No, don't worry, Jan. I'll do that for you."

Melinda took the roses while I walked towards Femi, holding my hand out to shake his when suddenly; he pulled me to him for a hug. Mindy reacted with obvious surprise.

"Hey! I thought you two just met last night?"

My mind was racing a mile a minute, thinking, *whoa, slow down there. He sure moves fast.*

But then I saw the mischievous twinkle in his eyes, and he reassuringly explained it as just a friendly hug. I pulled back blushing.

"You look beautiful, Janice."

I turned, looking into his expressive eyes, and saw the look of admiration. He helped me put on my coat as Melinda said,

"Have a good time, you two."

"All right, Mindy," I answered. "See you later."

"It was nice meeting you, Femi," she added, as she extended her free hand. He shook it graciously.

"The pleasure was all mine," he warmly replied.

As Femi released her hand, Melinda stood rooted to the spot thinking, *He is so different from Dele. This guy has class...*

We walked downstairs to his car. He opened the door for me, and then ran around to the driver's side. His car smelled of fresh roses.

"Nice car," I said, making small talk to mask my nervousness.

He smiled a thank you and turned on the ignition. As an African song began to play on the cassette, I sat back, feeling more at ease. He had a way of making me feel comfortable.

"Where are we going?"

"First, I am taking you to dinner, and then we go to a movie. How about that?"

"Sounds nice," I said. "Where are we eating?"

"I made reservations at Chez Paul on the north side. Do you like French food?"

"Yes," I said.

"Good. Then we will eat and go to see a movie."

I looked at his hands on the steering wheel. They were strong, yet gentle. I saw no ring.

He caught me looking at him and smiled. We reached a stoplight and he gazed at me briefly. His eyes seemed to be saying, "Janice, you are so lovely." I caught his look and held it ... just for a second ... then the light turned green. What I saw gave me insight into his feelings for me. His eyes were truly like a window to his heart. I had to caution myself again — *slow down, Janice. You just met him.* We reached the restaurant and were seated by the maitre'd. The waiter brought Femi the wine list, and we ordered. During the meal, we talked a little about ourselves and a lot about work. After eating, we sat drinking coffee and he told me about Nigeria. I'd always been curious about Africa, the land of my ancestors. As Femi spoke of Nigeria, his eyes took on a faraway look.

"My home is a small town called Ekiti. It is still a village, something like a farm town or a suburb, but more rural. My father also has a house in Lagos. I intend to make that my permanent address some day. Lagos is comparable to Tokyo in cost of living, New York in traffic, and Los Angeles in diversity."

"What an interesting way to put it, Femi," I said, sipping my coffee.

I tried to imagine New York filled with African women in their colorful cotton wrappers, carrying baskets with fruit and vegetables on their heads, and the taxi drivers

26

honking their horns. In that way, New York and Lagos are very similar. He spoke so passionately about his country that I was carried away by his enthusiasm that the government would one day be for the people. Our eyes met again, and I felt warm all over, but I attributed some of this feeling of warmth to the coffee; but, in my mind, I thought, *God, he is so good-looking.* Little did I know that his thoughts were the same as mine.

Femi paid the check, left a generous tip, and we proceeded to the movie. During the movie, which was a romance, I felt his warm hand over mine. Then he leaned over and I felt his hot breath in my ear when he asked if I was I enjoying the movie. Like I could concentrate with this man next to me! I closed my eyes and when he touched my ear gently with his lips, I shivered.

"Are you cold, Janice?"

The way he said my name made me shiver more...

"Yes," I replied in a husky voice. He immediately put his arm around me.

We left the movie around 11 p.m. As soon as we were in the car, he asked, "Where do we go now, Janice? It's still early."

I suggested we go for a walk down Michigan Ave. We drove to the Magnificent Mile and parked. He helped me from the car, and then we began slowly walking. Talking came naturally now, and we began teasing each other and holding hands. When we stopped in front of Bloomingdale's, he pulled me to him tightly.

"Janice ..." he began, his breathing coming soft and quick. Whispering, he confessed, "Janice, you take my breath away."

His swift action caught me off guard. He took the back of my neck in his hands and pulled my face close to his. As he looked deep into my eyes, our lips touched. His kiss was moist and tender. When I felt his tongue push gently into my mouth, to my surprise, I answered with passion. My limp arms went around his neck as his hands moved up and down my back in circular motion. We were locked in a passionate embrace, oblivious to everything. After a few moments that seemed like hours, we pulled apart, reluctantly, as he looked at me tenderly.

"Janice, I really like you."

"You do?" I asked, staring dreamily at him. "I like you too, Femi."

The honking of a taxi horn broke the spell. We walked back towards the car in silence, holding hands. Before we reached it, I asked him, "Femi, tell me more about your life."

"There is not much to tell, Janice. I am just a simple African man, who has just met an exciting American woman."

Then suddenly his mood changed. His brows came together, his eyes almost closed into slits, as if he were thinking of another place and time.

"Femi? Femi?" I called to him, bringing him back to the present without him ever answering my question.

"A penny for your thoughts?" I asked.

He sighed, laughing, as he put his arm around my waist. We walked back to the car slowly, enjoying the time together, then drove home in silence. Putting my key into the lock when we finally reached my apartment, I asked,

"Would you like to come inside for a glass of wine, Femi?"

"No, not tonight," he answered quickly. "We will go out again soon, Janice. I'll call you."

Then he took me in his arms and kissed me, but not as passionately as he did downtown. He pulled away, and we said goodnight. I went to bed thinking about my date with Femi. *I don't really know him yet. Are we moving too fast? Maybe he has another girlfriend.* Oh, well, that would just be my luck. The last man I dated turned out to be married and had two children. He had his lie so straight, I never saw through it. This time I was determined that I would never fall victim to a man who had obligations to someone else.

The weeks following our first date were so much fun that I forgot about the other side of Femi that I had gotten a glimpse of on our first date. He never showed that mood again. He was the perfect gentleman: taking me to the latest shows, sightseeing, dancing, and dining. He courted me with roses and wine. I loved every moment we spent together. We began to talk about everything and found we had so much in common. Femi never approached me for sex; we discussed it, but it was not the major reason we were attracted to each other. We enjoyed so many of the same things. It surprised me that someone raised in Nigeria assimilated into American culture so well.

Melinda and Bill had finally set the date for their wedding and had begun to prepare for it. It was to be in June, and Melinda needed all the help I could give. She wanted it to be a special wedding that everyone would remember. Her mother, my Aunt Dotty, came to Chicago from New Orleans to help us. Aunt Dotty was disappointed that they were not going to be married in New Orleans because most of our family was there.

29

But Melinda insisted on having the wedding here. I was with her the day she tried on her wedding gown. I sighed, hoping that maybe one day this would be me trying on the wedding dress. My sadness must have been obvious to Melinda.

"Jan, don't look so sad," she said, while the dressmaker fussed with her veil.

"I'm not sad, Mindy," I protested.

"Well, you look like you are, girl," she insisted. "Don't worry. Femi will ask you soon. After all, you two have been seeing each other for a few months now, and he is such a nice man. And, so good-looking!"

Yes, I thought thinking of Femi and what happened on our last date. He had invited me for a ride to the lakeshore. Lately, I found myself afraid of being alone with him. Even though we were both adults, able to decide whether to be intimate or not, the time and place never seemed right for us. In the car at the lakeshore, we began kissing, and before we knew it, we were petting heavy. His hands were all over me. I was touching his body and feeling like I was losing control. He pushed me on the seat of the car and unbuttoned my blouse. When his hand caressed my breast, I shivered with excitement. As he kissed it, I tingled with pleasure.

Oh, yes, I wanted him. My hand slid gently to the crease in his lap. He took a deep breath as I touched his maleness. He was all man. I was so aroused, just about ready to give in. *Move cautiously, Janice; let him make the moves*, a little voice inside my head kept telling me. Our kisses became more intense as we slid further down on the car seat. I squirmed with pleasure, but I knew that somehow we had to stop.

"Femi, Femi, please, not now; not this way."

"Why is it, Janice, that every time we get ready to make love, you want to stop?"

I knew that he was angry, as I searched for the right words to calm him down. "It's just not the right time, Femi," I pleaded, contradicting myself. "When we make love to each other, I don't want it to be on the back seat of a car."

He pulled away angry, and I could not blame him. Femi refused to talk to me on the way home. There was so much sexual tension between us it scared me. He didn't even walk me to the door; he just curtly said good night.

Three days had passed since I spoke to him. I was worried that I may have turned him off. On the way home after the fitting, I told Melinda about my fears.

"Oh, Jan, are you crazy? What do you expect him to do! Femi is all man; African men are very sexual, and they don't let women control them. You took away his power, Janice."

"But, Mindy, I really wanted him like I never wanted anyone before. He makes me feel so wonderful."

"Jan, don't you ever think about making love to him?"

"Are you kidding, girl? That's all I think about now, but he hasn't called me for three days. Mindy, I think I love him. I'm afraid, you know ... after Jeffrey ... I was devastated when I found out he was married."

"Janice, you didn't deserve that, but Femi is single and, girl, so desirable. I don't see how you have waited this long."

"Well, Mindy, sometimes it's not just me ... sometimes he's the one who says that it's not the right time, so I go along with him."

"That's strange, Jan. You're a beautiful woman, a bit stuck-up at times," she teased. "I can't understand why he would not just take you!"

My eyes became cloudy as I thought about what my cousin just said.

"Why don't you call him, Jan," Mindy suggested.

"I will, as soon as we get home."

When we arrived at the apartment, I went directly into my room. I stared at the phone for ten minutes, and then decided, *I'll take a chance; after all, what do I have to lose.* I dialed his number and waited. It rang, and then he answered,

"Hallow, Hallow!"

His accent was very noticeable today.

"Hello, Femi," I said slowly, unsure whether he would hang up on me or not. "How are you?"

My voice sounded nervous, despite the fact that I tried so hard to remain in control.

"I'm okay, Janice," he answered pleasantly. I swallowed, glad that he did not hang up.

"I haven't heard from you, Femi. Why?"

"Uh, I've been busy, Janice. I was going to call you when I found time."

"How about now, Femi. Do you have time to talk?"

"No, Janice. I wanted to put some space between us. I feel that you are not ready for love yet."

I was surprised by his revelation and attempted to defend my behavior. "But, Femi," I protested. "I do; I am!"

There was a long moment of silence. I could hear his steady breathing on the line. I held my breath, uncertain of what he would say next.

"Don't say anymore, Janice. Just come over here now!"

Then he hung up the phone. I just sat there in a daze, not knowing what to do. I didn't have the strength to refuse him. It was as if I became his slave and was at his command. I had to make a quick decision, and he made up my mind for me. I'd never been to his apartment before and wanted to look my best. So, I showered and changed into my black stretch pants and a big, silk shirt. I looked in the mirror, blushing, because I knew that once I crossed his threshold, there would be no turning back. I was finishing my makeup when Mindy came into the room.

"Going out, Jan?"

"Yes, Mindy, I am."

"How did that work out, I mean, you calling Femi?"

"It went fine, girl. I'm going there now. Keep your fingers crossed for me."

"Okay, I will, Jan. Think about what you said and try to have a good time."

Femi lived near the university in Hyde Park. It was only a few minutes from me. I found a parking space and entered the double glass doors of his building. When I rang the bell, he buzzed me in instantly. I became nervous as I took the elevator to the tenth floor. As the door opened to his floor, I took a deep breath. I walked down the carpeted hall and tapped on his door.

"Come in, Janice."

He greeted me as he swung open the door, smiling sweetly, welcoming me into his home. He took my hand, leading me into the living room. He was dressed casually, wearing a tee shirt and jeans. His feet were bare and soundless as we walked across the plush carpet. His apartment was just as I imagined it. He had a leather sofa, white with a black throw for accent. African art and kente cloth hung throughout the room, which smelled of sandalwood and spicy food. I sat down on the sofa. The room was dimly lit. A few pieces of Benin bronze statuettes stood on his cocktail table. I picked one up to examine it, and we began to talk about the piece and some of the others that were in the room. He explained about the history of each of the bronzes, fascinating me with the stories. The aroma from the kitchen was tantalizing and making me hungry.

"Are you cooking, Femi?"

"Yes," he said looking directly at me.

"I'm making a special dish from Nigeria, just for you."

His eyes were smiling at me as he talked, making me feel relaxed and comfortable.

"I didn't know you cooked. I thought African men were served by their women."

"No, not me ... How else would I eat, living alone?" He laughed, the happy sound filling the room. Then he took my hand and led me to the dining room, where the table was already set for two.

"In Africa, it is customary for the women to serve the men. Men rarely go into the kitchen."

I smiled and asked teasingly, "Are you saying that I should serve you?"

"No, no, Janice. When in America, we should share the responsibility; but in Nigeria, my mother would flip if she saw me doing this for you."

He laughed. His eyes held promise of things to come. I blushed.

"Well, what she doesn't know won't hurt her. I won't tell if you don't."

After seating me, he went into the kitchen and returned with a tray filled with food. My eyes opened wide.

"This is like the food at the party, Femi," I exclaimed excitedly.

Our meal consisted of rice, peppered chicken, fried plantain, and sliced cucumber salad. He also prepared coconut custard for desert. I ate with relish. This man had gone to all this trouble to prepare this special meal for me. What a treat!

"The food is delicious, Femi. You will have to teach me how to cook it."

"I'd be glad to, Janice," he replied, as he stood up to clear the table.

I helped him take the dishes to the kitchen. While I was standing by the sink, he leaned over my back. In his tee shirt, I could feel his strong, muscular body. He was wearing my favorite cologne. He gently put his lips to my hair, reflecting pleasure at the smell of my sweet perfume. I turned around and found his lips on mine. His kiss was tender and filled with promise. I was so happy. He had gone to such trouble to make me feel that comfortable. We returned to the living room, holding hands. Soft music came from the stereo as we sat on the sofa and talked. He stroked my hand gently.

"Janice, I've wanted to talk to you, but I needed some time to sort things out. I don't rush into things, especially a relationship with a woman. From the first time I saw you, I knew I wanted you, but I had to be sure you wanted me. The other night in the car, I lost control. I sensed you were not ready, and I tried to push you. I respect your feelings, even now. If you want to go home, you can, and I will understand ... but if you stay ..." he continued, softly massaging my hand, "I promise you will never regret it."

I looked at him with sincere love mixed with all the desire I had held back for so long. "Femi, oh, Femi, I ... I..."

And with that, I pulled him to me and kissed his lips softly. At first, only our hands and mouths touched, and oh, so tenderly and gently. He responded by pulling me into his arms and holding me in a passionate embrace. He kissed my neck with small nibbles that left me weak. He looked into my eyes; they had become floating pools of desire.

"Janice," he whispered passionately as he kissed me on the inside of my neck, then going lower as he unbuttoned the silk blouse I was wearing. "Your eyes are like fire."

I helped him, moving slow and easy as he removed my blouse, leaving me in my pants and bra. He kissed my shoulder; leaning down as far as his height would let him, and then pushed me back on the leather sofa. He gently removed my bra, never taking his eyes off mine, and then he cupped my breast as his mouth kissed it hungrily. All my desire rushed to my loins as I pulled off his tee shirt. He lay over me; the leather couch was soft under my body as I squirmed beneath him. We both knew where we were going, as I answered his every intimate advance. My hands explored his body, and I knew I was going to enjoy this man; he knew I was ready to go anywhere he could take me. He stood up, lifting me effortlessly, my arms around his neck.

He carried me to his bedroom with the style and grace of a panther. Our eyes never left each other as he laid me on the bed, and we both finished undressing. Then he began to kiss me on my neck, traveling down to my navel, going further down until I arched my back to receive him.

I sighed and drew in my breath, my hands playing in his hair as he took pleasure in pleasing me. When I could take no more, I pulled him to me and we became one. He was magnificent! So gentle and loving. I moaned softly as he moved deeper and deeper, accepting him into my depths. Our bodies moved in unison, with a rhythm that only lovers know. His sole purpose was to please me, and mine to please him ... There was no turning back as he put his hands under my body and drove us both to the end of the world. We both cried out, moaning, our passion spent. My hands were on his back, massaging, as he held me tight. Over and over, ripples of pleasure kept sending our bodies into motion.

He rolled over and lay beside me, breathing heavily. I had my eyes closed as I relaxed in total satisfaction. No words were needed, only the sound of our heavy breathing. He pulled me to him; the look I saw in his eyes was of pure love. He embraced me and whispered words filled with emotion.

"Janice, I love you."

My body shivered, for he said the words that I desired to hear from him for so long. I kissed him with passion, as I acknowledged his feelings.

"Yes, Femi, I know."

With that declaration, we began to make love over ... and over, until dawn crept over the windowsill. Then we just slept in each other's arms.

Chapter 3

I awoke to the shower running and hugged myself thinking ... *Umm what a man!* I got up naked and walked into the bathroom. Femi was in the shower, so I joined him. He turned around, surprised. I took the sponge and gently began to soap his back, the warm water running on our bodies. Soon he was like putty in my hands, and we made love again.

Later, we dressed, and then I went into the kitchen. Femi was in the living room reading the paper. I fantasized; *this is how I want my life to be — this picture of my man waiting for his breakfast.* I fixed breakfast, and we sat together eating, talking, laughing, and loving each other. It was Sunday, so we spent the whole day together. We went walking, holding hands, smiling, just feeling good being with each other.

When I went home, Mindy was out, so I lay on the sofa and thought how my life would be married to Femi. I love him, and I know he loves me. The differences in our culture did not even come into it. He was a man, and what a man! I knew that sooner or later, I would have to investigate his culture, but for now, I will just enjoy being with him. I was remembering what he said about his mother and the kitchen, but I pushed that thought out of my mind and filled my head with our lovemaking and the three words he spoke to me, *I love you.*

*****

Aduke came into my office bright and early Monday morning.

"Hello, Janice. Long time no see," she said, sitting in her usual spot on my desk, wearing a colorful cotton wrapper and matching head tie. She was cheerful as she sat smiling, fiddling with my papers.

"I've been busy, Aduke," I finally answered.

"Yes, I can see that," she said, her eyes twinkling mischievously. "I guess Femi Adegoke has nothing to do with it?"

I looked at her and blushed. "Well, in fact, he does," I answered.

"Janice," Aduke exclaimed, "when you are in love, the whole world knows it!" She smiled radiantly and let out a giggle. "He must be good."

I blushed an even deeper shade of red ... thinking, *yes, very good!* Wanting to change the subject, I began to ask her about her love life.

"How about your love life, Aduke? Are you still seeing Nelson, that Jamaican guy?"

"You know it, girlfriend," she said. "We always fight and get back together again. I am beginning to think that our African and Jamaican blood is too hot to be together."

"You know that Nelson adores you, Aduke. Why don't you stop stringing him along and get serious?"

"Janice, you know that I am not ready to settle down; besides, I have another friend hanging around. His name is Dominique, and he is very interested in me. Just be glad that you have someone like Femi. I mean, he is faithful, handsome, and trustworthy.... and handsome," she repeated, giggling.

"Okay, okay," I said laughing. You made your point. Just remember that he got someone good too."

"Yes, you are right," Aduke crowed. "You are beautiful and funny, and you will make a good African wife," she teased.

"And what does that mean?" I asked, eyeing her suspiciously.

"Barefoot, pregnant, and ten paces behind him!" she shouted jokingly, jumping off the desk and running out of the room just before my address book hit her. I laughed at her while I walked over to retrieve my book; but somehow, I kept having this nagging feeling about something she said. A little voice kept telling me *Check out his culture before you go too far.*

"Miss Bordeaux," my boss's voice on the intercom called, interrupting my thoughts.

"Yes, Mr. Dotson," I reply.

"Are those letters ready yet?"

"Yes, sir. I'll bring them to you right away."

*****

Femi and I met for lunch to discuss the graduation and Melinda's wedding, which was going to take place in two weeks. He was graduating with a Ph.D. in Engineering. We'd discussed employment opportunities in Chicago, but all he would ever say is that he would check into it. He was offered a full-time position as a senior professor at the university.

He said he was considering it, but that he had many other options, possibly even going back to Nigeria to work for his brother-in-law, who has a factory in Lagos. He complained about the racism in America, which he did not have to face in Nigeria. "In

41

Africa, you can go as far as your dreams and your money will take you."

That was a favorite saying of his. I got to know more and more about Femi, but I was still felt in the dark about his culture. One evening after work, Melinda and I were watching TV when I asked her about Dele and why they broke up. She told me in no uncertain terms that he wanted to have his cake and eat it too. When I asked her what she meant, she went on to tell me about his unfaithfulness and how she found out he had three other American girlfriends. Even though he professed to love her, he also said he loved them as well. Dele was enjoying the best of American women, because they all loved him unconditionally.

"I felt used, Janice." She continued, revealing the painful story about her relationship with Dele. "I gave our relationship two years, but when one of his girlfriends got pregnant and he said he had to marry her, that ended it for me. Well, even after all that, Jan, he still wanted our relationship to go on *as if nothing had happened*."

"Girl!" I said, appalled at his nerve, "you're kidding!"

"No, Jan, so I let him go. It wasn't until I met Bill that I began to heal and get over him. Dele did not want to let go. He kept calling and harassing me, Janice. I finally had to let Bill talk to him. Dele was so arrogant and sure of himself."

"What about the other girlfriends?" I asked, curious.

"They accepted his playing around. I guess they were desperate for a man ... any man."

"No," I said, "maybe they all really loved him, and it was hard for them to let go."

"Well, they're crazy," Melinda, replied. "Thank God Bill is nothing like Dele. But you know, Jan, sometimes I miss African culture — things like the food and the parties, but I wouldn't trade what I have now for anything. You see, I understand Bill; after all, he is from our world."

I began to think about Femi. I knew that Dele and he were from the same tribe, and now I was really curious about the culture. I called Aduke to get her opinion.

"Hey, girl, can you come over for some girl talk? There are a few things I want to ask you."

"Okay, Janice, I can come after the library closes, around 9 p.m."

"Great," I said. "See you then."

Aduke and I sat in my kitchen, drinking a cup of tea. From the look on her face, I knew she was curious as to why I asked her over, what I wanted to ask.

"Aduke, tell me about the woman's role in a typical Nigerian household."

She sat back in her chair, taken aback by my question. Finally, she said it depends on the family. Then I decided to remind her of Melinda's bad experience.

"Aduke, do you remember Dele, Melinda's old boyfriend?"

"Yes, I do Janice ... I know she had a real bad experience with him. Like I said, it depends on the family. Dele's father is a polygamist. He had many wives and many children." She went on to tell me about the culture and why Melinda got hurt. In Nigeria, when a man has more that one wife, there is tension in the household. Most of the time, the women fight among themselves over the husband, and they use the children to get back at him.

"Since I was not born in Nigeria, I was raised in a different way. My father has only one wife. But he never let us forget our culture."

Aduke continued, putting down her cup. "My brother Tunde was born in Lagos. From the day of his birth, he was king of the house. My parents denied him nothing. That is how it is in Nigeria."

"So, you are saying that males are given preferential treatment in Nigeria? It's the same in American culture, Aduke."

"Maybe, Janice, but sometimes it is how they expect to be treated, even by their wives. Men in Nigeria have the pick of the most beautiful women. In the old days, men married many women to prevent spinsters because of tribal wars when many of them were killed off. In some tribes, the men inherit the widows of the brother. Also some men marry multiple wives to have lots of children to work on the farm."

"In some families," she continued, "When the woman is barren, the men marry another woman instead of divorcing the present wife. They are supposed to ask the wife's permission before doing this, but sometimes they don't. Children are the crown jewels in our culture. In Nigeria, both Christian and Muslim men take multiple wives."

Aduke had captivated my interest. She continued ... "Today, the economics of the country make it difficult for a man to support multiple families."

"Did your father have more than one wife, Aduke?"

"No, my father loved my mother very much and never had reason to take another wife, but I know many who did."

I knew I had to ask her about Femi's family. "What about Femi, Aduke. Is his family a polygamist one?"

"Janice," she answered uncomfortably, "you should ask him yourself, but I will tell you this — Femi does not come from a polygamist house."

I breathed a sigh of relief at this information. This was a part of his culture I did not like. I'd heard stories about the unfaithfulness of African and Caribbean men, so I was a bit wary. But Aduke's explanation about the culture helped clear my mind on many issues. Yet, I wanted to know more. I inquired a little further. I wanted to know if the women were really kept barefoot and pregnant...

"Aduke, what about women? How are they treated?"

"In Nigeria," she began, "many women hold political office and have careers. Some are in television, business, or in education. The ones you see are educated. Many of the women in the village still follow the old ways, you know. They are hard to change. Many of them accept their fate as a part of their life."

After Aduke left, I went to bed thinking about all the information she had given me. Right now, I knew that Femi loved me and I him, and that is what mattered. Most important is that he does not come from a polygamist house. I would ask him about his culture later.

The weeks flew by and our romance blossomed, just like the beautiful roses of the church bow that Melinda and Bill stood under to take their vows. My mother and Aunt Dotty cried as she said, *"I do."* I was maid of honor, and as I looked over at Femi when the couple kissed to seal their vows, our eyes met and saw no one else at that time. The moment was as much ours as theirs. The reception was held in a hall downtown. I introduced Femi to my mother, and he promptly swished her off to the dance floor, charming her just as he'd charmed me. She was very impressed with him and happy that I had finally found someone to settle down with after Jeffery.

She thought I'd never get over him. I stood by Femi as Melinda and Bill cut the cake. I was holding his hand tightly and watching him to see his reaction. He only smiled and clapped with the crowd. We were dancing to the band when, suddenly, Femi took my hand to his lips and kissed it.

"Janice, you are gorgeous. You are more beautiful than the bride."

I blushed and thanked him for the complement. Many of Melinda's girlfriends stared at Femi; and a few even had the nerve to ask him to dance. I trusted him and let him go and have fun. Bill and I danced the last dance together before the bride was to throw the bouquet. All the single women, including mom, ran over to line up. Mindy stood at the top of the stairs and threw the bouquet over her shoulder ... It fell right into my hands as the others jumped up to try their luck at catching it. I beamed and smelled the fresh-cut roses as everyone came to congratulate me. Mindy ran to me and gave me a big hug.

"Girl, it's your turn next. I aimed the bouquet at you!"

I smiled at her, the tears in my eyes shining. "Oh, Mindy, I will miss you so."

Melinda and Bill were leaving to go on their honeymoon in the Bahamas. When they got back, she was moving in with Bill and setting up house. I was going to have to get a smaller place or find a roommate to help with expenses. I looked over at Femi and thought, *well, maybe not for long...*

My mother and Femi walked over to me. She took my hand and looked at me lovingly. "Janice, my dear, I hope it won't be too long before I am giving you away."

"I don't know, Mom."

Femi looked at me longingly and smiled. "I see you caught the bouquet," he quickly reminded me, "and if I'm not mistaken, your tradition is that you are to be married next, right?"

"Yes," Mom answered happily, smiling at the two of us. "Tradition says within a year, in fact."

I looked at the two people that I loved most in the world and said, "Well, maybe, but as you know, Mom, it takes two to tango."

"Umm," Femi said, smiling, "we'll have to see about that, Janice won't we?" he said, winking at me. My heart leaped two feet as I gazed dreamily at him. This was the first time he ever mentioned marriage. I was elated, and the thought made my mom happy as well.

Mom stayed at my house for a few days, and then she returned to New Orleans.

The apartment was lonely without Mindy or my mom. My spirits were lifted when I received a postcard from the Bahamas. Melinda told me she was so much in love, and they were having the time of their lives. She also missed me. Femi tried to make up for the loss of my cousin. Every evening after work, he and I had dinner. Sometimes we made love. Lately our lovemaking was so intense. I would question his fire, and he would put me off, saying that he loved me so much; he could not get enough of me.

About two weeks later, the week before graduation, we were watching television at his house when the phone rang. His telephone seldom rang while I was there, and I was curious. I found myself eavesdropping.

"Hallow, yes, yes. *Kini-nkan. Adupe.* Yes, yes," he started, and then he continued to speak in his language, which also was rare. First his conversation was soft and melodic, and then I heard a change in his tone to anger. All of a sudden, he banged the receiver down. I saw he was agitated, so when he returned to the living room, I asked, concerned,

"Is everything all right, darling?"

"Yes. No, it was my mother. She is coming to the graduation and is upset that I had not called to confirm the arrangements. She is coming with my father and my sister Bisola."

"What's wrong with that?" I asked, puzzled by his attitude. "I'll finally get a chance to meet your family, and after all, it's not everyday that their son gets his doctorate!"

"Janice, you don't know my family."

"Femi," I started diplomatically, "I'd like to meet them."

He smiled, but I sensed his uneasiness. Trying to calm him, I even offered Melinda's room for his sister. He looked at me, amazed.

"No, no; my sister is a classmate of Aduke, and she already made arrangements to stay with her."

"Great, then I will have them all over for dinner after the graduation."

He just looked at me pensively, and said, "Okay, we will see, Janice."

"Come on, Femi," I said cheerfully, "it will be fun."

I pulled him to me and kissed him sweetly. He began to relax and returned the kiss and embraced me passionately. We ended up making love, not like the last few times ... but slow, making sure we satisfied each other. Femi was almost apologetic with his lovemaking.

Chapter 4

The next few days after the phone call I did not see much of Femi. He always said he was busy preparing for his parents' visit. I called Aduke and she said that she was also too busy to talk, that she was getting ready for graduation. Her brother Tunde was arriving from London, and she needed to get her apartment ready for him and Femi's sister Bisola. Mindy was back from her honeymoon and had moved in with Bill. She called me from work and was describing her happy marriage. I was so happy for her. After I got home, I called Femi's house, and a strange woman's voice answered the phone.

"Hallow?"

"May I speak to Femi?" I asked courteously.

"One moment, please ..."

"Darling why haven't you called me?" I asked as soon as I heard Femi's voice.

"Janice, you know I have been busy with my family and the graduation preparations."

I knew the faculty had a gradation dinner for the teachers receiving their doctorates. And Femi had not invited me.

"I heard you were there, Femi. I saw Professor Langston at the office. Why didn't you tell me you were going? .... I wanted to meet your family."

Next, Femi quickly rushed me off the phone, evasively explaining, "I've got to run now, Janice. Mom is calling me. I'll call you later, dear," and he hung up.

I was so hurt and humiliated that he hung up on me. I began to cry, confused by his change of behavior since his family arrived from Nigeria. I thought we meant more to each other. I began to have doubts about our relationship. About one hour later, the doorbell rang. I opened to see Femi holding a bouquet of roses, looking like a wounded puppy. I embraced him, and we kissed.

"Janice, have you been crying?" he asked, as he brushed my tears away with his fingertips. His eyes held the look of love as he led me over to the sofa.

"Come and sit down so we can talk; I have something very important to ask you."

We sat on the sofa; he held my hand, facing me, gazing tenderly into my eyes....

"I was going to wait until after graduation, but I feel that this is the best time."

He pulled a small, velvet box from his pocket and handed it to me. I opened it. My eyes lit up like the glittering diamond in the engagement ring resting in the soft, velvet box.

"Femi, oh, Femi, darling," I squealed with delight. "What is this?"

He took my hand, kissing the slender fingers and looking into my eyes, as he spoke softly, "Janice, I've never loved or been loved by a woman such as you. I don't want to lose you, my dear. He slipped the ring on my finger. I want you to be my wife and share my life."

I shouted, "Yes! Yes!"

Tears in my eyes began to fall again. We kissed and made love that could only be made in heaven. Our passion was insatiable. He embraced me gently, while his lips kissed every part of my body. I was like a ship lost at sea, riding each wave to oblivion.

He claimed me over and over again, his manhood throbbing for release in my body. With each wave of emotion, we were lost in our desire to please one another.

I awoke, laying face down on my pillow, looking at my beautiful engagement ring. I lay there, admiring it and how the sun shone in a spectrum of color through it. I didn't even notice the note on the pillow next to me. It read, *My Darling, I have to leave. Always remember, no matter what, I love you.... Femi.* I lay back and remembered that this was not a dream. Femi had really asked me to marry him. I picked up the phone and called Mom in New Orleans. When I told her the good news, she got so excited that she started planning our wedding right then. I told her to calm down, that we had not set a date yet. After I spoke to her, I telephoned Melinda.

"Girl, you will never guess what happened to me!"

She claimed that she already knew. "I can hear it in your voice, Jan. Are you happy, really happy?"

"Yes," I answered, somewhat surprised. "Why do you ask me like that?"

"Well, you had me worried for a while, when you complained that he shut you out of his life since his family arrived here."

"Oh, no, that's all over now," I replied with more confidence than I really felt.

"They are all coming over for dinner after the graduation. I've got to go, Mindy. I have to get to work. Mr. Dotson may need some extra help closing out the school year."

"All right, Jan. Congratulations! Talk to you later."

I got up and prepared myself to go to the graduation ceremony. As I surveyed my image in the mirror, I saw my eyes had a sparkle and my cheeks glowed. I was radiant, as any bride-to-be should be. The campus was bustling with excitement. I watched from behind the stage as the graduating class took seats in the front rows. I could see Femi and Aduke sitting with their respective classes. There were visitors from all over the world. Some were dressed colorfully in the attire of their countries. Also present were famous dignitaries and university alumni. Even the President of the United States sent a representative to speak at the ceremony.

I could not tell who Femi's family was because there were many Africans present and most were wearing traditional attire. After all the speeches, they bestowed upon Olufemi Augustus Adegoke the honor of Valedictorian. This, he received, in addition to his Doctorate in Engineering. I beamed so proudly as the applause resounded in the hall for recognition of this honor. Aduke received her Bachelor of Science degree in accounting. She would be returning in the fall and entering the MBA program. After the graduation ceremony, a few selected graduates and their families were invited to a reception in honor of the alumni and guest speakers. I was having a conversation with my boss, Mr. Dotson, when Aduke came running towards me waving her degree. A strange woman wearing African attire was following closely behind her. She reached me and I gave her a big hug and asked where Femi was. Aduke was so happy.

"Look, Janice, I did it! I did it!"

Aduke looked positively regal in her cap and gown. The unknown woman stood by patiently, but not smiling, at our friendly show of emotion.

"Janice, I want you to meet Femi's sister, Mrs. Bisola Balogun."

She was tall, like Femi, and was beautiful, just like the pictures Femi had shown me. We eyed each other for a moment until she spoke in a strong voice with a very heavy accent.

"So, you are the one my brother is engaged to."

"Yes," I answered politely. "I am Janice Bordeaux."

"My brother has told me so much about you in his letters. My parents are anxious to meet you."

Aduke's brother Tunde joined us in the hall.

"Janice, this is my big brother Tunde," she said, as she happily introduced me to the brother I'd heard so much about over the years. Tunde and Femi were classmates in secondary school in London. There stood a man so like Aduke that they could be twins. They had the same mischievous twinkle in their eyes, the same smile, and I felt the same energy when he shook my hand.

"I've heard so much about you from my sister, Janice, that I feel I already know you."

He spoke with a British accent.

"However," he continued with a radiant smile, "she understated how beautiful you are."

His eyes never left mine as he continued the conversation about London, where he lived. I finally asked,

"Where is Femi, everyone?"

"He is coming with Mother and Father," Bisola said, giving me a strange look.

She makes me nervous, I thought to myself. But I shook it off, not wanting my fears to put a damper on the occasion. Bisola and Aduke were classmates at a private school they attended in London. She told me the stories about them being sent to boarding school instead of going to school in their country. It was not unusual for people who had money to send their children abroad to school from Nigeria. Bisola never finished college; she got married and had a family instead.

As we walked to the place where Femi and the rest of his family stood, Femi looked at me with a soft, tender gaze as he proudly introduced me to his mother and father. I held out my hand and Mrs. Adegoke took it slowly, shaking it firmly. Mr. Adegoke smiled as I welcomed them to America. Femi's mother was tall, but not at all as I had imagined. She carried herself with a royal air. Her medium-brown coloring set off her high cheekbones, so characteristic of Africans. But what caught my attention were the eyes that I saw — they were exactly duplicated in her son. Femi had his father's build and his mother's face. Mrs. Adegoke stood there with a grace that her years had earned her. She could not be more than 49, but she looked 30. She wore her traditional *iro* and *buba*, made from Venice lace, with a dignity that anyone would admire. She topped it off with a head tie that was tied to perfection. I felt underdressed around all of them. Mrs. Adegoke made me feel comfortable, in spite of the somewhat cool reception I felt from everyone else. My diamond ring glistened in the light and Bisola said,

"Umm, what a lovely ring. My brother, you have outdone yourself."

Femi beamed at the remark, replying with a broad smile, "Thank you, my sister."

His mother turned and looked at me with those same eyes as she walked over to her son and began to speak in Yoruba. I determined from her tone that she was

55

reprimanding him. Aduke, hearing their exchange, came over with Tunde and pulled me away from the family scene.

After a few minutes, Femi joined us, appearing flushed and uneasy.

"I'll see you at the house, Janice, after the reception." He pulled me to him and hugged me.

I whispered, "Congratulations, darling," and he kissed me in spite of the crowd. I could feel the family staring at my back. Femi looked at me lovingly...

"See you later, darling."

Aduke came home with me to help get the dinner ready.

"Aduke, what do you think of his family's reaction to me?"

She looked down at the dish she was stirring and began carefully, "Femi's mother is a formidable woman, Janice. She is the one responsible for her husband's success in business. In their village, he owns the largest company there. He exports palm oil and cocoa to other countries."

Femi had never discussed his family and what they did for a living with me, so I was impressed.

"Do you think they liked me?"

Aduke smiled and put her hand on my shoulder, explaining, "We Nigerians don't show a lot of emotion to strangers, Janice. Give them time to adjust to you. After all, you are American."

"What about his sister Bisola? I thought at least she would be friendlier."

"Well, she is another story, Janice. She is not a happy person at times because of her marriage, so she tends to take things out on everyone. Give her time; she will come around."

"Aduke, I feel that Femi is keeping something from me."

"Why do you say that, Janice," she asked, deliberately avoiding my eyes.

"I feel that his family was not happy about our engagement."

"Oh ... I see," Aduke said slowly, and then quickly changed the subject. "Come on, Janice, let's get this food on the table; they will be here soon."

We rushed to finish preparing the dinner. Melinda and Bill were invited, so they would be arriving in a few minutes. I'd just finished mixing the punch when the doorbell rang. It was Bill and Melinda, followed by Femi and his family. I led everyone into the living room and Aduke served drinks. I noticed that Aduke had a cute way of curtsying whenever she served Femi's parents. I asked her in the kitchen about it, and she told me it was tradition to bow before your elders as a sign of respect. Melinda and I laughed, surprised.

"You mean we need to bow to them?" Mindy teased. This was the first time I ever saw Aduke frown. She began angrily,

"Don't make fun of it. If you Americans showed more respect for your elders, maybe there would not be so much crime and violence here!"

"Well, excuse me," Melinda replied in a huff, but we both knew that there was some truth to her words.

"Stop it, you two," I intervened. "She didn't mean anything, Aduke. You know how she feels about African culture after Dele."

Aduke looked coyly at Melinda, who held her arms open to receive her hug and kiss on the cheek.

"Friends again?" I asked, as they both said, "yes" in unison.

We had outdone ourselves; we placed the food on the table and served buffet-style. Femi was the first to dig in as he showered on me a profusion of compliments. We served Creole and traditional Nigerian dishes that Aduke helped me with. Our menu consisted of shrimp jambalaya, étouffée, corn muffins, jollof rice, moyin-moyin, and goat pepper soup. Everyone ate with relish. I was glad that at least everyone agreed about the food, and it *was* delicious. I served cheesecake and coffee for desert. Mrs. Adegoke wanted my recipe for the jambalaya. I told her it had been in my family for generations and that I would be glad to give it to her since we were to be family soon. I noticed a change in her mood after I said that, and I wondered what was going on.

There had been a strong undercurrent from Femi's family all evening. He had tried to make them comfortable. He was the perfect host. I felt he was trying too hard. His father did not say much during the dinner. He just kept looking at me. I would smile at him, and he would nod in return. Femi, Tunde, Bill, and Mr. Adegoke retired to the living room after dinner, while all the women went into the kitchen to clean up. Mrs. Adegoke studied me from a chair, sipping a cup of coffee, as I tried to make idle conversation to lighten the mood.

"Bisola, how are you enjoying America?"

"It is wonderful. I'd love to live here. Aduke wants me to come and stay with her, but I have my children to consider."

Femi's mother was silent, looking at Melinda and me. I wondered what she was thinking about. As I reached to put the last of the dishes away, suddenly she sighed and asked,

"You really love my son, don't you?"

"Yes, I do," I said very deliberately, turning around from the cabinet to directly face her.

"Femi is the first man I've ever really loved."

Melinda broke in, "You have a very nice son, Mrs. Adegoke, and he has been good to Janice."

"Thank you, dear," Mrs. Adegoke replied politely, placing her cup gently on the table.

"I hear you just got married, Melinda. Is that right?"

"Yes, I did", she said, holding her hand so that her ring shone in the kitchen light. Bisola and Aduke surrounded her as Mrs. Adegoke and I looked at each other. She continued talking to me as though the others were not there.

"How does my son feel about you and your culture?"

"Shouldn't you be asking him that question, Mrs. Adegoke," I said shyly. "He says he loves me and wants to marry me," I continued confidently, wondering why she was asking me these questions.

Suddenly she changed the subject. "I like your home, Janice. You have very good taste. Are you from Chicago?"

"No," I answered, sitting down at the table with her. "I was born in New Orleans, Louisiana. My mom lives there."

"Really? I would like to meet her," she said, raising her eyebrows. "Don't you just hate the winters here?"

"Sure," I replied, "but I can live through it because there is nothing more beautiful than Chicago in the springtime."

"I see," she responded as we all returned to the living room to join the others. As we entered the room, Bill and Melinda said they had to leave and bid everyone good night. I didn't want Mindy to go and leave me alone with this family. As I walked them to the door, she whispered to me,

"Hang in there, Janice. The inquisition is almost over."

I smiled uncomfortably. Bill overheard her and said, "You should have seen my mother when she heard I was getting married to Melinda. She was cold as ice and now they are best friends."

He kissed Mindy's cheek to show his happiness with how that turned out. They left, and then I really felt alone.

I walked back into the living room, where everyone was deep in conversation. Femi seemed upset, and his father was looking out the window. They appeared to have just exchanged words — angry words. Aduke was noticeably uncomfortable and shifted uneasily in her chair. She began speaking in a defensive tone, in Yoruba,

"Why didn't you tell me? I'd never have introduced you to her."

Femi looked at Aduke menacingly and responded; "I didn't know I'd fall in love with her."

His mother got up from her chair and joined him, looking at him, trying to calm him down, saying in Yoruba, "Olufemi, you must tell her. It is not right, son that she not know."

Well, all this was just too much for me. I was the only one who could not understand the language, and I was beginning to feel that this conversation centered on me! After a few moments, all of them began to argue in Yoruba. Mr. Adegoke was furious, and Mrs. Adegoke was trying to calm him as well. I looked at Aduke for some help in understanding what was going on, but she turned her head towards the window, so as not to face me. I could see she was very upset and that whatever they were discussing was serious. Tunde walked over to Femi to try to intervene as Bisola yelled, *"Lola nko?"*

A hush fell over the room as if a forbidden word had been spoken and everyone turned their eyes as if to gage my reaction. I walked to the center of the room, wondering why this word, *Lola*, had caused such a silence. Femi was the first to utter a sound by clearing his throat, looking guilty.

"Sorry, Janice. We were just having a family disagreement."

"Why? This is supposed to be a happy occasion. You and Aduke just graduated. Isn't everyone proud of your achievement? I mean you are now Dr. Adegoke."

"We are sorry to spoil your dinner," Mrs. Adegoke said, as she gestured to hug her son.

"Aduke, my daughter, come over here."

Aduke got up and rushed to Mrs. Adegoke, and she hugged her as well.

"Yes, we are all proud of the two of you. No more talk now. Emanuel, I think it is time for us to leave."

Mrs. Adegoke walked over to me, taking my hand, "Janice, the dinner was wonderful. Thank you for all you have done."

After a short silence, Mr. Adegoke said to Femi, "Son, when do you plan to return to Lagos?"

My heart froze. Femi stuttered as he avoided my eyes.

"In a few weeks, Father." Then he added in his language, "As soon as I tie up little loose ends."

"All right, Son," his father said assured, and they shook hands. Bisola walked to the door and looked at me defensively.

"Thank you for the dinner, Janice," she said pleasantly, but uncomfortably. "Hope I see you again."

I reached out to hug her, but she pulled back quickly.

Mrs. Adegoke sensed my confusion and again took my hand and squeezed it.

"Let me know when you set a date, Janice. We will try to come over for the wedding. Come Emanuel."

Femi's father shook my hand coldly and turned to the door. "Thank you for dinner," he said politely and arrogantly as he walked out the door. Aduke and Tunde were the last to leave. She brushed past me without saying good-bye. Tunde thanked me, avoiding my eyes.

"Aduke, call me, girl."

She did not answer and hurried down the stairs.

They had all gone downstairs except Femi. We stood in the hall and looked at each other, neither of us speaking. The silence began ringing in my ears when he spoke apologetically.

"Thank you, Janice, for being patient with my family."

"You are welcome," I said, looking at the floor.

I walked back into the living room and sat down. I was tired. The day had been a long one, and the dinner had a surprising end. Sure, the food was great, but his family did not seem to like me at all. Femi walked over and put his arm around me.

"Janice, I love you, no matter what. You need to understand my culture. Our parents are like kings and queens. They are always in control of everything."

"It appears so, Femi. Your mother seems to control everyone. What was everyone arguing about?"

He put his mouth to my ear, and I could sense his need to be with me, but I was confused and needed some answers. I asked again,

"Femi, why was everyone upset?"

His voice held a solemn tone as he tried to explain his family's behavior. "Janice, my parents are angry with me about our engagement."

I looked at him, confused.

"I can't understand your parents' reaction. I mean, after all, you are 32 years old. Why do you need their permission to marry? I could see that your father did not like me. It was clear that he was angry and disappointed in your choice," I said, feeling badly, twisting the diamond ring on my finger.

"I feel like you are not telling me everything, and that something is going on I should know. What were you all arguing about in Yoruba?"

Femi became noticeably agitated and began pacing the floor. "Before you came into the living room, my father and I were discussing my eventual return to Lagos. I was shocked to hear the words coming from his mouth."

"Lagos! Lagos!" I said loudly. "You didn't tell me you were planning to return home so soon after graduation!"

"I know, Janice, but you knew that was always a possibility," he said arrogantly.

So, I thought, *so Femi shows his other side again. He keeps secrets.*

"Femi, we never discussed this. When you asked me to marry you, I never gave any thought to going to live in Nigeria."

I turned away from him and walked over to the fireplace. I felt I'd been a fool not to get more information from him in the first place. He was always very quiet when we were together. He never really spoke a great deal about his personal dealings outside our relationship. I respected his privacy, but since we were to be married, I needed to trust him, to know him, to understand him, even if we do come from different worlds. Had I foolishly let the joy of being in love and our wonderful lovemaking cloud my judgment?

64

No, better late than never. I needed answers *now*.

Moving over to the window, I looked out at the trees blowing softly in the cool summer night. The moon was shining on the street, and I looked at his car filled with his family waiting for him. I remembered the night Femi and I walked along Michigan Ave. That night seemed so long ago...

"Janice," Femi's masculine voice broke through my thoughts as he came over and embraced me. "Darling," he started softly, "are we fighting?"

Beep, Beep, the car horn was blaring, breaking the magic with impatience. Femi said,

"I've got to go now."

"Oh, yes," I said sarcastically, "Your parents are waiting."

At that, Femi's look darkened.

"You don't have to be insulting, Janice. We'll finish this conversation tomorrow. I'll pick you up around two in the afternoon."

I did not answer, but continued looking out the window. He rushed through the door; I heard his footsteps on the stairs. As I watched him, tears filled my eyes and began to run slowly down my cheeks. I cupped my face with my hands and sobbed bitterly, thinking, *Femi, I do love you so. What has come between us?* I went to bed exhausted and cried myself to sleep.

Early the next morning, Aduke phoned.

"Janice, how are you?"

"I am okay, Aduke. Where is your houseguest, Bisola?"

"She went out shopping with Femi and their parents. They are leaving tomorrow."

"Oh?" I said unenthusiastically. "Aduke, they didn't like me did they?"

There was silence on the other line as she chose her words carefully in fear of my reaction.

"Let me explain, Janice. In Africa, it is customary for the family to meet the bride of the son. In many cases, they choose one for him. That tradition is still being practiced today. Femi's mother was upset with him because he did not give her the chance to pick his wife."

"You mean, they don't let a grown man choose who he wants to spend his life with? What about you, Aduke? Will your family choose a husband for you?"

"Oh, no, no, no," she replied emphatically.

"In my family, we marry for love, and that's what I intend to do. There will be no bride price for me."

I had read about the bride price. In some parts of Nigeria, they still pay the family a dowry for their daughters.

"Aduke, what was wrong with you last night? You did not even say goodbye."

"I was embarrassed by his family's attitude towards you."

So, the argument was about me, I thought.

"Did you and Femi argue?" she asked, concerned.

"Yes," I declared sadly, "and yet, I still have so many unanswered questions. He is very evasive about many things."

"Janice, if Femi has anything to tell you, he will. Femi loves you, and you need to trust him."

"I know that, Aduke, but I still feel uncomfortable with the culture, especially when they speak your language in front of me. I feel just plain left out."

"It will be all right," Aduke said, trying to console me. "Well, love; I've got to go now. Keep your chin up, Janice, and I will call you later."

Chapter 5

I hardly slept at all last night. When I woke upon looking in the mirror, the dark shadows under my eyes told a story of their own. I carefully put on some makeup to cover them and was just finishing when the doorbell rang. It was Femi. We greeted each other cordially. He, too, looked tired; the strain of the past few days had taken a toll on him as well.

"Did you sleep well, Janice?"

"No, Femi, I did not. In fact, I hardly slept at all," I said curtly, turning away and continuing to get ready.

We left for the restaurant and said very little on the way. Once there, even while eating, we were uncomfortable. Neither of us wanted to be first to break the silence. I decided that I'd had enough, so I spoke while we were having our coffee. I asked him about his plans to return to Nigeria and how was I included in those plans. He reached over to my hand that was fiddling with the teaspoon and I looked in his eyes. They were blank. I could not read him as I normally did.

"Janice, I love you, and I know that I have not been fair to you these past few days. My family is leaving tomorrow, and then we can get back to normal."

"Normal? Normal?!"

My voice became louder as I repeated *"NORMAL"* with emphasis! The people in the restaurant began to stare. My nostrils flared, and my lips curled as I tried to hold back the anger that threatened to boil over. I did not want to make a scene in the restaurant. That was not my style, so I got up from the table and said,

"I'm leaving, Femi. When you decide that you are ready to discuss us, give me a call!"

I pulled the engagement ring off my finger, put it on the table, and then ran outside to hail a cab. Femi sat there embarrassed, trying to decide whether to remain or run after me. The waiter brought the check, but Femi just sat there as if in a trance.

"Sir, sir," the waiter spoke to him. "Is everything all right?"

"Oh, yes," he said distracted, and then he picked up the ring, threw money on the table, and ran after me. While I was waiting for a cab, it started to rain. So on top of everything else, I had to get wet too. I saw him coming and took off running down the street, faster and faster, with him in hot pursuit. He caught me easily, holding me by the shoulder.

"Janice, Janice, please listen," he begged "... I don't understand why you are behaving this way."

I was so grateful for the rain because it hid the hot tears that I was crying. We stood there in the rain getting wet. I had no answer for him. I only wished that we could understand each other. Maybe our cultures were incompatible. I finally broke the ice and said,

"Femi, Femi — God —" I cried in anguish. "Why are you so daft? Can't you see I'm hurting?"

He looked at me with confusion. We just stood there, our clothes soaked, and then he touched my cheek with a trembling finger. I was shivering more from emotion than from the cold rain. When I found my voice, I said,

"Femi, let's go."

With that, we ran to his car and drove in silence to my apartment. Once inside the warm, dry living room, he stood there, as if in shock, unable to move, dripping on the carpet, as I rushed into the bedroom to get some towels. He removed his shirt that was plastered to his body. It showed his ever-present muscles and fine physique. I stripped to my underwear and wrapped a towel on my hair that hung loosely, dripping down my back. I quickly pulled on a caftan, one he gave me. He was sitting on the sofa, wrapped only in his towel.

"Give me your clothes," I said and took them to the kitchen to dry on a chair. I returned to the living room and asked,

"Do you want a robe?"

Not that I had one that would fit a 6-foot man. He said no, and then suddenly, as if he regained his senses he shouted,

"Janice, please. I do not understand why."

I sat across from him, my eyes looking at the empty place on my finger where the ring had been. I shivered and continued to stare at him.

"Femi, I feel so lost. It's almost as if you abandoned me. You left me out of every plan and activity that you have had since your family arrived. I feel like a fifth wheel, always in the way. So I decided to make it easier for you. Now you don't have to explain anything to anyone."

He began to move closer; I put up both hands to stop him.

"Janice, please let me explain. I'm sorry; I am so sorry. I never meant to hurt you.

I apologize for my family's behavior towards you."

"Femi, why didn't you tell them how you feel about me? Are you ashamed of our relationship?"

"No, Janice, no. You mean everything to me." His voice quivering with emotion, "I love you as I've never loved anyone before."

His face bore the look of sincerity, but I was not convinced. He moved closer to me, took my hand, but I resisted. He pulled harder with a determined look in his eyes, then with one swift motion, he removed the towel from my hair, and it fell freely, curling around my shoulders. His eyes bore deeply into mine as his hand slid behind my neck, pulling my face closer to his lips.

"Janice," he whispered softly into my mouth, his lips touching mine. "Do you doubt my love?"

I closed my eyes, drawing in my breath as a single tear ran slowly down my cheek. I opened my mouth to receive his kiss, our tongues touched with desire and need as he explored my mouth; my hands went to his chest, so smooth, so inviting. As his kiss became more urgent, his hands found their way under my caftan, seeking my breast. He stood up, all six beautiful masculine feet of him, and the towel fell away. I could see that he was ready to make love. He picked me up while smothering my face and neck with kisses as he carried me into the bedroom. He removed my caftan and laid me gently on the bed and repeated, "Janice, how can you doubt my love?"

Femi began to kiss my forehead, then each eye, his tongue slid down my neck to my breast and on until he reached the other secret places of desire on my body. I arched my back with pleasure as he took total control of me. His kisses set me aflame with passion, until I begged breathlessly,

"Femi, Femi. Don't stop, darling."

"I don't intend to, Janice."

We both burned with insatiable desire, both locked in a struggle to please each other, and receive the maximum pleasure as well. He entered my body and our rhythm was in unison, first slowly, then faster and deeper, our emotions running amok. I moaned with each wave of motion, as the goal of our lovemaking was achieved together.

"Say you love me, Janice," he shouted at its peak.

"Yes, yes, Femi. I love you!"

"Say you want me, Janice. Say you want me."

"Yes, Femi. I want you," I affirmed, and then he began speaking his language.

Any woman alive with a man who makes love to her in this way can understand what he was saying at this moment. I clung to him in ecstasy repeating his name over and over again.

We continued making love through the night and when I awoke in the morning, he was gone, and on my finger was my engagement ring. Femi left a note on the pillow that read: *I had to take my parents to the airport. Be back soon. Love, Femi.* I lay back and thought of our passionate lovemaking. I was tired, but it was a good feeling, and I soon drifted back to sleep.

Later that day, Melinda came by. We were sitting in the kitchen having a soda and

I was filling her in on the events of the past few days.

"Jan, would his change of attitude have anything to do with a woman?"

I put my glass down, almost choking on the drink.

"What makes you think that?"

"Well, some African men can be promiscuous. Remember what I went through with Dele."

"Yes, I agree, but Femi is different."

"How different, Jan. I didn't even know that Dele had another woman until I fell in love with him!"

I could see Melinda was becoming upset with me by the tone of her voice.

"Jan, I cannot bear the thought of you going through what I went through. Don't let good sex get in the way of your good sense. Whatever happed to my sensible, conservative cousin?"

I sat back and thought about what she said. *What if some of these things were signs that there may be another woman?* I broke the silence.

"Mindy, at the dinner after you left, the family was arguing, even Aduke was involved. I have never seen her so mad before. Bisola, Femi's sister, said a word that sounded like a name I heard spoken before. It sounds like the woman who works in the African studies department. You remember her, that Nigerian lady who married Professor Madison."

"Oh, yes, Jan. Isn't her name *Lata, Leila,* or something?"

Oh, my God, I thought as the realization came to me. *LOLA, that is the name she said, Lola! Oh, God. How had I been so stupid? Had I let love blind me to this?*

"Oh, Mindy. Lola ... Lola." I said the name over and over.

"Didn't you ask him, Janice?"

"I tried to Mindy, but he kept evading all of my questions. I can't believe he would do this to me. I was so honest with him."

"Well, Jan. It won't hurt to ask him. Make him be honest with you, girl. Don't be kept in the dark like I was with Dele."

"I'll ask him," I said distracted. "I will ask him as soon as he calls me."

I shooed Mindy out, although she didn't want to leave me so upset. I sat there thinking, trying to put the pieces together. Lola. Could she be the reason for the change in him? I'll ask him when he comes tonight, but the rest of the day, all I could think about was who Lola was.

The doorbell rang, and I knew it was Femi. I had taken a long, hot bath and tried to relax after Mindy left. Our conversation and the realization that his family had been discussing me and another woman name Lola really unnerved me. I dressed in a comfortable caftan and slippers and answered the door.

"Hello, darling." Femi appeared a bit agitated and nervous. I could sense his discomfort.

"Want a drink?" I asked.

"Thank you, Janice. I'll have rum and Coke."

I mixed the drink, and then sat down on the sofa with him.

"Well, Femi, how did it go? Is your family gone?"

He stirred the drink with his finger, and then drank a large portion of it before answering.

"My parents send their regards Janice."

Femi was in his own world of thought. He sat quietly, sipping the rest of his drink, not looking at me. I sat there next to him, watching him, waiting for him to speak, but he was deep in his own thoughts. He was remembering the scene that his parents made on the way to the airport. It was very disturbing to Femi, especially when his mother reminded him of his days in London and the English girl he tried to bring home.

"You must to tell Janice about Lola. It's unfair to keep her in the dark," his mother scolded him.

"Yes, son," Mr. Adegoke jumped in. "Think of the family honor!"

Bisola had listened intently as her parents berated her brother, and then she broke in.

"What's wrong with you, brother? This is not like you at all. I know you love this woman, but she is not Nigerian. She can never understand our culture!"

"So what?" Olufemi responded with annoyance. "Are you saying that if she were a Nigerian, it would make a difference?"

"No, brother, but at least she would understand the culture, and it would be easier for her to accept becoming a second wife."

Mrs. Adegoke spoke softly to her son. "Olufemi, Lola is a good wife. She has waited patiently for two years for you to return to Nigeria. Think of how this news will destroy her."

"I already told her, Mother. I wrote her a letter, explaining everything."

It was as if all hell had broken loose in the car. His father was first to react.

"Eh, eh, haba! My God, what a way to tell someone, Son! I am very disappointed with your methods!" his father fumed.

"Olufemi, you didn't," Bisi cried. "My poor sister-in-law! What were you thinking about?"

Femi kept his hands tightly on the steering wheel, gritting his teeth before answering.

"I felt this was the best way, and I will tell Janice in my time. We are not married yet, and it may not work out."

"Yes, that is true," Mrs. Adegoke started. "But do not wait too long, Son. Janice is also a good woman, and she deserves to know the truth."

With that, the discussion was closed as they drove into the international terminal at O'Hare Airport.

*****

"Femi, Femi," I called, bringing him back to the present. "What are you thinking about?"

"I was just thinking about my parents, Janice. Come over here. I want to talk to

76

you about my culture."

"First, Femi, I have some questions to ask you. Mindy was over last night, and I was thinking about something that happened at the dinner party."

"Go on, Janice," Femi encouraged me to continue.

"Who is Lola?"

He dropped his glass to the floor; the remaining ice, rum, and coke ran onto the carpet. We both jumped up at the same time to get a towel to wipe up the spill. Avoiding my gaze that was fixed intently on him, he wiped up the spill, and then I took the glass to the kitchen. We sat down together. I touched his hand and asked softly again,

"Femi, who is Lola?"

He jumped off the sofa and began to pace the floor, visibly agitated by the mention of that name. Then he began slowly, his voice shaking,

"Her name is Omolola. She is a woman from the village of Ilesha, someone that my parents wanted me to marry. They had arranged for me to be with her when I finish school and returned home."

I sat back on the sofa, stunned by this revelation.

"Janice, until I met you, I never knew what true love could be like between a man and woman. I have never felt like this before. I do not want to live without you. I carry you in a special place right here," he said, pointing to his heart, then to his head. He continued, "You are in here too. I sleep, eat, and live you, Janice."

I was too stunned to speak. Femi continued passionately as he knelt down in front of me, taking my hands in his large ones.

"With you, Janice, I see a whole new world for me, different from the one my parents wanted. In our culture, the son is like the center of the universe. No matter how hard I try to tell my family my wishes, they want me to do things their way."

Femi went on to tell me about the English girl he brought home to marry, and how they had rejected her.

"Was Bisola's marriage arranged too?" I asked, curious to know if he was the only one to be told who to marry.

"Yes, that is exactly why she never finished college! Always remember, Janice. I love you, and no matter what you hear, always ask me first."

"Femi, what about Lola. Do you love her?"

"I love you, only you, Janice, and I want to spend my life with you."

Looking into his eyes, misty with tears, it was impossible not to believe him. I pledged to him that,

"I love you. You are all the man I ever want or need in my life. Without you, I go back to the lonely existence I had before I met you. It was written before time began that we were to meet and fall in love. Together we can face any obstacle that your family may place in front of us. Yes, together we can ...."

Even though he cleared the air about Lola, something inside me kept questioning Femi's answer. I felt I had to be strong like him and support his decision to stand against his parents. At least now I knew why they didn't like me. It all seemed crystal clear.

"Femi, let's plan our wedding."

"Janice, you know I have to go back to Nigeria. I have a job waiting for me with my brother-in-law Taju. Also, my father is getting old and wants me to learn about the business that I will be taking over when he retires."

"So, if we get married, I have to live in Nigeria?"

"Just for a while, anyway, until I get things going as I plan. You can travel home as often as you like, I assure you."

This sounded too good to be true. I could say goodbye to my 9 to 5 job. Life in Nigeria would be a lot different for me than in America.

"So, when will we get married?"

"How about in July?"

"Femi! That's next month. I have so much to do. I've got to call mother and Melinda and ..."

"Whoa, Janice, slow down." Femi's arm encircled my waist. "Right now, all you have to do is to love me."

We spent the rest of the day making love, only stopping to satisfy our appetite for food.

We continued on throughout the night. There was no stopping now — we had finally set a date for our marriage.

I went to work and spoke happily to everyone I met. Aduke came into my office, asking me to join her for lunch in the cafeteria. I told her that we had set the date for the wedding for July 15th. She was very excited for me until I told her that Femi wanted us to return to Nigeria after the honeymoon to live.

"Girl, I knew everything would work out. I am glad to see you smiling, Janice, since after last week."

"Oh, you mean his parents? I know that they don't like me, and Femi explained the reasons why."

"Why?" Aduke asked a curious tone in her voice as her eyebrows rose. "What did he tell you?"

She sat stiffly in the chair as I began to tell her the story about Lola and his marriage arrangement.

"That is what he told you, Janice?"

"Yes, Aduke," I said, wondering why the color was draining from her face.

"Janice," she said nervously, "I've got to go now, but I will meet you in the cafeteria at lunch time."

Aduke could not wait to get out of the room. Standing outside the door, she leaned on the wall. *Damn, damn, damn, that Femi. How could he make up such a lie? I must speak to him.* She walked to the phone in the lobby of the business building, where she dialed the number to his office in the engineering dept.

"Hello, Femi? I need to speak to you ..."

"Aduke," he answered. *"Ba-womi.* I am free now. You can come over to my office."

Aduke ran across campus to his office. She was filled with anger and frustration, wondering what she could do to stop a tragedy in the making. She took a deep breath before knocking on Femi's office door.

"Come in," Femi's masculine voice happily responded. Aduke began to speak before he could offer her a chair.

"Olufemi," she nervously started. "I just left Janice, and she tells me you two have set the date of your wedding for July 15th."

"Yes, that's the day," Femi acknowledged, pretending to be busy shuffling papers on his desk, not meeting her eyes.

"Olufemi, *tani, kilo-de'?* How can you lead her on this way?" she repeated in English.

His happy mood vanished with this direct question. "I don't know what you mean," he answered evasively.

"You don't?" she said angrily. "What about your wife, Lola?"

He banged his fist onto the desk so hard Aduke jumped, startled at the ferocity of his gesture.

"What about her?"

Aduke was trembling when she answered him, "You didn't tell Janice, did you?" she asked accusingly.

"No, no, and no again, Aduke. And neither will you! I love Janice!"

"Yes, I know you do," she said, her voice tinged with sadness.

"No, you don't, Aduke," Femi continued with emphasis, his voice shaking, adamant that he be understood. "I love her as I have never loved anyone in my life!"

Aduke sat down, defeated, and said "Lola *nkọ?* What about Lola?"

"I still care about Lola, but in a different way."

"How different, Femi? They are both women with the same parts!" Aduke said vehemently.

"Yes, but it is how they use them!" he replied arrogantly.

"I see, Femi. How crude. So it's sex that you like Janice for."

"No, Aduke, you misunderstand. With Janice, I fell in love with her, and with Lola, she fell in love with me. Aduke, my marriage to Lola was arranged by my parents, and though I grew to love her, I did not fall in love with her the way I did with Janice."

"So, my African brother, you want to have your cake and eat it too!"

"If that's the way you see it," he said with arrogance.

"Femi, my friend. Janice will find out and grow to hate you."

"Why should she?" he asked chagrined. "She will see that I could have done this no other way."

"Is there is nothing that I can say to stop you, Femi?"

"Ah, Aduke, my friend," he began in a dangerous-sounding tone, "Don't try anything .... Stay out of this, I warn you. Don't interfere. After all, you are the one who introduced us."

"Yes, I did," Aduke, agreed. "But, I didn't know that you were married."

"Oh, stop saying that. Tunde knew."

Aduke stood up, shocked.

"You mean, my brother knew? Oh my God. Why didn't he tell me?"

"He didn't want anyone to get hurt once he found out about Janice and me. You see, Aduke, if you tell Janice, she will be hurt, and you will be blamed."

"Does Lola know about your plans to marry Janice?"

"Yes, I wrote her a long letter."

"How is she taking the fact that her husband is a liar and a cheat?" Aduke spat at Femi.

"Aduke, be careful. After all, I am your senior," he said angrily.

"Femi, when do you plan to tell Janice?"

"I don't know; maybe when we get to Nigeria."

"Nigeria! Femi, are you mad? You cannot wait. If you don't tell her, I will!"

Femi stood up and walked towards her menacingly. "No; Aduke, remember — she will hate you for introducing me to her, as well as you keeping the truth from her all this time."

Aduke sat down in her chair, her ego deflated.

"You see? That is why I refuse to marry a Nigerian man. You do not know how to treat women."

"Really, Aduke?" Femi asked smugly. "Or is it because you are afraid to be a second wife?"

"Damn you, Olufemi Adegoke. I can see you for the person you really are. I have been so blind!"

"What I am is a man desperately in love with a woman and wants to protect her from harm."

"Sure, my friend, I will keep your secret. I love Janice, too, but I know she will never understand a culture that is so unfair to women. I am meeting her for lunch today in the cafeteria."

"Maybe I will join you, Aduke. Shake, truce?" Femi asked, extending the olive branch of peace. They shook hands, even though Aduke knew she was making a terrible mistake. She loved weddings, and she had to admit that she had never seen Janice so happy. Now, come to think about it, she had never seen Femi so happy either.

Making her way to the cafeteria, feeling like a co-conspirator, Aduke saw Janice standing in the tray line.

"Save me a seat, Jan," she called to her friend.

I carried my tray to the table loaded with today's special, meat loaf with rice and gravy.

Mr. Dotson, my boss, was eating with some of the other department managers nearby. He waved at me, smiling, and I waved back. Aduke sat down and told me she saw Femi and that he might be joining us. One of Aduke's admirers, who hailed from Senegal, came to the table and sat with us. He appeared very dashing in his double-breasted suit that accentuated his physique. He had a very strong French accent, which gave him a very distinguished air. The way he was looking at Aduke told me that he was in line with the rest of her suitors. His name was Dominique; he was an archeology student and had just returned from an expedition in Egypt. He was sharing with us all the details of the trip, when I saw Femi walk into the cafeteria. A warm glow spread over my eyes, and they began to twinkle. Aduke did not miss my reaction. Femi joined us after he got his lunch. He was also impeccably dressed in a black suit; powder-blue shirt, and matching tie. We were the only two women in the cafeteria with two of the most handsome men on campus sitting with us. Dominique went on talking about paleontology after speaking to Femi. Femi reached over and kissed my cheek, our eyes were glued to one another.

"You can see that they are in love," Dominique said, looking at Aduke.

She toyed with her food and remarked, "Yes, some people have all the luck."

During our lunch, we talked about our wedding plans and Aduke agreed to be my bridesmaid.

Later that evening, Melinda came over to help me make decisions about the wedding.

"I am glad you reconciled with Femi, Janice. I hope he was able to answer all your questions about his life in Nigeria."

I looked up from my list of things to do and said,"Well, sometimes, Mindy, I still have doubts, but I love him so much that I push them aside."

"Just keep your eyes and ears open, Jan, Where will you be honeymooning?"

"We are going to Europe."

"Really, girl? I am so happy for you," Mindy said, her voice filled with excitement.

"Yes, on our way to Nigeria ..."

"Nigeria?" Mindy said startled. "What? You mean you are going to leave the U.S.A.? What about your family here, Janice?"

"Melinda, calm down. Femi is going home. He has a job there, and he needs to help his father with his business. After all, he is the only son."

"What about you, girl? You are your mother's only child. I don't think she will want you way over in Africa!"

"Mom will understand, Mindy. You know she likes Femi, and all she wants is my happiness. She can come to visit me, and so can you. Femi told me I could come home as often as I like."

Melinda got quiet trying to absorb all of this. "What about the political instability? You know they just had a coup!"

"Femi says that the political unrest rarely affects the average citizens."

"You seem to have all the answers, Jan. I just hope you know what you are doing."

"Come over here, Mindy," then I hugged my cousin.

"Trust me. I love him, and he loves me. I would follow him to the ends of the earth."

"Yeah," Mindy started, her voice filled with skepticism. "Well, Africa is at the other end of the earth."

And with that, we both laughed. I conveniently left out the information on Femi's girlfriend Lola. I guess I did not want to give her more ammunition than she already had to try and change my mind.

The days flew by so rapidly that I barely had time to get everything ready. The invitations went out the next week, and my mother flew in from New Orleans to help with everything from caterers to the gown. The reception would be held in the same hall that I met Femi at, and the wedding would be in the university chapel. The girls at work surprised me with a bridal shower. I received a lot of racy, lacy lingerie and other sexy gifts, as if I needed any. Our sex life was not one that needed any prodding. It was wonderful, but Femi had to practice abstinence when my mom came to stay with me. I missed our lovemaking, and I know he did too. I would have two bridesmaids, Aduke and Sandra Mason, who worked in the next office. We had been friends for a few years. Melinda was to be matron of honor since she was married, and Bill would be her escort.

Tunde Bakare, Aduke's brother, was best man and Dominique Hassan would also be an usher. I picked up my wedding dress from the dressmaker. It was beautiful with lots of lace and chiffon. I would wear a bridal cap with a long train, and my bouquet would be baby breath and African violets. The bridesmaids were wearing yellow gowns and wide brim hats trimmed with daisies. It was to be a perfect summer wedding. The men would be in white tuxedos and have yellow carnations and yellow ties. Femi's tie would be violet with a matching cummerbund to accent my bouquet.

Two days before the wedding, Tunde and Femi were sharing a beer at his house when the phone rang. It was his sister Bisola.

"Bayoni, how are you, Bisi?"

"Femi," she started quickly. "I just got news of the wedding. Did you tell Mom and Dad?"

"Yes, sister, I wrote them a long letter explaining my feelings and telling them of my plans and asking them to come, and if they cannot, then I ask for their blessing."

"Olufemi, you know how they feel about you marrying a foreigner ... Lola came by to see me. She was devastated by what you are doing. My brother, you have not been fair to either of them. Did you tell Janice about her?"

"No, I have not ... I love Janice, and know that she would never agree to marry me and come to Nigeria if I have another wife!"

"I know, Olu, but I believe that you are making a tragic mistake and could end up losing the two of them. Have you thought of that?"

Femi thought about his sister's words and said, "No, I did not think of that, and I will not let you ruin my happy wedding with your gloomy thoughts. We are getting married in two days ..."

"All right, Olufemi. I only hope you know what you are doing. I love you, Brother, and you have my blessings."

"Thank you, Sister. Please try to convince our parents. I will see you in about a month, Bisi, after my honeymoon."

"Brother, I implore you. Please tell Janice about Lola before you come home."

"I will not discuss this again, Bisi. Just drop it," he said with anger." I know what is best for me!"

A defeated Bisola hung up the receiver and went to say special prayers for her big brother. He would need them. Femi returned to his beer and Tunde said,

"I couldn't help over hearing your conversation, Femi. Was that Bisola?"

"Yes, Tunde. She wants me to tell Janice about Lola before we get married."

"Man, oh man," Tunde, cried in sympathy. "That's no good. Janice would never agree to marry you if she knew about Lola. You know foreign women ... had a girlfriend in London like that. I knew she would never agree to marry me and go to Nigeria under those circumstances."

"But, man, sometime I feel so deceitful," Femi said sadly. "I mean, it's hard when you are torn between two women. I gave Lola the option of leaving by telling her first."

"What?" Tunde asked surprised. "You mean you told her? How did she take it?"

"Not so good, actually," Femi answered. "Bisi just told me she was devastated."

"She will get over it," Tunde said. "After all, she is a Nigerian and is from of our culture."

"I hope so, but I know that Janice would never forgive me."

Tunde walked over to the fireplace and leaned against the mantle, looking at a picture of Janice.

"Femi, you may underestimate her. She appears to be a very strong woman. I don't think she would leave you, man, but she may not forgive you for a long time. I know if I were a woman, I wouldn't."

The two men stood silent, each thinking their own thoughts while finishing their beer...

Chapter 6

You could not have asked for more beautiful weather on our wedding day. Melinda and my mother assisted me with my dressing. I looked like a fairy princess on my way to the ball.

"Janice," my mom cried, "you look so beautiful! I wish your father were here to see you."

"That's okay, mother. Uncle Henry will be here to give me away. Melinda's father gave her away and said he was honored to do the same for me."

"It's too bad that Femi's parents couldn't make it," she said sadly.

"Well, Mom, I said they were just here for his graduation, and they sent a telegram. We will see them in Lagos."

With that comment, my mother sat in a chair, a look of sadness on her face; she buried her face in her hands crying, "Oh, God, my baby is going to be so far away."

"Aunt Edna!"

Melinda rushed over to her aunt, trying to console her.

"Don't cry; be happy for Janice!"

My mother then rushed over and held me and kissed me, holding my face in her hands.

"Mom, I love him, and he loves me, and I trust him ... I will be all right; after all, I am 27 years old ... I had to get married one day. Look, you live in New Orleans, and I'm in Chicago. We don't see each other that often anyway ... This way, you will get the

European trip you always wanted. You have to go past there to get to Nigeria!"

"All right, my daughter," she said blowing her nose. "Whatever you want. After all, I have dreamed of this day for many years."

The limousine was waiting as I looked around my apartment for the last time before I took my vows. When I return, I will be Mrs. Janice Marie Adegoke. It sounded good to me as I rushed out the door with Melinda holding my train. By the time we reached the church, the guests had already arrived. The bridesmaids and ushers took their places as the organ began to play the wedding march. Uncle Henry and I stood at the doorway, waiting for our cue. He whispered in my ear,

"Janice, you are beautiful. Two weddings in less than a year. I'm really lucky."

I laughed as we began to walk down the aisle towards the altar. My eyes scanned the crowd, but they saw no one except Femi at the altar, standing tall and proud. He looked splendid in his white tux. I followed Aduke and Sandra as Melinda carried my train. People were whispering that I looked like I was floating on a cloud of lace, silk, and chiffon. As we said our vows, our gaze never wavered ... We exchanged rings and sealed our vows with an endearing kiss. Everyone was clapping and cheering as we ran down the isle to the door and were met by a shower of rice. I looked at Femi and him at me. We smiled for the cameras as we entered the limousine to drive to the other side of the campus for the reception. No expense was spared for the reception. We even had a live band. After all the announcements and toasts, Femi and I opened the floor to the first dance. All the men wanted to kiss the bride. I was flattered. My mom was radiant. One of the professors at the university, Dr. Alex McKinnon, appeared very interested in her. *Mom needed someone now.* I heard her crying as I said my vows in the church. The music played, people danced, and the champagne flowed. Aduke rushed over to me, giving me a big hug,

"Janice, you are so lovely. God, I hope I look this good when I get married!"

"Aduke, all the men you have trailing behind you — it won't be long girl ..."

Someone came at that exact moment and whisked her off to the dance floor. Then Dominique came and asked me to dance. While he held me gently and looked into my face, smiling, I was too happy to notice the disappointment in his eyes when Femi came over to claim me. My new husband put his arm around me possessively and whispered,

"You are mine now ..."

"Yes, darling," I said. "I am yours totally, explicitly yours!"

As the reception progressed, I danced with many of the men. I saw Femi talking to my mother and Professor McKinnon; I was walking their way when Bill and Melinda cut me off.

"You are gorgeous, Janice," Bill remarked, admiring me.

"Your wedding was almost as good as ours," Mindy said with envy.

I laughed and challenged them on that.

"Now, you know mine is bigger, and I have more gifts than you, plus my cake tastes better," and we all laughed.

The time for the bride and groom to leave was drawing near. My boss, Mr. Dotson, came over to the table.

"I am really going to miss you, Janice. I have never had such an efficient assistant. Where will I find another you?"

"I think, Mr. Dotson, I have just the person for you; my cousin Melinda is looking to change her job." At that moment, Melinda ran up to us.

"Did I hear my name?"

"You sure did, Mindy. This is my boss, Mr. Dotson, and I told him you would like to try for my position."

"Thank you, Janice. You're such a great help to me."

"Melinda," he said, turning to my cousin, "drop me your resume on Monday. I will see what I can do for you. Congratulations again, Janice."

Many of the guests were wishing me good luck when Aduke came rushing over to me and asked when I was going to throw the bouquet so the single women could have a chance to catch a husband. At that point, I walked to the middle of the room with a crowd of single women behind me. I closed my eyes and threw the flowers over my back...

Whoosh ..." I got it! I got it!"

Aduke jumped over the crowd and grabbed the bouquet. Femi threw his bride's garter, and Professor McKinnon caught it. I thought to myself, *Way to go, Mom. Looks like you might be next.* Aduke had many men to choose from.

Her present steady, Nelson, could have some stiff competition from Dominique. Dominique would probably romance the pants off her while with Nelson; she would have to run after him.

Femi and I decided it was time for us to leave. I kissed Mom good-bye, and she hugged Femi. We would be leaving tomorrow afternoon for London, the first stop on our honeymoon.

Mom held me tight and whispered, "My baby-girl. I love you, and I will miss you dearly."

"Oh, Mom," I cried. "You know I will miss you too."

"Don't worry, Mom," Femi said politely. "I will take good care of Janice."

"You'd better." Femi held us both and spoke his accent slightly heavy after the champagne.

"My two girls, you are both mine now. Mama, I will take good care of your precious jewel. To me, she is more precious than gold. I will treat her as such."

"Femi," she complained, "Nigeria is so far away!"

"It is only a minute by phone. Think of her as setting a precedent. She will be the first Bordeaux to travel to Africa, the land of her ancestors."

I looked at my charming husband and for the first time, I felt really sure I had made the right decision. I would be the first in my family to go back to Africa, the continent that my ancestors were taken from and forced into slavery. It's an honor not only to be Mrs. Olufemi Augustus Adegoke, but that I am the first one in my family to travel overseas. Our children will truly be the first generation of true African Americans. The thought was thrilling, especially about the children. Femi and I never really talked about having any. We would have plenty of time to do that while on our honeymoon.

We stood on the sidewalk and waved good-bye to all our well-wishers, who then returned to the festivities. We sat exhausted in the limousine. I lay my head back on the leather seat, too tired to feel sexy. Then I looked at the ring on my finger and smiled. Femi was very quiet. He reached over and took my hand and poured me a glass of champagne. We toasted our wedding and were both relieved it was over. Getting married was not easy. I wondered if people have a big wedding to please others or themselves.

We arrived at my apartment, all full of boxes packed and ready for moving. Femi kicked the door open and picked me up in his strong arms, carrying me over the threshold. It felt good to be off my feet as he dropped me on the bed. He fell next to me; I saw he was as tired as I was. He closed his apartment last week, so he had no more packing to do. Tunde was taking care of the small details and seeing that all our personal effects and furniture was shipped to Nigeria. Those things would meet us there when we arrived.

I sat up on the bed and Femi undid the small pearl buttons on the back of my gown. As I stood up, it floated to the floor, leaving me standing in my stockings and bustier. He began to unfasten his tie and took off his jacket, vest, and cummerbund and was standing in his shirt and silk boxer shorts. I liked him just like that; he and I both began to laugh at the same time.

"Let's go to bed, Mrs. Adegoke," he said, calling me by his name for the first time.

"Okay, darling. I'm tired, too. We will have plenty of time to make love on our honeymoon." I watched him remove the rest of his clothing as I took all mine off and slid between the cool sheets.

"Femi?"

"Yes, Janice," he answered as he joined me on the bed.

"We need to consummate the marriage, to seal it."

"Umm-hum ..." he mumbled, as he began dozing off. I shook him, and then tickled his ear with my tongue; he shivered as he felt my warm moist breath on his neck, and he began to moan softly. I ran my fingers gently on his chest and his breathing became heavy ... I thought he had gone to sleep when I felt his hands grab me.

"What are you doing, woman?"

"I am making love to my beautiful husband."

"Men are not beautiful," he said.

"Yes, they are."

As his large hands reached out to touch my body, they made a path to the secret places that he knew only too well. I took control of the moment by climbing onto him. Surprised by my move, he lay there, feeling the passion of my slow movement. When he could lie still no longer, he joined in as the rhythm became fast and deliberate. Our intensity rose until he could stand no more, and we climaxed together in unison, declaring our love for each other. We slept in each other's arms, a lover's sleep waiting for the dawn of the beginning of our lives.

In the morning, we were both rushing to get to the airport to catch our plane to Paris, the first stop on our honeymoon. I took a last, long look around my apartment, saying good-bye to a place that I had shared with Mclinda since I came to Chicago. I said my tearful good-bye as Femi and I took a taxi to the airport. We checked our luggage and sat down in the international waiting room. Femi took my passport and examined it, making sure all my visas were in order. I looked around the international waiting room, amazed at the number of people waiting to travel to many different destinations. There were quite a few waiting to board our flight. I was thrilled with the prospect of going to Paris, London, Rome, and Amsterdam. I looked at my husband and asked,

"Femi, how does it feel to be married 24 hours?"

He took my hand, oblivious to the people in the room, and kissed it. Taking it gently to his face, he held it softly. No words were needed at that moment, for all was said through the tender look in his eyes. Over the intercom, someone was announcing the boarding of our flight. My heart began to beat with excitement as I picked up my carry-on luggage and walked towards the gate to board. I took one last look outside the window at Chicago. *I won't be seeing you for a while, old friend. Take care.* My new husband took my hand, and we entered the plane. The flight from Chicago to Paris was excellent. We sat next to a couple that was visiting Paris for the fifth time. They were telling us all the good places to eat and sights to see.

I was anxious to get there since I had never traveled out of the U.S.A. I didn't know much about Europe, only what I was taught in school. I had so little time to read the travel brochures because I had to prepare for the wedding. We arrived in record time and entered a taxi to our hotel near the Champs-Elysées.

Femi spoke fluent French. I could understand some since I spoke a little, but I mainly spoke Creole. I felt like royalty the way I was treated as soon as we arrived at our hotel. It was as if my American passport made me a true American. For the first time in my life, I really was proud of the good ole U.S.A. Paris was exciting and wonderful for Femi and me. It was a time of delightful discovery and romance. We made love every day, sometimes all day. We were like any typical couple on their honeymoon. I pushed all the thoughts of Lagos and his family out of my head and just enjoyed this time I had alone with him. After Paris came Rome. Our honeymoon went from *Magnifique* to *Magnifico*. We traveled to all the old ruins, visited the Pope, and saw the leaning tower of Piza. I felt as if I was living the history that I was taught in high school. I bought Italian gold and shoes, while Femi loaded up on suits. He bought me gold engraved bangles and told me this is what Nigerian women like to wear. Nigerians come to Italy to buy gold to sell in Nigeria.

"I thought that they had gold in Nigeria."

"No, Janice. They have the finest quality gold in Ghana. The problem with Africa," he continued "is that we have all the raw materials and no industry to process it."

I saw things I had only dreamed of in the past. After a romantic week in Italy, we traveled on to London. Femi has many friends and relatives in London since he graduated from Oxford University. We were to stay with his cousin Bankole. He was married to an English woman name Patty. She was a gracious hostess and was pleased to have one of her husband's relative's visit. She had been to Lagos a few years ago, so I was eager to sit down and discuss it with her. One evening after dinner, the men went off to a pub. Patty and I sat down in front of the fireplace. London summers can be cool. Sipping a cup of tea, she told me all about her visit to Nigeria.

"The weather is very hot and humid, and the people are very friendly."

I asked her if she had met Femi's family. She told me that the only person she met from his family was his sister Bisola, but that she met many other relatives from her husband's extended family.

"You know that they have a large extended family, Janice?"

"Yes, I heard. So how did you like it over there?" I asked.

"Well, it was okay. Actually, I would prefer to live over there, but Bankole refused to stay. We may go after the baby is born. Can I be frank, Janice?" Patty asked, softly wishing to confide in me.

"His family was not too keen on having me marry into the family. Bankole says that they will come around after I have the baby."

I asked her why they did not accept her. She told me point-blank, "Because I am English and white!"

I silently thought to myself that at least I wouldn't have that problem. I told her that I had already met his parents.

"That's good," she said, "because if the family does not like you, well, it can be hard on you."

Patty and Bankole were expecting their first child in a few months. She was a pretty woman, about 25. She and I became instant allies and friends. When the men returned from the pub, rather drunk, Femi wanted to make love, but I turned over and pretended to be asleep. I began to have thoughts about us having our own baby. *Soon my husband, soon, I will make you a daddy, too*, and with that thought, I soon fell asleep.

Bankole and Patty took us to see all the sights: Buckingham Palace, 10 Downing Street, the House of Parliament, Liverpool, Soho, The London Tower, and we took a tour of a real castle. On our final day in London, they gave us a small farewell party at their flat. They invited other couples and friends. It appeared that most of Bankole's friends were married to English women. I only saw one Nigerian couple there, and the wife was not too friendly. Most of the women were white, though a few were of mixed race. They commented that I looked mulatto because of my fair skin and long brown hair. I assured them that I was not. They all were very happy to meet an American Black. They remarked that I was nothing like the images that they saw on television. I began to wonder what their idea of an African American was. I was sure they all held a negative opinion, because they all watched CNN. The party lasted through the night. The next day, when we ready to leave, I thanked Patty and Bankole for their hospitality, and they promised to visit us in Nigeria soon after the baby was born.

We arrived at Heathrow airport for the flight to Amsterdam, where we were to spend a quiet week in a hotel in the heart of the Holland. As our plane began its descent to Schiphol International airport, you could see the fields of colorful tulips in bloom. It was the most magnificent sight I'd ever seen — tulips of every color and shape everywhere. I was amazed that they came in so many colors. The airport van took us to a small guest inn. In Europe, I found out you had to request an American-size bed, as most of their hotel rooms had only single beds. I longed for my king-size mattress.

Femi said we would have all the comforts of home once we reached Lagos at Bisola's house. The Dutch food made me long for Patty's home-cooked meals and London. I didn't care for the heavy potatoes and carrots mixed with sauerkraut. To make up for my lack of appetite for the food, the city of Amsterdam was beautiful and so colorful. Never had I felt so free.

There is something wrong with America, if I have to leave the country behind to feel this way. That is why Femi says he wants to go home. I cannot say I blame him. Once the people here knew I was from America, skin color no longer mattered anymore, only your passport.

The days in Holland were short and our nights long. Femi and I lay naked on our bed at night, not touching, just enjoying being in each other's presence, talking about our love and building our life together. I would remember our honeymoon for the rest of my life. On our last day, we packed and prepared to travel on to Lagos. My heart beat fast as we walked through the airport to board our flight on KLM. I looked around the duty-free shop for a last souvenir to send home to my mother. I had mailed her a postcard on every stop. While we were in flight, Femi surprised me with a little gold locket. It was exquisite, with the words engraved inside, "Janice & Femi Forever." I asked him to put it on me. As he did it, he stopped to kiss my neck. I looked at him,

"Femi, I will always love you."

The flight would arrive in Lagos in five hours, and then we would begin our new life as husband and wife. I couldn't wait.

Chapter 7

The Muslim call to prayer was loud: it resonated from the speaker in the minaret, even slightly overriding the sounds of the taxi drivers honking their horns and bus conductors yelling, *Oshodi, Oshodi* at the bus stop. Sounds could be heard of a cock crowing in the yard and a child selling food in the street, calling *moyin, moyin — ati eko*. She got up, immediately made her bed, walked to the kitchen, and opened the window.

The poignant sounds and smells of Lagos filled the air. A woman and man were fighting in the courtyard, their curses ringing out. The smell of garbage, burning wood, and food frying made her nostrils tingle. Lola shut the window quickly. *"E'karo,"* she says and begins frying plantain and egg, fanning herself in the tiny, hot kitchen. After eating her breakfast, she bathed. As she was getting dressed for work, she heard someone knocking at the door ... *"Tani, tani?* (Who's there?),*"* she called.

"E'mi, Jide (It's me, Jide).*"*

"Good God, Jide, you are early," she said, opening the door.

"Well, I thought I would get a head start this morning on the traffic. But I see you are not ready yet. How are you today, Lola?"

"I'm fine, Jide. I got a letter yesterday."

"Oh, what did your long-lost husband have to say this time?"

She laughed, "Did I say it was from him?"

"Who else, Lola?"

"Jide, Jide, my friend," she teased, "what would I do without you?"

She went into the bedroom to continue getting ready. "I'll be right out; there is some plantain and egg on the stove. Have some."

Lola stood before the mirror, admiring her image. She was 5'5", medium-brown skin, and almost copper in color. She had almond-shaped eyes and a long, slender neck. She wore her hair in braids, hanging long down her back. Her graceful figure was like that of a dancer, which included long, shapely legs and a small waist.

As she put on her head tie and applied her lipstick, the beautiful African woman slipped into her sandals and returned to the parlor.

"I'm ready, Jide."

Mrs. Lola Adegoke stepped into the early morning sunshine in the city of Lagos, Nigeria. Every morning, Jide, her husband's friend, would pick her up and take her to work or wherever she needed to go.

"Jide," Lola asked gaily, "can we stop at the post office today? I want to mail a letter to Olu."

Lola waited for his answer and began to think that lately his replies have been fewer. She was a good wife, who did not question her husband. She knew that one-day, Olu would return to Nigeria and they would continue to live as man and wife. It was time she had a baby. Her hand brushed lightly over her flat stomach.

Lola lived in a one-bedroom flat in Oshodi. It was a far cry from the three-bedroom house, with boy's quarters, that she and Olu shared together before he went to America. He told her this sacrifice was necessary in order that he had enough money to finish his education. She often wondered why he would not ask his father for money, but she never dared to question him. He promised her a mansion upon his return, and they would have a fancy car with a driver to carry her around.

Lola rushed out of the post office after mailing her daily letter and re-entered the car. The Lagos traffic was atrocious. With so many people and so many cars, the government instituted odd and even license plate driving days. Jide had to have two cars so he could drive everyday, which defeated the government's purpose of limiting the number of vehicles on the road. She held onto her head tie as Jide maneuvered the car into the traffic.

She worked at the Ministry of External Affairs as secretary to the director of Planning. Jide looked at his beautiful friend, who appeared so cool and calm for a woman who had not seen her husband for over two years. *Olu is a good man,* he thought. *He will return soon.* Jide dropped Lola at her office. She walked slowly up the stairs, smiling and spreading good cheer to all.

"*E'karo, sir, e'karo, ma* (Good morning, everyone)."

Alhaji Mohammed Yaro, her boss, was not in yet. She prepared tea for him and looked through the mail, hoping for a letter from Olu. On her desk was a picture of her husband. She sat down and picked up the picture.

"Oh, Olu, *eku-jo meta — oju- yin- niyi* (I do miss you, so please, hurry home)."

The air-conditioned office was very comfortable after a hot night in her flat. Lola knew that things would be better for her when her husband came home. *No more suffering and pretend smiling for me,* she thought. She sat there looking at his picture, remembering him — so strong, good-looking, and such a good lover. He could make her shiver with desire. She closed her eyes remembering the passion they shared, and it made her lips moist. A tear fell from her eyes; she brushed it away with her finger.

The wedding ring shone brightly on her finger as she daydreamed about her wedding to Olu. Then Alhaji Yaro arrived, so she shook herself back to reality.

"Sannu, Lola (Good morning, Lola)."

"Sannu, sir (Good morning, sir). *Lafiya*? (How are you?)" Lola arose and took her boss his tea, bringing with her the mail and messages.

"Lola, you look lovely today. Isn't that a new wrapper?"

"No, sir. It's the same one I wore last week," she said blandly.

His eyes were all over her, savoring the curves she had under the wrapper.

"Have you heard from your husband lately?"

"No, I haven't," she answered suspiciously, never knowing what he would say next to try to aggravate her.

Alhaji went on sarcastically, "I'm sure he is busy with all those beautiful American women. You know, America has some of the prettiest, most sophisticated women in the world."

Lola turned, stunned, and looked at the boss who was baiting her. She was angry that he would assume that Olu was unfaithful! He did not even know him!

"Sir, I'd appreciate it if you would not make references to my husband's fidelity in the office."

"But Lola, you are such a beautiful woman to be wasted on a man who won't even take the time to write."

With that, Lola ran from the room. She did not want Alhaji Yaro to see her tears. She ran into the ladies' room and pleaded silently, through her tears, *Olu, Olu. Is he right? No, I could not even bear the thought of you and another woman. I miss you so. Please, please, hurry home*, she prayed, then wiped her eyes.

Alhaji Mohammed Yaro was attracted to Lola, even though he already had three wives. His religion allowed him one more, and he wanted Lola. Every day he had to exercise self-control when she walked into the office. He wanted to take her right there, on the floor. It took a while for him to recover after being so close to her.

That Mr. Adegoke is such a fool, he thought, *to leave this beautiful woman alone with no one to hold and caress her at night. How I'd like to make love to her*. Alhaji Yaro was deep in his thoughts when the phone rang. Lola was just returning to her desk.

"Long distance for Mrs. Adegoke," the operator said. He called Lola on the intercom. "You have an international call on line two."

"Thank you, sir." Lola cleared her throat before she spoke.

"Hello, Lola. *Ekaro, se'dada, ni, adupe?* (How are you, Fine I hope?)"

She beamed with happiness as she answered, "Olu, I was just thinking about you. Congratulations, darling, on receiving your doctorate degree. I wish I had been there to see you graduate," Lola chirped excitedly on the phone.

"So do I," he replied. "Are you alright, Lola?"

"Yes, I am fine, Olu; just lonely and missing you terribly."

"I called to let you know that my mother and father will be arriving tomorrow."

"Good. I will go and see them," she replied.

"Lola, I am sending something for you and Jide, so pick it up from them. By the way, have you received my last letter?"

"I got one yesterday, but you wrote it three weeks ago. I have not checked today's mail yet, darling. When are you coming home, Olu?" she asked, caressing the phone lovingly.

"Soon, Lola, soon." She sensed something in his voice. He appeared very distant.

"Olu, is everything alright?"

"Yes, Lola, just missing you. Shouldn't it be okay?"

"Oh, yes, yes, darling," she replied. But she was not convinced.

"I have to go now, Lola. Oh, by the way, Bisola is coming tomorrow, but on a different flight. She is stopping off in Rome for some shopping."

"Okay, Olu. I will try to see her as well. Darling, I miss you desperately; please hurry home. Lola is waiting for you. I love you."

"Me too, Lola," he replied quickly, not returning her endearment in his usual way. His tone was casual, like the words of his last few letters. She sensed that something had changed, but shook the feeling off, determined that it would not spoil her day. "Lola, give my regards to Jide and others," he continued, trying to keep things cheerful.

"Alright, my darling," she said. "Take care ... *Odabo* (good-bye)."

Then the line went dead. ... Lola sat there as if paralyzed. Something had changed.

Was it something in his voice? He did not tell me he loved me. Alhaji Yaro buzzed on the intercom, bringing her back to the present.

"Yes sir?" she replied.

"Lola, will you come here please."

She got up and fixed her head tie and wrapper, thinking, *Could Alhaji be right? No, no, not her Olu.* She entered his office and sat down.

"Lola, was that call from your husband?" he asked prying.

"Yes, Alhaji, he sends his regards to you."

"You seem upset. What did he say?"

Lola became angry at his questions, knowing full well what his motive was. "Nothing, sir," and she rushed out of the office.

That evening at home, Lola sat on her sofa, thinking about her phone call. A lonely tear slid down her cheek. *I've been a good wife,* she thought. *I have waited patiently for Olu to return, and I will continue to wait, no matter how long it takes him to come home.*

With that thought, Lola stood up and brushed the tears from her eyes and stretched. Her body, firm and ripe, needed Olu. *Kilo se'?* (Olu, why have you forsaken me?)

*****

Early one morning there was a knock at the door.

"Tani? (Who's there?)" Lola answered, not expecting anyone.

109

"E-mi Bisi. (It is I, Bisi.)"

Lola rushed to the door, her slippers flapping on the tile. She opened the door and to her surprise, there stood Olu's sister, Bisola. They embraced, jumping and laughing.

"My sister, how are you? How was the journey?"

Bisola walked into the parlor and sat in a chair, still tired from her international flight.

"I want you to tell me everything, Bisi. How is Olu? And what about Mom and Dad?"

"Hold on, sister-in-law; wait till I catch my breath." Bisola, holding Lola's excited hand, tried to calm her down, then began to tell her about the graduation and showed her the pictures.

"I wish I could have been there." Love and beauty shone brightly on Lola's face as she looked at the picture of her husband receiving his doctorate degree. There were many strange people in the photograph.

"Who is this, Bisi?" she asked, pointing to a photo of Professor Langston.

"I think that is one of his professors," she replied.

Lola continued to look at the pictures until she came upon one with the whole family in it.

"Look at Aduke and Tunde. They look so different. And who are the other women in the picture?"

Bisi took the picture, thinking that she had been careful not to leave in any pictures with Janice in the bunch. But evidently, this one slipped through.

"They are just some of the people that work at the university," she answered as casually as possible.

Lola was remembering Alhaji's comment about the beautiful American women; the thought gave her chills as she looked at the picture.

"There are many beautiful women there," she said admiringly as she looked at the photograph, and then put it away.

"I wish I had been there," Lola said dreamily. Bisola looked guiltily at her sister-in-law, thinking how she really had the right to know everything. But she thought, *who am I to tell her? I am sure my brother would never forgive me. He was already angry that I mentioned Lola's name at Janice's house.*

"Bisi," Lola said softly, "a penny for your thoughts."

Bisola blushed. "Oh, it is nothing."

"How are your children and Taju?"

"They are all fine, Lola. I heard that Taju has been spending time in the village with his other wife while I was away."

"Is that so?" Lola said, surprised.

"Yes. I married this man because of my family, and look at him now — he is not even loyal to me."

"Bisi, I am so sorry," Lola began, trying to console her sister-in-law.

"I know it has not been easy for you having to share your husband. Yet, you are

111

blessed with two lovely children. I mean, look at me. Your brother has been gone for over two years, and I have no baby to love. When he comes home, that is the first thing I am going to do."

"What is that, my sister?" Bisi asked.

"Have a baby, Bisi! Have a baby!" With that, even Bisola laughed at the innocence with which Lola made that statement.

"Come, my sister," Bisi said with some relief. "Let's drown our sorrows with some shopping at the market."

The two women left Lola's flat, each dressed in a colorful wrapper. They decided to go to the Central Market on Lagos Island.

The driver maneuvered the car through the narrow roadways leading to the open-air market. You could smell the food from the vendors, hot and steaming. There was fresh fish and vegetables arranged neatly in each of the trader's stalls, and people hawking their wares on their heads. The two women were not interested in buying groceries, but in indulging their taste in clothing. They arrived at the clothing section, walking slowly through the stalls of women selling colorful *ankara* cotton prints and lace material imported from Europe.

"What will you buy, Bisi?" Lola asked, unable to make a choice.

"I don't know yet," she replied, fingering some white lace material.

"This would make a fine dress, don't you agree, Lola?"

"Yes, it would be lovely, and how do you think this cotton would look on me?" Lola asked, holding a colorful material of red and green hues in front of her.

Suddenly, a different voice responded, "That will make a good wrapper, Lola." Lola turned, startled by the voice that answered her instead of Bisi's.

"*E'kabo*, Kemi? (Is that you, Kemi?)" Lola asked with pleasant surprise.

Kemi Afolabi was a good friend of Lola's. They had known each other since they were children. Both were from the same hometown.

"Kemi let me introduce you to my sister-in-law, Mrs. Bisola Balogun."

"Pleased to meet you," Kemi said cheerfully. Lola told her that Bisola had just returned from her husband's graduation in America.

"How nice," Kemi said. "How is Olu?"

"He is well, Kemi, anxious to come back to Nigeria and his wife," Bisi lied. "Listen, Lola, I've got to run now, but I'll see you later."

"Okay, my sister," said Lola. "*O'daro.* (See you later.)" Kemi and Lola hooked arms and walked towards a food vender.

"Let's eat some yam, Lola," suggested her chubby friend, who could not pass up the delicious scent of the food in the market.

The women took their lunch and sat down under a shady palm tree, eating the yam with relish and finishing it off with a bottle of orange Fanta. The ocean breeze was blowing cool air, but it was still hot and humid.

"So your husband has finally graduated, Lola," Kemi said through a mouthful of yam.

"Why didn't he take you with him? It would have done you good if you had gone with him instead of slaving on that job. You could have taken a course or two yourself."

Lola looked at her chubby friend, who was very critical of everything and everyone, and answered quickly, telling her that Olu said that there would be no place for her to stay, and we needed to save the money.

"Anyway, I like my job at the ministry," she answered defensively.

"You mean with Alhaji Yaro," Kemi remarked sarcastically. "Is he still chasing you?"

Lola blushed, looking down, admitting, "Worse than ever. The man is determined that I should leave Olu and become another wife in his harem!"

"I heard he already has three wives," Kemi teased, "but listen, he has a lot of money too."

"So all you can think of is money, Kemi? What about the other women?"

Kemi smiled and thought about what she would do if Jide were to have another woman. Kemi and Jide were engaged to be married.

"Jide would never do that to me, Lola."

"Are you sure, Kemi?" Lola teased her friend, her brown eyes glowing with mischief.

Kemi put a chubby finger to her cheek thinking out loud, "Come to think of it, I did see him the other day with a beautiful woman in his car."

"What did she look like?" Lola asked, trying to hide her smile. "Was she tall and good-looking?"

"Yes, and she looked a lot like you, Lola Adegoke!"

They both laughed at that and continued eating their yam, watching the people walking by in the afternoon heat. After lunch, Kemi began on a more serious note.

"When is Olu coming home, Lola?"

"He said soon — I spoke to him last week — but he has to tie up a few loose ends. I'm worried, Kemi. Olu was so evasive, and he sounded so different over the phone."

"Look, my friend, you have not seen him for a few years, and maybe he has been messing around."

"Heavens, no! God forbid. He loves me, Kemi." Lola was frightened at the thought. "He's true to our marriage."

"Come on, Lola, grow up," Kemi said, exasperated. "Olu is a grown man. How many Nigerian men do you know that are faithful?"

Lola tried to think, "Well, there is ... uh ... and uh ..."

"See, cannot think of any, can you?"

"Jide!" Lola yelled, and Kemi laughed.

"He'd better be," she said. "You know, Lola. Those American women may have mesmerized Olu with their charms. You know they are so different from us."

"Kemi, stop it, I don't want to hear anymore, and you are beginning to sound like my boss."

"Lola, I am trying to get you to wake up and stop being so naive."

"But, but ..." and the tears began to fall. "Kemi, Olu must return. I love him so."

"Here, Lola, take my handkerchief and dry your eyes, girl. He is coming back. After all, he is your husband."

At that point they took a taxi home.

Chapter 8

The next day, Lola boarded a taxi to take her to Surulere. She was going to visit her in-laws in Lagos. Her anticipation was high since they had requested to see her. She decided to wear the dress that Bisi had brought her from Rome. She looked like a page from a fashion magazine. Her dress, matching shoes, and accessories brought out her copper color, so that as she left her flat, she attracted a lot of attention. Her hair was hanging in braids, uncovered today, since the dress she was wearing was western-style clothing.

She rode quietly through the traffic, still disturbed by her conversation with her friend Kemi at the market. It really upset her, and she had a hard time sleeping. Lola had tossed and turned in her bed, dreaming about Olu and other women. A herd of goats blocked the road as the taxi tried to go around them. Lagos was a mixture of both old and new traditions; sometimes like now, the two would clash. It was not uncommon for a herd of cows to be on the freeway. She reached her destination and paid her fare.

Lola walked sprightly to the door and rang the bell. The houseman welcomed her inside. Lola greeted her in-laws in the traditional African way, by kneeling down on the floor, respectfully.

"You must be thirsty after your long ride," her mother-in-law insisted.

"Yes, Ma, I am. It is very hot today."

"Kubi! Kubi!" Mrs. Adegoke called her maid.

"Come and bring coke and Fanta for us to drink."

The maid returned with two bottles of soft drinks, and Lola settled down in an overstuffed chair. Her mother-in-law had gone into another room and returned with a large box.

"This is for you, my dear, from the two of us."

Mr. Adegoke sat quietly on the sofa, looking at his daughter-in-law. His wife also gave Lola a letter from Olu. Lola fingered the letter, anxious to leave and read it in private.

Olu's mother said, "Lola, you are a good wife. I know you must miss your husband very much."

"Yes, yes, Ma."

Olu's father just sat by the window, still looking at Lola, not speaking. Mrs. Adegoke continued talking, seeing that her husband seemed to be at a loss for words.

"Our son made a wise decision when he married you."

At that comment from his wife, Mr. Adegoke closed his eyes and frowned, thinking to himself, *Oh, my son, why do you want to hurt this girl?* He pursed his lips and opened his eyes, still thinking, *I never thought my son would do this to a woman.*

Mrs. Adegoke broke into her husband's thoughts, "Emmanuel, are you alright?"

He cleared his throat before speaking. "Yes, dear, I am; just a slight headache. Lola, Olufemi is well and sends his love. He should be returning to Lagos in few weeks. We just wanted to say hello, and see how you are getting along before we return to Ondo state," Mr. Adegoke said, thoughtfully.

"Thank you very much," Lola said happily.

"I want to ask you, sir. Is everything alright with Olu?"

"Why do you ask, my daughter?"

"When I last spoke to him, he sounded worried. Surely all he has to do is pack his belongings and come home to me. I am so lonely; even my job is no longer fulfilling. I long to see him. Can't you tell him to come home now?" Lola asked, her eyes filling with unshed tears. Mr. Adegoke, touched by her display, got up and walked over to her. He put his large arm around her. He was a tall man, like his son, and towered over his daughter-in-law.

"It is not that simple, my dear. Olufemi has a lot of business to take care of before he comes home."

He held his weeping daughter-in-law, looking guiltily over her shuddering shoulders at his wife, who sat down, feeling defeated, wringing her hands. Lola continued to sob,

"Sir, it has been two years since I last saw my husband. What is keeping him in America?"

Mr. and Mrs. Adegoke exchanged knowing looks. Mrs. Adegoke rose and took Lola into her arms.

"There, there, my daughter," she cooed, as she attempted to comfort her like she was a small child.

"Oh, Mom, Mom. I do love him. I am sorry I lost control."

"It is okay, my daughter. It is to be expected of you, who have been so patient."

"I think I'd better be going now," Lola said as she blew her nose with her hanky and wiped her eyes.

"Emmanuel, will you call Lola a taxi."

Mr. Adegoke stepped out into the air. It felt good to be away from the tension in the parlor. *It is so hard being a father*, he thought to himself; *sometimes your children can downright disgrace you.* Mrs. Adegoke walked Lola to the gate and the waiting taxi. Her father-in-law gave her five hundred *naira* and said,

"Lola, be patient. It will soon be over, and Olufemi will return to you."

"E'se (Thank you), Father."

"You are welcome, my dear. Olufemi is a good son; he will not disappoint you."

Lola entered the taxi saying, "Good-bye; have a safe journey to Ekiti."

Mrs. Abimbola Adegoke took her husband's hand for support, "Oh, Emmanuel, what have we done?" He looked at his wife, sharing her concern.

"God will provide, dear. We have done all we can do."

"Emmanuel, we didn't tell her about Janice!"

"It is not our place to be our son's messenger!" he said angrily.

"Lola is a grown woman and a dutiful wife," Abimbola said sincerely to her husband, continuing, "I agree that we have no right to destroy her love for our son, but Emmanuel, we have betrayed her by keeping silent. I feel so guilty."

"No, my wife, we have not — our son betrayed her by not seeking her permission to marry another wife!"

"You are right, as always, Emmanuel. We'd better leave it in God's hands."

The taxi sped along the highway, seeming to take forever. Lola sat back in the corner, looking out the window at the familiar landscape, seeing nothing, only thinking about Olu. His letter was the same as the one she got last week. It was very short and said nothing of his plans. She arrived at the flat carrying the box and met her friends waiting outside.

"Hello, Jide and Kemi."

"Lola, where have you been?" Kemi asked. "We have been waiting outside for 30 minutes!"

Lola smiled at her girlfriend's impatience. "I was visiting my in-laws. They are going back to Ondo state tomorrow, and I went to greet them."

"Did you ask about their wayward son?" Kemi asked, her voice tinged with sarcasm.

"Haba, Kemi," Jide said, taking up for his friend Olu. "Don't say such things, woman; Olu is not wayward."

"Then why is he not at home with his wife making babies?" Kemi asked, laughing.

"Will you two stop it and come inside," Lola said, trying to coax her friends to stop bickering.

"Oh, no, you don't, Lola. We came to take you out this evening. Shina Peters is playing at the National Theater, and I've got tickets!" Jide dangled the tickets under Lola's nose. It pleased him to see her beautiful eyes glow and a bright smile on her face showing her dimples.

121

"Jide, my brother, I love you. You know how I love Shina!"

"So hurry up," Kemi said, pushing her friend inside. "Get changed so we can go."

Lola ran inside the bedroom and put on her new lace wrapper and *buba*. She looked in the mirror, satisfied with what she saw, pulled on a new head tie and wore gold trim slippers. Then she picked up her matching bag and ran into the parlor.

"Was that fast enough for you?" She stood in the middle of the room, modeling her new outfit.

"You are fantastic, Lola," Jide complimented. "Olu is a lucky man."

"Yes, he is," agreed Kemi, "and he had better hurry home before he loses you to another man. Is that the lace you bought at the market the other day?"

"Yes, I was saving it for Olu, but I rather wear it now."

Jide put his arm around Kemi and whispered into her ear, "Guess what? You are beautiful, and I am a lucky man as well." Then he shouted, "We are all lucky people tonight!"

*****

The weeks drifted by and still no word from Olu. Lola had to force herself to the office each day. This morning was particularly difficult because today, Alhaji Yaro was extremely persistent. Early this morning, he cornered her and said, with his eyes devouring her from head to toe,

"Lola, you look so lovely today, and your perfume smells so sweet. Have you heard from your loving husband?"

Lola smiled, "No, sir, I have not heard from him, but he will be home soon."

"So you say, so you say," he replied sarcastically, then returned to his office.

Lola took a deep breath and went to her desk to finish typing some correspondence when she found a box with a pretty ribbon on her desk. *It's not my birthday*, she thought, *so who would be giving me a gift?* She carefully opened the box; inside were a pair of gold earrings. They appeared to be 18K gold and had an intricate design unlike any she had seen before. Her eyes shined with the glitter of the gold. She looked around suspiciously, wondering who would give her such an expensive gift. Looking for a card, she felt someone standing behind her, his hands warm on her shoulders, asking,

"Do you like them?"

Lola felt like a mouse cornered by a cat.

"They are beautiful, sir," she answered nervously.

Her boss, Alhaji Mohammed Yaro, hails from the northern states of Nigeria. He came from the Hausa/Fulani tribes of Kano state. He bore the aristocratic look of royalty. A strikingly handsome man, tall like the Fulani, fair-skinned, with soft, curly hair. His mother was a member of the Kano royal family. He was born with a silver spoon in his mouth, and usually got what he wanted. For him, money was no object. He didn't earn his position in the ministry; an uncle in the government gave it to him. He was educated at Oxford, in England, and had homes in Lagos, Kano, and in Paris. His long, slender fingers slowly massaged Lola's shoulders and neck, and then he slid them carefully down her arms. She stiffened, saying,

"Sir, sir, please don't."

"Lola! ..." his voice was soft and excited as he whispered in her ear, "You know how much I care for you. ... These earrings are just a token of my affection."

Lola shivered, "No, sir, I cannot accept them. You know that I'm ... I am ... married!"

He nuzzled his face into her neck, and that brought Lola to her senses. She pushed back the chair with such force that it knocked her boss off balance. Seizing this chance, she bolted to the door. Standing there holding the knob, trying to catch her breath, she looked cautiously at her boss, afraid of his next move. Alhaji Yaro caught himself before he fell.

"Lola, my dear, you know how I feel about you," he pleaded, as he advanced slowly towards her.

"Sir," she cautioned him, "you know how I feel about this. You are a married man with three wives."

"You are right, Lola, but give me a chance with you. My family chose my wives, you know, for me. You know my culture and religion allows multiple wives. I want to bestow on you the honor of being one of them," he said passionately.

"Oh, really," Lola responded with sarcasm.

Alhaji continued to advance towards her with a mission in mind. He reached her, towering over her, looking splendid in his *baba riga* made from guinea brocade. He put his arms around her, pushing her back into the door. She was beginning to weaken, as it had been such a long time since she was this close to a desirable man. Her boss was a very handsome, persistent man, and she was a woman who had been too long without her husband.

God, it felt good to be held, she thought to herself.

"Lola, Lola, I want you," he whispered the heartfelt words into her ear. "My dear, how long has it been, one year, two, since you have been loved by a man? It's so unfair that such a beautiful, desirable woman be unappreciated for so long."

Lola had her face in his chest. It was so hard to resist him, but her heart belonged to only one man. Alhaji's arms caressed her waist and his lips touched her ear, and then slid to her neck. A shiver went through her body, awakening the smoldering fire that had been cooling, and was now beginning to ignite. Lola raised her head to look into his eyes and receive his kiss when — *Buzz, buzz* — the phone began to ring, jolting her back to her senses. She broke away and raced to the phone, leaving Alhaji standing there. Her heart was beating very rapidly as she lifted the receiver.

"Hello, yes, hello, Bisi. When?" she asked with great interest as she reached for a pencil and pad to scribble the message down. The excitement was apparent in her eyes and voice.

Alhaji stood at the door, a crooked smile on his lips as he watched his secretary talking on the phone.

"Yes, flight arriving from Amsterdam at 2:45 p.m. on Thursday. Thank you."

Lola replaced the receiver and picked up the box with the gold earrings. She walked over to Alhaji, who stood there waiting as if he already knew what the call had been about.

"Sir, I need the rest of the day off," Lola said, handing him the box.

There was a knock at the locked office door, and Alhaji opened it. It was the mailman, bringing today's letters. When the mailman left, Lola said,

125

"Sir, I cannot accept these."

"Why?" Alhaji asked dully.

"That call was from my sister-in-law. My husband is arriving tomorrow, from Europe."

Alhaji's smile faded for he knew that his chances for an affair with her had ended.

"I told you he would return," Lola said triumphantly.

"I guess you were right, and I was wrong," he admitted, taking the earrings back.

"What would my chances have been if he didn't come back?"

"Well, I don't know, sir. Maybe I would have gone out with you, but I never could have married you."

"Why not, may I ask?"

Lola began to remind him again of his other wives and that she refused to become a part of that type of marriage. She went on to explain her views on polygamy and how it is sometimes very unfair to women.

"I beg to disagree with you, Lola," Alhaji interrupted strongly. "It protects women from being alone."

"That is a man's point of view, Alhaji," Lola continued passionately. He looked arrogantly at her and said matter of fact,

"Lola that is *the only* point of view that matters in Nigeria!"

He quickly turned and walked into his office with all the dignity he could muster and shut the door. Lola straightened her wrapper and sat down to sort through the mail. A letter from Olu was among the business correspondence. She held it to her heart; as she carefully opened the letter, her hands shaking. It began:

> Dear Omolola,
>
> It has been a long time since I wrote you last. I am sorry I have been so busy. First, I want to tell you that I love you. The graduation was a success. By now, you should have seen my parents and sister. Please give them my regards. Omolola, I am writing you now because something happened while I was in America.
>
> I met an American lady, whose name is Janice. I am bringing her back to Nigeria with me. We are married. I have decided to have two wives. I believe that there will be room in my life for the both of you.
>
> I am sorry to break it to you this way, Lola, but there was no time to do it otherwise. It just happened. I fell in love again. See you when I come home.
>
> Love,
> your husband Olu

When she first started reading the letter, Lola's heart began to beat with desire and affection for her husband. .But as she continued reading, she found herself catching her breath and holding it, afraid to read on. She took a deep breath and continued reading. When she finished, she just sat at her desk, her hands trembling, her arms shivering, her lips parted in shock. Her eyes blurred from the unshed tears that filled them and then they began to run over. She wiped them roughly with the back of her hand. Her tears spotted the page of the letter, making the ink run.

Lola sat in her chair stunned, re-reading the words **I have decided to have two wives**, — just like that — no discussion. *I waited for you, Olu, two years*, she thought, *two long and lonely years, and this is the thanks I get for being faithful.* She looked at the wedding ring on her slender finger, turning the band around. She angrily asked herself, what is this for? She took the ring off and threw it at the wall, grabbed her purse, and ran out of the office, down the stairs, and into the street. As she kept running, her head tie came loose. She ran like a madwoman, not caring if anyone saw her — running, screaming, and crying. She kept running until she fell in the street. A stranger asked her,

"Can I help you, Ma?" She just kept screaming and tearing at her hair, "Why, why, Olu, why?"

Most people stayed away from her, thinking she was either possessed by the devil or demented. She was sitting on the curb when a hand touched her gently, and she heard the sound of a familiar voice.

"Lola, Omolola, what has happened to you?"

"Kemi, Kemi, Kemi," was all she would say.

"Lola, what has happened?" Kemi demanded, shaking her friend. Kemi was on her way to meet Lola for lunch. When she saw her running down the street, she followed her, but Lola was too swift for her chubby friend. Kemi sat on the curb, trying to catch her breath, holding her friend's head in her lap, trying to understand what had happened. She saw the letter in her hand and took it. Upon reading the disastrous news, she exclaimed, *"Kai, Kai, now wayo*, that devil. How could he do this to you? No word until now — just this letter? Oh, God. Oh my God, Lola! I have got to get you home."

Kemi struggled with her hysterical friend, trying to get her on her feet. She hailed a taxi and pushed her into the cab with the driver's help. Lola just kept moaning,

"Olu, Olu ..."

"Where to, Madame? Luth hospital?"

"No, take us to 22 Adame Street in Oshodi."

The taxi sped towards Lola's flat. She was semi-conscious and lay in Kemi's lap mumbling,

"Olu, why? Olu why?"

Humph, Kemi thought, *what kind of man would hurt his wife this way?*

Kemi paid the fare and, with the help of the driver, got Lola into the flat. They lay her on the sofa, and then Kemi went into the kitchen for a towel and cold water. She began sponging her delirious friend's face and forced her to sip some water. Lola gagged and was almost sick when Kemi spied a bottle of wine and poured a glass.

"Here, my friend, drink this. It will make you feel better."

Lola slowly sipped the wine. It felt warm and soothing in her throat. As she finished the glass, Kemi poured another. She felt her body begin to relax. Soon the shivering stopped and some of her pain began to subside. There was a knock at the door, and Jide rushed into the room. He looked at Kemi for an explanation.

"Kai, Kemi, kilo-se'? (What happened, Kemi)? I got a call from a friend who works at the ministry. He was concerned when he saw Lola running and screaming in the street."

Lola looked at Kemi and Jide then put her hands on her head and began crying hysterically again, *"Eg-bami-o! Eg-bami-o!"* wailing in the Yoruba women's age-old way of expressing grief. She began pulling at her hair and clothing, tears streaming down her face repeating,

"Olu, why, why?"

"What has my friend done, Kemi?" Jide asked. "Is he dead?"

"No, no, Jide," Kemi said, trying to speak over Lola's wailing.

"Look at this letter he wrote to her."

While he read the letter, Kemi tried to console her friend. She held Lola's slender body, racked with sobs. When he finished the letter, he stood there silent, thinking that it all added up.

"I can see now why Olu delayed his return. I cannot believe it. I cannot believe that he would do this to Lola, and with an American woman."

"Oh my God! What a disgrace to you, Lola. My heart goes out to you."

Then suddenly, Lola stopped crying.

"Heart," she said vehemently. "What is a heart? Your friend, Jide, has taken a dagger and cut mine out and fed it to the vultures! Heart!" she laughed dangerously. "What heart?"

"Lola," Kemi said, frightened by the behavior and tone of her words. "Lola, are you alright?"

Lola looked straight ahead, eyes burning like a madwoman and said passionately, "I do not know why Olu has chosen to take this path, but I am going to find out what happened in America to change him so."

"How will you find out, Lola?" asked her friends...

"Tomorrow morning, first thing, I am going to see my sister-in-law Bisola and see if she can shed any light on her brother's change of attitude. Until then, I am going to rest. I will need all my strength to get to the bottom of this."

Lola got up and walked unsteadily to the door, opening it. "Thank you, Kemi and Jide. I will be alright, but I need to be alone now."

Her friends looked at each other, unconvinced that Lola would be all right. However, they saw she wanted to be alone and they left. They knew Lola was a strong woman and were sure she would do no harm to herself. After they left, Lola showered and lay in her bed alone, feeling really alone for the first time since Olu left for America. Her ring finger was sore where she had pulled off her wedding band with anger. She turned her head into the pillow and thought; *maybe if I had given you a child, this would not have happened. You could have waited, Olu.* The broken woman cried herself to sleep, curled into a little ball in the middle of her bed.

Chapter 9

The taxi drove through the heavy traffic to Ikoyi, where Bisola and Taju lived elegantly among the affluent in Lagos Island. The couple lived there with their two children. Taju owned several businesses that processed raw materials into products used by the country. He was a wealthy man and also had interests in Europe. The taxi sped past luxurious mansions. They belied the poverty that was rife in Lagos. The beggars and homeless people nearby stood out in stark contrast to the opulence of Ikoyi.

Lola was anxious to reach her destination. She had many questions to ask her sister-in-law about her husband. Bisola had made a good marriage and she knew it, though sometimes she wished she could have finished school like Aduke. But she banished the thought because she had two lovely children and a rich husband. She was relaxing poolside with the children when her steward informed her that she had a visitor.

Bisi pulled on a caftan and rushed to the parlor. After their formal greeting, Bisola said to Lola, "Sister, you look tired. Have you been sleeping well?"

"I could sleep better, Bisi, if I had been told the truth!" Lola answered in anger, gritting her teeth. Bisola held her breath for an instant. Then she placed her hand on Lola's shoulder.

"What truth?" she asked.

Lola shook off her hand so violently that Bisi was stunned by her reaction.

"What is this, Bisi?" She took Olu's letter, torn and tearstained, from her handbag.

"What happened to Olu in America?"

"What do you mean, my sister?" Bisi said cautiously.

"Here, read this!"

She thrust the crumpled page into Bisi's hand. Bisi read it and slumped onto a sofa.

"Oh, Lola, I am so sorry."

Lola was angry and hurt. Her eyes were blazing. "You knew? You mean, you knew all along?"

Bisi stood up. Her mouth fell open and shut, but no words came out ... "I ... I ... I ..." she stammered, before finding her voice.

"I did not feel that I should be the one to tell you," she finally said, wishing the ground would open up and swallow her. "My brother should have told you the truth, not I," she said apologetically.

"Bisi, Bisi, you kept this from me. And that lets me know how much you really care for me," Lola exclaimed, feeling abandoned and betrayed.

"So the wife really is always the last to know."

Bisi began to talk more openly about the trip and graduation. "Listen, all I know is that we were invited to dinner at this friend of Aduke's house after the graduation. The *oyinbo* (foreign American) had prepared this elaborate dinner for the family. Olufemi and Dad had a very heated argument at dinner about you. Olufemi was adamant that he was going to have the two of you, and he would not leave America without her."

Lola sat down in a chair, feeling gutted. "What does she have that would turn Olu's love away from me?"

"Lola, I don't think she even knows about you," Bisi said ruefully.

"Really?" Lola asked surprised. "Well, she should know better than to take another woman's husband!"

"No, Lola, I do not think she knows about you at all!"

Lola's eyes became wide with amazement as Bisola's words sank in.

"You mean she does not know he is married?" she asked, incredulously.

"Yes, that is exactly what I mean, my sister!"

Lola sat back in the chair bewildered. She looked at her bare ring finger sadly. It was as if she did not know the man she was married to anymore.

"Look, Lola, I am sorry about the terrible way my brother has treated you; but believe me, we did not intend to keep you in the dark. We love you, and we believe that he should have told you about the woman before now."

"How long has he been with her, Bisi?" Lola asked sadly.

"I think since early April."

"They will be here tomorrow, Bisi. Do you believe that they are really married as he said in his letter?"

"I do, Lola. Janice does not appear to be the type of woman who would travel across the world without a commitment."

Bisi carefully omitted the fact that her brother and Janice had a very big wedding and were coming to Lagos on the last leg of their month-long honeymoon. At the mention of the English name, Lola looked closer at Bisi.

"Her name is Janice?" Lola asked. "What does it mean? What is she like Bisi?"

Bisola rose and went into her room, returning with the photographs she had shown Lola on her last visit.

"Remember this picture, Lola? Janice is the one next to Olufemi."

Lola took the picture. Her hand began to tremble as she looked at Janice.

"She is lovely," she said, as she stared at the photo of the woman with the long, light-brown hair and fair complexion. There was no denying that Janice was beautiful.

"I can see why he wants her," she said softly.

All the anger had gone from her voice and was now replaced with dismay.

"Bisi," her voice began to break, "how can I compete with this woman? She looks cultured and educated. What does she do; does she work?"

Lola's tears began to fall uncontrollably.

Bisi cleared her throat, "She works at the university that Olu graduated from. She has a lovely home and was a gracious hostess, even though we were not very friendly. She went out of her way to be nice. Lola, it was a shock to see my brother with another woman."

Lola sighed deeply and gave the picture back to her sister-in-law.

"What are you going to do, Lola?"

Lola walked over to the window, looking out at the garden. She turned to Bisi and asked,

"What would you do?"

Bisola took a few seconds to answer, searching for the right words to say to her sister-in-law. "I understand how you feel, Lola. Remember, I am a second wife, and even though I knew about Taju's other wife, I still did not want to share him. I am able to manage because Taju keeps her away from me in the village. So I don't have to live with her. Still, it is not easy. Everyone knows that I am the *Iyawo* (junior wife), and she is the *Iyale* (senior wife)."

"Bisi, Janice is not one of us ... She is not Nigerian! I do not even know any Americans. I have decided to go home for a while to see my mother."

"Do you think that wise, Lola? I mean, after all, they are arriving tomorrow. You need to talk to Olufemi about this."

"No, Bisi," Lola said, her voice trembling with emotion, "I cannot face them now. I want to see my mother and talk to her about this. I need her comfort and advice, Bisi. She will tell me what I should do."

"Please, let my driver take you home, then."

Bisi walked over to Lola, and the two women hugged.

"I know it is hard, Lola, but it is a part of our culture. Our men have done this to women for centuries. We just have to either accept it or leave them. You are lucky that you have no children yet to complicate matters."

Lola pulled away and asked, "Do you really believe that I am lucky, Bisola? Maybe if I had a child, he would have taken me with him to America. I feel as though I have lost everything. I was naive and foolish to believe that Olu and I could be separated for so long without him finding another woman. I am surprised that it took this long."

"No, my sister, it is my brother who is the fool."

The two women walked to the car. As Lola got in, Bisola said, "Take care, my sister, and have a safe journey."

"Bisola, please, do not tell Olu where I have gone."

"Are you sure, Lola?"

"Sure or not, I am not ready to see him." With those final words, Lola went home to prepare for her journey.

She was packing when Kemi and Jide came over. The three friends sat in the parlor, discussing her journey home.

"How long will you be gone, Lola?" Jide asked.

"I don't know yet."

"Will you call us and let us know?"

"Of course, I will. You two are my good friends."

"What will we tell Olu?"

"Please do not tell him where I am."

"Lola, you know that he will know you are with your mama," said Kemi, concerned by Lola's decision not to meet her husband.

"Kemi, I need time ... time to get over this shock."

"I know. It is a terrible thing to happen, Lola," her friend began angrily, "But that *oyinbo* is the one to blame; after all, she knew that Olu was married, and she went after him anyway!"

"No. You are wrong, Kemi. She does not know about me."

"Kilo-she'?" Jide asked, surprised at this new information.

Lola continued softly, her features devoid of emotion.

"He never told her about me and neither did my in-laws."

Kemi felt so badly for her friend that all she could do is look at her with deep sympathy.

"Is there anything we can do for you?" Jide asked, trying to be helpful.

"Yes, you can take me to my office. I need to ask Alhaji for some time off."

Jide picked up her suitcase, and they walked to the car. They arrived at the ministry and walked upstairs to the office. Lola did not greet anyone in her usual way. She was embarrassed, certain that everyone had seen her reaction to the bad news she received from her husband. She sat at her desk. Olu's picture was there. She took it and placed it in the drawer, and then she buzzed Alhaji Yaro on the intercom.

"Sir, may I speak to you?"

"Yes, come in, Lola."

She entered his office and took a seat facing Alhaji. Looking down at her hands, she asked him for some time off. Alhaji reached into his desk drawer and fished out her wedding ring.

138

"Here, Lola, I found this on the floor in your office."

He handed the ring to her, but she hesitated briefly before taking it.

"Lola, I heard what happened. I was worried about you," he said sincerely.

"I guess everyone knows what a spectacle I made of myself."

"No, Lola, only a few people saw you."

Tears welled up in her beautiful, expressive brown eyes. He walked over to her. It tore at his heart to see her like this. She rummaged in her purse for a handkerchief. He gave her his. Lola swiveled her chair towards him, keeping her head down.

"Sir, I still cannot believe what my husband did to me. I have been a good wife, waiting patiently for his return."

He stood in front of her, putting his finger under her chin and raising her face to look at him. "Lola, sometimes men do not appreciate what they have until they either lose it, or until they know they can never have it."

She returned his gaze and touched Alhaji's hand on her chin. He pulled her to her feet, holding her by the hands. He just stood there breathing heavily, looking at her face as if memorizing her every feature.

"You do not deserve this, my dear," he said with passion. "You are a very special person. One day, your husband will realize the mistake he has made and come to his senses."

"I hope so, sir," Lola said, averting her face from his longing gaze.

"How much time do you need, my dear?"

"I need at least a month."

"Take as much time as you need, Lola; your job will be here when you return." He let go of her hands.

"Is there anything else you need — money, anything?"

"No, sir, but thank you."

"Where will you go?"

"I will be in Ilesha with my mother for a while."

"Where will your husband be?" he pried inquisitively.

"He will probably be in Lagos with his new wife ... Thank you, sir. I have to go now. Some friends are waiting for me."

Alhaji escorted her out of his office to where Jide and Kemi were waiting for her. They greeted him in unison.

"Sannu, Alhaji."

He returned their greeting and turned to Lola. "Remember, if you need anything at all, just call."

"Thank you very much, sir. I will."

On the way to the bus station, Lola was silent, but Kemi had taken note of Alhaji Yaro's deep concern.

"Lola, you are crazy to let a good man like Alhaji get away."

Lola was not listening. She seemed lost in her own thoughts.

"Did you get a message to your brother, Lola?" Jide asked.

"Yes, he will meet me at the station."

"While you are gone, I am going to talk to my friend Olu. Sure, he may have made the choice to have another wife, but he should have consulted you."

She just looked at Jide with thanks. They reached the motor park, where the smell of fried fish and *suya* drifted through the air. A young girl was selling oranges, and Lola bought a few for her journey. She joined the other passengers in the queue to board the bus.

Kemi embraced her friend. "Take care, Lola. Please don't be away too long. I will miss you." Jide also hugged her and said,

"Keep fit and safe journey. Greet everyone at home for me." Then he pushed an envelope into her hands.

"This is for your mama, Lola, and God bless."

As the bus turned onto the highway leaving Lagos, Lola sat back in her seat and thought about her marriage to Olu. They had been blissfully happy before he decided to go abroad to earn his doctorate degree. Their lovemaking had been exciting. Just the touch of his lips could arouse her. To her, Olu had always been the most handsome man alive. She had seen him many times in her village when he was on summer break from school accompanying his father on his visits to the store. Her mother managed the village shop for Mr. Adegoke.

She had fallen in love with Olu after seeing him standing there counting the crates of soft drinks. She asked her mother who he was and she told her. There was a spontaneous spark between them that grew as she matured. Her mother was pleased that Olu had taken an interest in her only daughter. Later on, after she entered secondary school in Ibadan, she learnt that her mother was arranging her marriage. She had feared it would be to some old, rich man and was delighted when she was told it was to be Olufemi Adegoke. Lola's mother was a shrewd businesswoman, who made the store into a profitable venture.

Mr. Adegoke was so pleased that he made her a partner. Lola and her brother Segun never wanted for anything. They were among the few children in the village who had new shoes and clothes every holiday.

After her graduation, while Olu was home for spring break, they were formally engaged. Olu's father paid a good dowry for Lola, who was everything that he wanted in a wife for his son. Olufemi had been too wild at school in London, dating English women. Mr. Adegoke could not countenance a white woman giving him grandchildren, spoiling their pure African line. He wanted his son to marry as he did, within his tribe and culture.

He chose Lola, an educated girl, not too worldly, but sophisticated enough to keep Olu at home. He knew she would be an obedient wife and give him many grandchildren. His wife kept talking about love and romance and letting Olufemi choose his own wife, but she even backed down when he came home one year with a white, blond-haired, blue-eyed English woman. Mrs. Adegoke felt that this woman would never accept African culture and would lure her son back to England. They threatened to disown Olufemi, and in the end, he backed down and broke off his relationship with the woman.

When Lola and Olu met again for the formal engagement, he was sure he would

142

not like her. But he took one look at her large, almond eyes, full lips, and copper skin and his memory re-ignited the spark that had flickered a few years earlier.

Lola had grown up and blossomed into a beautiful, graceful woman. Any man would have been proud to have her. After receiving his Masters Degree, he returned home from England and they were married. Their wedding was the biggest that the district had seen since Lola's mother and late father had sealed their nuptials.

Lola sighed as the bus reached the village. Her brother Segun was leaning against his white Peugeot 505.

"Segun, Segun," Lola called.

He turned, saw her, and rushed to her side, picking up his little sister and hugging her. They continued the traditional greetings as he took her suitcase and loaded it into the car.

"It has been too long, big brother."

"Mama will be glad to see you," he remarked happily.

"When she heard you were coming, she prepared all your favorite dishes."

"Wonderful," Lola lied. "I am famished."

In truth, she had not really eaten since receiving Olu's letter.

They drove up the dirt road of the village to the bungalow that her mother shared with her brother. Shuffling, taking off her dusty shoes at the door, Lola walked into the cool house. The African afternoon sun was very hot, and it was always humid in the southern part of the country.

"Mama, Mama, *e'kasun* (good afternoon)." Lola kneeled down before her mother as she came into the room. Then she got up to embrace her.

Her mother, Titiloye, bore the tribal marks of the village on each cheek. It was easy to see from whom Lola got her beauty. Her mother, even at 48 years old, was a fine example of African womanhood. The only difference between them was their coloring. Lola had her father's copper tones, whereas Titiloye was a fine, deep, mocha-brown.

Her mother held her and said, "It has been so long since I last saw you. You are thin, and you look tired child."

"Yes," replied Segun, who towered over the two women and wrapped his arms around them.

"Come and sit down and tell me about Lagos."

Lola curled up on a familiar sofa with her feet under her. She knew her mother and brother would not be happy with the news she brought. When she told them what had happened, her mother exclaimed,

"Ah, ah; *kini kilo-de'?* (Why? Oh why?), my poor child." Then she embraced her weeping daughter.

"It is going to be alright," her mother said, soothing her.

Segun was beside himself with anger. He stormed out of the house without saying a word.

"Come, my child. I will fix you a bath, and you can relax. When you are finished, we will eat dinner and talk some more."

The older woman was greatly disturbed by the news. She wondered why Emmanuel and Abimbola, Olufemi's parents, had not informed her of this matter.

Lola sat on the porch. The crickets were chirping in the night, and a dog could be heard barking in the distance. She felt for her ring, recalling that she had never put it back on when Alhaji gave it to her. Titiloye came into the parlor, looking for her daughter, and joined her on the porch.

"Daughter, we have to talk. Tears have no place here, Lola. Right now, you need to draw on the strength of our ancestors. This is not a new thing. This is a very common occurrence in our culture. Polygamy can be a curse or a blessing for the African woman. It is our way of trusting our husband's judgment, even if we do not agree with him. I do not agree with the way Olu did this, but I cannot condemn him for it. After all, he did not say he no longer wants you or asked you for a divorce, did he?"

"No, Mama, he did not; but it hurts so badly, and I feel so betrayed."

"My dear, your father died before you were four years old, but I am certain that he would have taken other wives as well. You see, after you were born, I could not have any more children. Your father wanted many sons, but he died before he could take another wife to give him them."

"Mama, would you have accepted his women?"

"Why not? What else could I do, I already had two children. It's our culture and the way my mother raised me!"

"That's the old way, Mama, and anyway, Olu's other wife is not a Nigerian."

"Does that really matter, Daughter? She is still a woman."

Lola was shaking with anger.

"Mama, I cannot accept this. Things are changing today for the African woman."

"Omolola," her mother cut in, "Things are not changing that fast. Remember your marriage to Olufemi was arranged, and his father paid a handsome dowry."

Lola fell silent. She felt that her mother did not understand. Then she said, "Mama, how can I share a man with this woman? I told you, she does not even know about me."

"When is he coming home, Lola?"

"They will arrive in Lagos tomorrow."

"Where will they be staying?"

"Probably in Ikoyi with his sister."

"Lola, I thought you had more common sense than this," Titiloye scolded her daughter. "After all, he graduated almost two months ago."

"But, Mama, I trusted him to do the right thing and come home to me. All this is a terrible shock to me. What shall I do, Mama?"

Lola's mother sat down to think about what her daughter should do.

"First, Daughter, you need time to prepare for this woman. Second, we will have to summon all the strength of our ancestors for guidance. Right now, my child, you need to go and rest."

Lola said good night to her mother and went to her room. It was just as she had left it before moving to her husband's house. She lay on her bed, wearing only a wrapper, rubbing her flat stomach, thinking, *I'll never have a child now. Oh, Olu, why did this have to happen?*

Chapter 10

The plane touched down at the Muritala Mohammed International Airport in Lagos. Bisola and her driver, Adisa, were waiting for her brother and his new American wife, Janice. Bisi thought to herself, *Poor Lola, I wonder how she is doing at home?* Olufemi and Janice were walking from customs with a baggage handler pushing a cart loaded with their luggage. When they reached the outside, Bisola came over to them and welcomed them home.

The brother and sister continued greeting each other in Yoruba. I stood there, taking in all the strange and wonderful sights before me. People everywhere, hurrying from place to place. The beauty of blackness overwhelmed me. I felt as if I had finally retraced the steps of my ancestors and was home for the first time.

"Janice, welcome to Nigeria."

Bisola walked over to me and took my hand. The three of us walked towards the car. There was too much luggage, so we had to hire a car to carry it. I could not take my eyes off the masses before me with all the people wearing colorful clothing. Even the buses and small taxis carrying passengers to unknown destinations fascinated me.

Women and children carried parcels and goods on their heads. I was amazed at the sizes of loads that they could balance at one time. So this was Lagos. I had read so much about it. I had seen pictures, but nothing prepared me for the beauty of the place. The smells and sounds of Africa — I had so many questions to ask about the exciting and different sights. Being from New Orleans, I was used to the sight of palm trees, but never had I seen so many different varieties.

As the car drove towards Ikoyi, I caught a glimpse of the red flame trees in bloom. The traffic was very heavy. I sat back in the Mercedes and leaned on Femi's shoulder. He looked lovingly at me and smiled, asking, "Enjoying your first taste of Africa, dear?"

"Yes, I am. You never told me how beautiful it is here."

"This is our beginning, darling."

I'd sensed a change in him. It seemed the closer we got to Nigeria, the quieter he became. He was speaking to his sister in Yoruba; I may as well get used to him doing that. We soon arrived at Bisola's home. I was impressed as we drove through the electric gates into the circular driveway. My, it was grand.

I guess it was true what Aduke told me about Bisi's husband being rich and successful. I was anxious to meet this man. The steward rushed to open the door and welcome us into the cool interior of the house. Joseph, the steward, was from Ghana, as were many of Bisola's servants. He showed us to one of the guestrooms near the rear of the house, overlooking the pool. The room was decorated tastefully and had a private bath and entrance to the gardens. There were touches of European and African elegance.

I heard the sound of children playing in the pool and walked to the sliding patio door to see two children, a boy and girl, playing in the water.

"I hope you will be comfortable here, Janice," Bisola said, smiling. "Let me introduce you to the children."

As she walked out onto the patio, the children came running, shouting, "Mommy!

Mommy! Uncle Femi!"

A young girl around seven years old ran to Femi and held him around his waist. He picked her up.

"My, how you have grown, Ajoke," he bragged. "Janice, come and meet my niece and nephew."

I was formally introduced to Ajoke and Taju Jr., a serious young man of ten years.

"Hello, children."

They were staring at me with awe.

"Children, children," Bisi said,"it is not polite to stare. You must forgive them Janice. They are not used to Americans."

"I understand, Bisola. I am pleased to meet both of you," and they ran back outside to the pool. I was tired from the trip and just wanted to lie down and peel my clothes off. *The humidity is similar to New Orleans,* I thought.

"Okay, you two. I will leave you to get settled. If you need anything, just ring for Joseph."

Bisola closed the door, and I sat down on the bed. Femi joined me, kicking off his shoes, and sat down. He kissed my lips and whispered, "Welcome to my country," in a way that made his accent sound so sensual.

His next kiss was returned with fiery passion. All the fatigue I felt a few seconds earlier turned into burning desire. I knew we would not stop with one kiss. He rolled over me on the king-size bed. Then he stripped off the traveling suit with fervor as I assisted him with his disrobing. We made love slowly and deliberately, trying to satisfy each other's needs.

Our lovemaking lasted until the sunset and the air outside began to cool. I opened the window and let the ocean breeze blow into the room. We took a bath together, soaping each other, then rinsing, savoring the feel of each other's skin. After our bath, there was a knock at the door, and Femi asked me to hurry and dress for dinner.

I joined the family in the dining room. There were two men present that I had not met. I joined Femi, standing at his side, and was introduced first to my new brother-in-law, Tajudeen Balogun. We shook hands, and he welcomed me to Nigeria. The other gentleman kept staring at me as if he saw a ghost. Taking me by the hand, Femi introduced me to his friend, who extended a shaky hand.

"Janice, I want you to meet my good friend Jide."

"Pleased to make your acquaintance," he said very formally, as he bowed politely, quickly releasing my hand. Then he walked away as if he were afraid of me. While Jide was distant, Taju was very comfortable with me and kept making jokes about Nigerians. My brother-in-law was nothing like I had imagined. He was youthful and exuberant. Bisi was really very lucky to have him ... his jolly demeanor made the evening a joyful occasion.

Everyone, even Femi, treated me like a porcelain doll. They spoke very little in their language out of respect for me. Femi escorted me into the den for drinks after dinner.

"I think you will enjoy Lagos, Janice," Taju said, handing me a drink. "You must have Femi bring you to the factory, its state-of-the-art."

"Will you, Femi?" I asked.

"Certainly, darling." Then I thought I saw Jide wince at the endearment.

Bisola joined us and asked about the wedding. She wanted to see the pictures.

"I have them in the bedroom; I'll go and get them."

While I was out of the room, the mood changed. Jide pulled Olufemi aside and said, "Well, my friend, you have really gone and done it now!"

Femi looked at his friend arrogantly and said, "And would you have done it differently, Jide?"

"Yes, I would have. This, Olu devastates Lola. How could treat her this way?"

"I did what I had to, Jide. I am not in the mood right now to discuss it. Janice will return in a minute."

Jide would not be put off like that, and he continued angrily. "I have not seen you for two years, and I am sadly disappointed that the man who left here has not returned," Jide said, his eyes downcast.

"Jide, I still consider you my friend, but I would appreciate it if you would not get involved in my personal life."

"What are friends for, Olu, if not to advise each other when they are courting disaster?"

Olufemi's face took on a tired, drawn look of a man many years older.

"I know what I did is not ethical, but I love Janice." Olu thought for a moment,

"And Lola, well, I love her, too, in a different way."

Returning to the den with the photo albums, I asked Taju and Bisi where Femi and Jide were.

"They are in the hallway," Bisi answered, looking nervously at Taju. "I'll get them," she volunteered.

Bisi walked in on the angry discussion that Jide and Olufemi were having.

"Janice has returned with the wedding pictures. I think you should talk about this at another time." The two men followed her back into the den. You could feel the tension in the room; everyone's mood seemed to have changed. I particularly sensed a change in attitude from Jide. I could tell he and I did not hit it off. Bisi and I sat on the sofa, while the men stood around us. Femi and I explained each and every picture. I sat back, looking at Jide, wondering what had I done to offend this man. This time I know I saw him wince as Femi proudly described a picture of us exchanging our vows. Taju asked to refresh my drink. I passed him my glass, and Femi continued describing the pictures. Jide said something in Yoruba to Femi, and I watched Femi's face change. *I must learn that language,* I thought, sipping my drink. Then Bisola exclaimed,

"Oh, Janice, your dress is so stunning. Was it your mother's gown?"

Both Jide and Femi glared at each other; I had a feeling that this evening would soon be over.

"No," I answered, distracted, as Femi got up and went into the hall with Jide close behind.

Taju joined his wife and me on the sofa. I sat sipping my drink, pretending to be

153

comfortable. Suddenly, we heard voices rise in anger. Femi shouted,

"*Kilo-de,* Jide? Why should you ask me this question?"

Their language was frank and to the point. They continued in Yoruba.

"Where is she, Jide?" Femi demanded. "I called the flat and got no answer."

Jide thought to himself, *I promised Lola that I would not tell him where she is.* Olufemi was so angry that Jide decided that it was best to give in to his demands. The mood in the room was quiet; everyone seemed to be holding their breath, not sure of what was going to happen next. Taju broke the ice.

"Janice, let me freshen your drink."

I looked at my glass, still full.

Taju and Bisi sat together on the sofa, pretending to look at the albums. I began to strain my ears, trying to hear what was going on in the hall. Even I could understand some of what they were saying, as they mixed their dialogue with English occasionally.

"Where is she, Jide?" Femi demanded.

"She went home to Ilesha."

"Why didn't she wait?" Femi said in anguish.

Jide knew he would be testing his friendship when he answered Olu's question. "She did wait, for over two years, my friend, while you gallivanted in America!" He then took a deep breath, preparing for Olu's onslaught, but instead, Olu said,

"Jide let me explain."

Olufemi apologetically went on to tell his friend about how he met Janice and fell

154

in love. He was alone for two years and needed someone. He did not set out deliberately to find a woman. Still, it did not explain why he didn't tell Lola about Janice.

"What do you intend to do about Lola?"

Olufemi was faced with the most difficult dilemma of his life.

"I don't really know, Jide. I never really thought about being a polygamist. My grandfather had three wives, but I never thought I would follow in his footsteps. I know it would be wrong to put Lola aside. I still care about her, in a different way than Janice. The time that we spent apart made my love for her soften."

Jide cut in, "That may be true, my friend, but it made her love grow stronger."

Olufemi looked with anguish at Jide, his eyes asking for help.

"Olu, I feel that you should have waited to marry Janice. She can never understand our culture. It was hard enough on Lola; think of how Janice will take this."

"That is my point, Jide. It is why I didn't tell her ... I wanted her to see the beauty of Nigeria and our people."

Jide walked over to the window, looking out at the garden, the two of them unaware that we heard them.

"When will you see Lola?"

Olu looked at the floor and answered, "Whenever she is ready, Jide."

With that, the two men returned to the den and sat down. Femi avoided my eyes, and Jide gave me a superior look. I was totally taken off guard. I could only understand a few words, but I do know whatever they were talking about involved Lola. Taju

155

announced that Femi would be working at his factory and would have his orientation tomorrow. Bisi asked me what I would be doing tomorrow. I replied, whatever she wanted since I was her guest. Jide stood up and announced that he was leaving. He wished everyone good night as he walked to the door; looking at me in that strange way he had been doing all night. Femi patted him on the back, and I invited him to be our first dinner guest once we got a house. Then the four of us continued talking about Femi's new job and all the perks that came with the position. By then, I had moved from the sofa and was sitting alone in a large, white leather chair, looking around the comfortable, elegant room thinking, *I could learn to like living like this!*

While we prepared for bed, I asked Femi, who, incidentally, had been very quiet the rest of the evening, about Jide.

"He kept giving me strange looks. I wondered what his problem was."

"Oh," Femi laughed," he is probably jealous that I have the most beautiful woman in the world as my wife."

Then he grabbed me and pushed me on the bed. We made delicious love all night long.

Chapter 11

Lola arrived at the store where her mother worked and aimlessly attended to a few customers. Unknown to her, her mother was observing her behavior. Titiloye was worried about her only daughter.

"Omolola," her mother called.

"Yes, Mama?"

"I want to talk to you. How did you sleep last night?"

Before Lola could answer, Jide drove up to the store and entered.

"Ekaro Iya Segun."(Good morning, mother of Segun*)*. He prostrated himself as a show of respect for Lola's mother, greeting her in the traditional way. Suddenly Lola perked up seeing Jide, running towards her friend, glad to see him.

"Jide, what are you doing here?"

He went on to tell Lola that her husband and his new wife had arrived.

"Jide, you drove all the way up here to tell me that?"

"No, Lola, I have much more to tell you."

They left the store and walked to the bungalow that her mother and brother live in. Segun was fixing his breakfast in the kitchen.

"Kini-Kong, Segun," Jide greeted his friend.

"Se'dada, ni, Adupe? (I hope all is well?) Please sit down."

May I offer you something to eat?

"No, thank you, Segun. I got something to eat on the way here."

All of the Shodeye family was anxious to hear what news Jide brought from Lagos.

"Jide," Lola began, "how is Olu?"

"He's fine, Lola."

She was glad to hear of the good health of her husband.

"What about the woman?"

Jide felt sad, telling Lola about Olu's other wife. He did not hold back anything. "I cannot lie; she is beautiful, more beautiful than her photographs." His eyes took on a thoughtful look as he remembered having dinner with Janice and the others.

"America has been good to your husband. He looks very well."

"Did he ask about me?"

"Yes, Lola, he did."

"Damn, damn that Olu," Segun cut in. "I hate the position that he has put you in, Lola!"

"Calm down, Segun; it's alright," Lola said, trying to console her brother. Jide was beginning to get angry at Lola's attitude towards the news of Janice and Olufemi. He felt that she should at least show some anger.

"Lola, you should be there! You are his wife. She knows nothing about you!"

Lola grasped her neck in horror at the tone of voice that Jide had used with her. Jide continued with vengeance.

"Olu is behaving as if you do not exist!"

"Maybe that is how he wants it," Lola came back at Jide, and it was at just that moment Titiloye walked into the room. All the young people turned in her direction as she looked at her daughter and began voicing her disappointment.

"No, Daughter, you sound as if you have taken the attitude of defeat. I agree with Jide, that you should be there. You should have welcomed the woman into your family!"

Then Segun, who had been unusually quiet, said, "No, Mama. I disagree with you; Lola would only get hurt if he rejected her."

Jide walked over to Segun, facing him as he said, "I do not think that he would reject Lola ... I really do not ... but it is not fair that the woman does not know about her."

Jide went on to tell everyone about Janice, how she appeared to be kind and thoughtful. He also did not leave out how much she appeared to love Olu.

"I saw a picture of her at Bisola's house," Lola spoke suddenly. "She is a beautiful woman."

"That picture does her no justice," Jide broke in.

"She has pink lips and her eyes sparkle ... and when she speaks, everyone listens."

Lola sat back down and felt a sinking feeling in the pit of her stomach, and then she looked at her mother and tearfully exclaimed, "Oh, Mama, what shall I do?"

Segun was the first to speak, and he was angry at his sister's apparent weakness where Olu was concerned. "I'll tell you what to do — you should confront your husband and ask him why he did this to you in the first place, instead of hiding behind Mama's skirts!"

"Segun, my son," Titiloye began in earnest, "That is not the right way, not with anger; you must use diplomacy."

Segun was fuming and shouted, "Olu did not use diplomacy when he took another wife!"

"I know my son," Titiloye said, as she tried to cool her son down.

"Two wrongs do not make a right. Can't you see you sister has suffered enough? It would be worse if she were to alienate herself. Olu must face her, so she must be prepared for him."

Titiloye continued to tell Lola that she did have choices.

"What do you mean, Mama?"

"You see, my child, you can stay with Olu and try to work things out with the woman, or you can leave and look for another husband. After all, you do not have any children yet, and you are still young and beautiful," she continued, touching her daughter's face.

"But, Mama, I love Olu. I cannot face my life without him."

Titiloye held her daughter, rocking her and repeating, "I know, my child, I know."

The suddenly Segun broke the mood and shouted, "Lola, you need to go to Lagos to be with your husband, instead of running away like a coward!"

"Segun," his mother said softly, "be gentle with your sister."

Then Lola jumped out of her mother's arms; it was as if a total transformation had occurred. A strong, determined woman had miraculously replaced the crying little girl too afraid to stand up to anyone.

"No, Mama, Segun is right," she said bravely. "I must go. I will let them settle down first, then Mama, you will call a family meeting at Olu's father's house at Ekiti, and so we can discuss this issue before the whole family."

"I think that is a good idea," Jide spoke again. "I mean, after all, Lola gave him over three years of her life. He owes us all an explanation."

It was settled that the family meeting would be in Ekiti and Titiloye would make all the arrangements. Jide spent the night in Ilesha at their house. In the morning when he prepared to leave, he asked Lola "Won't you come with me? I'm sure you can work things out."

Lola had already made her decision and repeated, "I will let the family decide, Jide."

"Any message for Olu, Lola?"

Lola thought a moment before she told Jide to just tell him hello. With that, he got into his car and drove out of the village, leaving a cloud of dust behind him on the road.

*****

The factory Taju owned was in the Isolo Road Industrial Estates on Lagos Mainland. He produced a number of products. Femi possessed the skills that he needed to train the workers. After a tour of the complex and introductions to the staff, Femi and Taju returned to Taju's office. Sitting down, Taju asked his brother-in-law about his father's offer to take over his company.

"He wants you to go to Ekiti to run the business, Olu."

"I know, but I am not ready to settle down there. It is too quiet, and I don't think Janice would like living in the village." Taju cleared his throat before going on to ask about Lola.

"Bisi has been very concerned about that situation. She has been nagging me to talk to you about it, but I felt it was too soon."

"Well, I thank you for your consideration, Taju, and to answer some of your questions, I did not ask to be in this situation, but if I had told Janice about Lola, I would have lost her."

Taju nodded his head in agreement as Olu went on passionately, "Can you imagine what it would be like to lose an angel?"

Taju smiled, saying, "Olu, I do understand; remember, I have another wife in the village. I keep her there because Bisi cannot stand to be near her."

"My brother," Taju went on to ask, "how can a Nigerian woman and an American woman live together?"

Femi thought a moment before he gave his answer. "I do not intend for them to live in the same house. They will have separate homes with equal amenities," he explained confidently.

"What about you, Olu? How are you going to deal with two beautiful women? Many a man would like to be in your place," Taju commented, trying to make light of the serious situation.

"My brother, I will take it one step at a time. First, I must talk to Lola to see if she still wants to stay married to me, then I will talk to Janice and tell her the truth."

"Good luck, old man," Taju said as they left the office for home.

*****

Janice and Bisola walked through the Falamo shopping center to a few of the high-priced boutiques. The two fashionably dressed women got a lot of stares as they walked into the ice cream parlor to get cool, when a strange woman walked up to them and spoke to Bisola in Yoruba.

"E'kaubo, Kemi," Bisola said to the woman, who looked rudely at me and continued to speak directly to Bisi. Their discussion became heated as I interceded with,

"Is there a problem?" I asked concerned.

My sister-in-law replied nervously, "No, no, no, Janice. This is my good friend Kemi, and Kemi; this is Olu's wife, Janice."

I stood up to shake her hand, but she did not offer me hers. I pulled my hand back, stung by her cold, icy glare.

"Pleased to meet you," she blurted out rudely. Then she muttered something in Yoruba and left. Bisola took out her handkerchief and wiped her face, sweating.

"Who was that woman?" I asked. "She was so rude."

Bisi laughed uncomfortably, not meeting my eyes. "Yes, she was," Bisi said, continuing to eat her ice cream. She never told me who she was, and I let it go at that.

Lagos was fascinating! As our car drove across Eko Bridge, I watched a ferry go by on the lagoon. Since it was early afternoon, the traffic was light for a change. The ocean view was fantastic as we sped towards the mainland. We visited some government offices and the marina. We also went to the Apapa Amusement Park and the wharf. Lagos was truly a cosmopolitan city.

Later at home, we ate dinner with the family. I became friends with Taju Jr. and Ajoke. They seemed to trust me, so I taught them how to play monopoly and other board games. After dinner, I spoke to Femi about my day and mentioned the woman Kemi that Bisi and I met at the market. I told him how rude she was to me. He informed me that she was Jide's fiancée and was probably jealous.

"How was your first day at the company, dear?" I asked.

"I will answer that after I kiss you."

He pulled me to him, his warm mouth covering mine. I could hear the children giggling with glee at our open show of affection. We pulled apart and Femi winked at them. Afterwards, we walked out into the garden for a while, enjoying the tropical evening breeze. Holding hands, we began to talk about our future. Femi told me about the benefits package with Taju's company. It included a house and car.

"Janice, I don't want you to work right now. I just want you to get used to Nigeria."

"But, darling, I'll get bored staying home; after all, I am a career woman."

He told me in no uncertain terms that he did not want his wife to work; he wanted me to make a new career of being his wife.

"Bisi will keep you company until you meet others and make friends of your own. I will have her take you to our house in Ikeja tomorrow, then you can go shopping for anything we may need."

I was excited about the prospect of having a home of our own and being able to decorate it. I had seen a few things already that I would like to buy.

"Money is no object, Janice." Femi went on to tell me about his salary. "Taju is giving us the blue Volvo."

"Fantastic, Femi," I said happily. "Your family is very generous. It is nothing like America — I mean a job, Volvo, and a new house — it's just too much!"

"Just wait, darling. You will see many things in Nigeria that you cannot compare to the U.S.A."

"Femi, I have never asked you about money. Is your family wealthy?"

He told me about his father's business, and that he was also a chief in the village. One of the companies his father owns processes raw cocoa and sugar cane. He also has some stores in smaller villages. As Femi spoke, his thoughts drifted to the fact that Lola's mother managed one of his father's stores, and that he owes Mama Lola an explanation.

In bed, I lay back on the pillow, holding Femi's hand and dreaming of the house I would see tomorrow.

"Femi, how many children do you want?"

He said he wanted a big family, with ten children; I sat up with my eyes and mouth wide open in surprise, shouting, *and "Ten* children!"

"Yes," he said laughing, looking deep into my eyes, then pulled me to him and kissed me.

"Janice, I want only two children, a boy and a girl."

I breathe a sigh of relief since we were in perfect agreement. His lips trailed along my cheek to my neck, as his hands caressed my breast. He lay over me, nibbling each ear lobe gently and whispered, "Let's start making one now."

"Umm," I moaned softly and stretched. "What a wonderful idea."

Then we kissed, deeply this time. His breathing became heavy, as he sprang into life like a lion. We made complete love, not leaving out anything. Our passion was indescribable. It was so hot and intense, that, in spite of the air conditioner, the bed became wet with our sweat. As our labored breathing began to relax, he rolled off me. I was filled with an intense pleasure that was so fulfilling.

"We must do this every day, Femi, when you come home from work. You were like a tiger, *grrrrrr!*" I growled into his chest. He lay there, looking at me and wondering how a man could be so lucky.

"Janice, I must never lose you. I love you so."

I jumped up and got into the shower, and he followed. The cool water felt good on my hot, sticky body. We bathed each other, and before long, we were making love again. He held me against the shower wall, lifting me up off my feet. This time it was short and sweet. We were both so exhausted that we slept soundly.

Bisi took me to the house in Ikeja the next day. It was a large house, with four bedrooms and three baths. It had a pool, servant quarters, and was surrounded by a lush tropical garden. She explained as we toured the rooms that this was to be Taju's other wife's home, but she preferred to live in the village. I wondered how much of a preference it was, seeing the distasteful look on Bisi's face. I couldn't wait for the arrival of our furniture and other things at the new house. I knew just how I wanted to decorate it.

Later that evening, we had dinner with the whole family. The dinner menu consisted of fresh fish stew with rice, garden salad, and fried plantain. Their cook was marvelous; he even prepared a fruit trifle. After dinner, we sat in the den, drinking wine, discussing the new house and Femi's job. Later that evening, I decided it was time I called my mother. It had been some time since I had spoken with her. I missed her very much. She was so glad to hear from me. She had received all my post cards. I had taken a few pictures and told her I would send them to her. It all seemed too good to be true, that I could be this happy. I never thought that I would find a man who could satisfy all my wants and needs. I was not superstitious, but being from New Orleans, I was careful. I kept having nagging doubts in the back of my mind that something was going to spoil my happiness. I dismissed the negative thoughts as I looked across the room at the man I had married.

Chapter 12

Femi received a message from Jide that his father requested his presence at a family meeting in Ekiti next weekend. He asked for everyone to be there except me. They wanted to discuss Lola's situation and did not want me to know yet. Femi was disturbed by this news and invited Jide to join him and Taju for lunch.

"Well, brother-in-law, you know that it is our culture to have two wives," Taju began earnestly, "and you did not handle it very well."

"Yes, my friend," Jide cut in, "you could have done this in a different way. After all, Janice still does not know about Lola."

Femi felt like a caged mouse. He had invited them to lunch to give him advice on what to do. Instead, all they told him is what he did wrong.

"Jide and Taju, I know what I am doing. Janice is so happy; I don't want to spoil things for her. Right now, she is getting the house ready for us to move into."

"What about Lola?" Jide asked.

Femi answered that he was going to the meeting, and everything would be settled there.

"You are so unfair to her, Olu," Jide said, perturbed.

"Life is sometimes unfair," Taju reminded Jide.

"Yes, but to Lola, who is so innocent in this?"

Olu tried to change the subject by asking Jide about Segun, Lola's brother. Jide told him that Segun was helping out at the store and driving a taxi.

"He is very angry with you, and how you treated his sister. You should be careful what you say to him."

The three men finished their lunch and returned to work. Olufemi sat back in his chair, unable to concentrate. Looking out the window, he saw a woman who reminded him of Lola. He knew it would not be easy deciding what to do. *I didn't mean to hurt anyone.* He covered his face as the shudders began. He cried for Lola, Janice, and himself. Even he did not have all the answers.

Bisola, Taju, and Olufemi left for Ondo state that Saturday morning, leaving me with the children. They told me it was a family emergency that required their presence. I was glad when Femi told me that I did not have to go. I was not ready to face his parents yet. I enjoyed the children, and we spent the day swimming in the pool. I would miss Femi though; this was our first separation. We said our good-byes, as the Mercedes drove through the security gates. They would return Sunday night.

Mrs. Adegoke prepared her home for the children's visit. It was the largest house in the village, built in the colonial style of the British. It had a long balcony with an awning to keep out the hot afternoon sun. A fence ran around the house, separating it from the rest of the plantation. Surrounding the house were palm trees and tropical flowers of red, yellow, and green. Lola's mother, Titiloye, had arrived Friday with her daughter and son Segun.

"Emmanuel? Emmanuel?"

"Yes, my dear," her husband answered.

"The children should be arriving soon. Is everything ready for the meeting?"

Emmanuel told his wife that the houseman, Sunday, was arranging the chairs.

"I am so worried," Mrs. Adegoke, said expressing her feelings. "I never thought that it would come to this. Lola and Olufemi were so happy before he left for America."

"Well, dear, things change. You know that they were apart for a long time, and a man has needs."

"Humph!" she made an angry noise. "Needs, needs — look at the trouble our son's needs have gotten him; two wives and one of them a foreigner!"

Mr. Adegoke sat down; the room had the air of defeat about it.

"I know my wife; I tried to advise him, but he is as stubborn as a mule."

"Oh, well," his wife replied, "I hope this meeting will not take long. You know that it is really up to Lola, Emmanuel. She just has to say yes or no."

The doorbell rang and Sunday went to open the door; at the same time, Lola and her mother entered the room.

"Remember, my daughter, listen to your husband and be strong," Titiloye reminded Lola. Segun was outside, waiting to meet the car as it drove up. *He has some words for his brother-in-law,* thought Titiloye, after she searched the house for her son.

"Bimbo, have you seen Segun?" she asked Mrs. Adegoke.

"I think he went outside to meet the car."

I had better get him before he makes trouble, Titiloye thought as she hurried outside, but she was too late, for as she reached the front door, she heard a commotion outside. Segun and Olufemi were engaged in a loud argument. Taju and Bisi were pleading with Segun to stop and come inside.

"Well, my deceitful brother-in-law," Segun began angrily, "did you leave your *whore* at home?" Olu was furious at his blatant disrespect for Janice, and without thinking, he jumped at Segun, swinging his fist, just missing him.

"O, ti to', Segun, *now wayo, kilo-se',"* Taju shouted as he stood between the two men.

"We are all here to settle this!" Taju shouted over Segun.

"We cannot settle my sister's honor!" he returned with determination. "Get out of my way," he shouted. "Let me fight him!"

There was no stopping Segun. He had been holding back all this time and with that, he swung at Olufemi, his fist connecting with his jaw. Segun was a taller man with a slim build compared to Olufemi's large, muscular build, but he had the anger of a bull. Olufemi fell back on the ground, stunned by the quick blow, but by this time, all the family came running out of the house. Lola stood screaming as Segun jumped on Olufemi, who was trying to get up.

"Ah! Ah! Stop it, Segun, stop it!" Taju, who had been pushed aside, yelled at him, but could not stop him. Bisola was yelling, "Ye, ye, ye!" with her hands on her head as the two men went at it. Olufemi hit Segun in the stomach, and then kicked his legs from under him, losing his balance as Segun fell. The two men rolled on the ground, exchanging blows. Suddenly, Mr. Adegoke yelled,

"Stop this at once!"

With the sound of his commanding voice, everyone got quiet. You could hear the sound of their heavy breathing as the two men got up and squared off for another round. Emmanuel Adegoke raised his hand; the two men dropped their fists and prostrated before the patriarch. Abimbola and Titiloye stood silent, and Lola was sobbing in Bisi's arms as the head of the family spoke,

"Ki, ki, kilo de' (What has gotten into you?) Segun, you impatient boy, and Olufemi, what are you thinking?"

Olufemi stood up, keeping his eyes lowered as he would if he were ten instead of thirty.

"Father, I'm sorry, but he hit me first!"

Segun, grinding his teeth in anger, also rose, shouting, "You deserved it!"

"Enough, both of you," Mr. Adegoke said. "Go inside and get cleaned up; the meeting will be in one hour."

With that, the two men turned into boys and obeyed without question: for in Africa, when the father has spoken, *he has spoken.*

Olufemi ran into the bathroom, his nose was bleeding and his lip was swollen. *Wow*, he thought rubbing his jaw, *that Segun has a sharp right hook.*

Segun went into another bathroom, accompanied by his mother, to cool off and tend his own wounds, thinking vehemently that Olufemi would not get way with this, that he would pay for hurting Lola. The women went inside to assist the servants preparing refreshments. No one wanted to look at anyone else. Bisola and her mother hugged each

172

other and Taju joined Mr. Adegoke in the parlor. Titiloye went to Lola after seeing to her son's wounds and told her Segun was all right. Lola was crying, so she took her to wash her face.

"Mama, what is wrong with my brother?" she asked, distraught. "I did not even get to greet Olu."

"Come with me, Daughter. I will take you to where he is; you two need to talk before the meeting."

Titiloye led her daughter to the outer room, where Olu was. She knocked and left her daughter. Olu opened the door, wearing his singlet and trousers. He was preparing to change his clothes and opened the door, surprised.

"Omolola," his eyes softened.

"Hello, Olu." Lola was fighting to control her emotions. She wanted to rush and embrace him, never letting go, but instead, she walked in and sat on the bed. It was a few moments before she spoke.

"Olu, I am sorry," she said in a small voice. "I did not mean for it to be this way. Segun is angry."

"Sh, sh, Lola. I know."

Olu looked at the beautiful wife that he had not seen for two years. The years apart had made her even more desirable. Suddenly, all the memories of her came rushing at him. Lola stood up, searching the eyes of the man she married; they just kept looking at one another, as if trying to read the other's mind. Lola broke the spell and burst out,

"Why? Olu, why?"

His lips hurt as he tried to find the words to answer her. Tears were spilling over from her expressive eyes, making them sparkle like amber; her lower lip trembled as she lost control of the emotions that she held pent up for two years. Again, she repeated the question, sobbing,

"Why? Why did you hurt me so?"

Olufemi balled his sore fists and beat at his sides. "Oh, Lola, I didn't mean to hurt you."

He walked over to her and held her body; she was shaking so badly that he was afraid. He took her chin in his hand and lifted her face to his. It reflected the Heart and Soul of African Beauty. Her full lips trembled; her eyes closed, ringed with the long, wet lashes; her nostrils flared as he wiped her tears and held her.

Her hands gripped his back as he lifted her off her feet. Then he sat on the bed, holding her on his lap like a baby, sobbing. Soon he began to cry with her, because he had hurt her so deeply. He was a sensitive man; he knew this would not be easy. He could see that Lola still loved him so. She ran her fingers through his soft hair, touched his face, her mouth hungry and wanting to claim what was hers. She kissed him; no man alive would have resisted that kiss, filled with so much desire. Their mouths melded as one. He began to respond slowly, for he had gotten used to another's kisses, but the memory of Lola was strong as he held her tightly, taking her breath away. Her wrapper fell silently to the floor. He reached under her *buba* (blouse) to touch her firm breast. She arched her hips in pain for it had been so long, too long. Olu was like a man lost in the desert, dying for water, and had just found his oasis. Lola's head reared back, crying,

174

"Olu, Olu, it has been so long."

Her braids fell free from her head tie. Her body was moist with the heat of passion and was ready for him as he lay over her on the bed. She arched her hips, begging him to enter and love her like he used to. Femi felt his desire rising as he removed his pants, so that all was between now was their memories. As he touched her body, she moaned softly, guiding his hands where she wanted them to go. He began kissing her everywhere; she responded like a woman insane, her head moving from side to side as he entered her slowly, but deliberately, unable to contain his own passion any longer. She bit her lip as the painful thrusts burned into pleasure. The lovers continued to move to a rhythm inside their heads. The beat of their drums was as intense as their desire to please one another. As their passion exploded into pleasure, Lola screamed with electric intensity that shook her to the core. It was so powerful that Olu could not hold back any longer and joined her in oblivion.

She held him, her nails scratching his back as she moaned with each wave of pleasure. She was afraid that if she let him go, he would be gone. When he could speak he said,

"Lola, how could I have been so selfish to think only of myself?"

Lola was lost in the renewed passion that she had just experienced and mumbled, "You are mine, Olu, and all mine."

They washed in the bathroom and redressed in silence. The others were assembled in the parlor, and the women were scolding Segun, especially his mother Titiloye; she was upset that her son had been disrespectful to his sister's husband.

175

"You must apologize, Segun," she said angrily to her son.

He refused, saying that the only people he owed an apology to were Mr. and Mrs. Adegoke, for fighting in their home. The family sat in the parlor, waiting for Olu and Lola to come and join them. They walked into the room, their faces still flushed from their lovemaking. No one, especially her mother, missed that fact. Segun stood there, staring at the couple in disbelief. Titiloye smiled a knowing smile that maybe Lola had come to her senses and had taken control of the situation. The pair sat with their respective families. Mr. Adegoke spoke first.

"Let us begin the meeting to settle the matter of my son Olufemi's marriage to Omolola." Segun, being the man of his family, began to speak.

"Sir, my brother-in-law has been unfaithful to my sister by marrying another woman without even telling her."

Titiloye broke in, "This has caused my daughter great harm. It broke her heart, as she trusted her husband."

When she finished, Mr. Adegoke said, "Then it is for me to ask you, Omolola, what do you want? Do you wish to remain married to Olufemi, or get divorced and go on with your life, given that my son intends to have Janice as his second wife?"

"Sir," Segun broke in rudely before his sister could answer the question, "the *oyinbo* (foreign woman) does not even know about my sister. It is not fair that she be asked to decide, without knowing if the other woman will accept being the second wife and sharing Olufemi."

Mrs. Adegoke had remained quiet until now and she said gently, "Now, now, Son, no one is talking about first or second wife, but if Omolola still wants to be married to my son."

Everyone murmured in agreement. Lola stood up and the room fell silent.

"My family, since I am the one who is the topic of this meeting, it should be I that come up with the terms of agreement. I am very unhappy about the situation, but I know that Olufemi loves me."

Lola looked at her husband across the room and smiled.

"He may love the other woman as well, but I am convinced that he still loves me too."

Segun cut in, looking directly at his sister. "Lola, remember the *oyinbo* (woman) has no knowledge of you."

Lola continued eloquently, speaking to the group, while looking at her brother. "I know, but it really doesn't matter as long as I have Olu's love."

With that, Segun began shouting. *"Kai, haba,* Lola. Do not be a weak fool, letting him disrespect you and your marriage!"

Titiloye Shodeye spoke in a commanding tone to her son. "Silence, Segun; that is enough; you are out of order!"

Olufemi was quiet up to that point, but he'd had enough of Segun's foolishness. "Segun, why can't you let Lola make up her own mind?" He added that he was tired of him speaking disrespectfully of Janice as well.

"Disrespect? Disrespect her?" Segun's voice took on a menacing tone, and then

he stood up, pointing his finger at Olufemi as everyone got on guard again.

"You disrespect her intelligence by not letting her know what a liar and a cad she married. I have had enough of this charade," Segun continued in anger.

"Lola and Mama, if this is what you want, then you can have it. I am finished."

This time, everyone tried to calm Segun, but to no avail. Titiloye rushed towards her son, speaking in a soothing voice, *"O ti toe,"* but Segun was on his feet. *"Joko, joko,* my son. Sit down and let Lola finish."

"No, Mama, she has said enough."

And with that, he stormed out of the house. As he entered the courtyard, he was thinking, *I will not stay with people who do not have my sister's best interest at heart; they only want to protect their son and his woman.*

Titiloye excused herself and joined her angry son outside, pleading with him. "Segun, you represent your late father here. *E-jo, e-jo*, please, Son, do not leave."

He ran towards his taxi.

"Never mind, Mama; I'm going. I've had enough!"

"Segun," Titiloye called to her wayward son, "Lola needs you now!"

He turned before entering the taxi, looked at his mother, and said sarcastically, "Lola does not need me, Mama. She has reunited with Olu!"

Titiloye could not say anything to convince her son because she knew that he spoke the truth.

"I'm sure, Segun, that he will be good to her as he was in the past."

That was more than Segun could take; he jumped into his taxi and sped away towards Ilesha without saying good-bye. While driving, he was making plans. His mind was made up. *I'll go home, pack a bag, and drive down to Lagos and reach there before 10 P.M., if I go quickly. Before this day is over, Janice Adegoke will know about my sister!*

Returning dejected to the meeting, Mrs. Titiloye Shodeye felt all of her 47 years. She knew that her son's attitude had disgraced the family, and she had to remain strong to be able to salvage what pride she had left.

"Where is Segun, Mama?" Lola asked.

"He went home," she lied. She really did not know where he went.

"Home? Why?"

Her mother told her that Segun could not stay around to see her give in so easily to Olu. Lola was despondent. Titiloye explained to everyone that her son had left for the day and would not be returning. Mr. Adegoke began speaking to Lola,

"You can continue, Omolola."

Lola began speaking with confidence. "I have decided that if Olufemi's other wife will accept me being married to him, and then I will stay."

"Fine; then it is settled," Mr. Adegoke responded warmly to this. "Now my son, when will you tell Janice?"

Olufemi cleared his throat before answering, "When we return tomorrow, sir, and Lola will come with me."

179

"Do you think that wise, my son?" his mother asked him. "To expose Lola to Janice so soon?" Olufemi looked at Lola and smiled.

"The sooner, the better; then we can all get on with our lives."

Titiloye stood up and directed her question to Emmanuel, "Where will Lola live?"

Taju spoke up. "I have given Olufemi my house at Ikeja. Janice has been preparing it for them to move into."

"I can live anywhere, as long as I can see my husband regularly."

Bisola turned to her father, "The house that my husband gave Olufemi is a palace. Lola must have one that is at least similar, if not equal."

"Your point is well made, Daughter," Emmanuel answered Bisi.

"I have a house in Surulere, Lola; you know the one that I stay in when I am in Lagos? It is on Bode Thomas Street. How would that suit you?"

Lola hid her true thoughts and feelings. She really wanted to say she wished to live in the same house with Olu and Janice, and share their life. She was afraid that she would be left out. Instead, she lowered her eyes and said, "Thank you, sir; that would be fine."

Lola sat back in her chair and closed her eyes, taking a deep breath. Olufemi called her name softly. "Lola, Omolola, are you alright?" She opened her eyes and whispered,

"Yes, Olu, I am now."

"My daughter," Titiloye asked, "do you agree with the decision to live apart from your husband?"

Lola looked at her husband, "Yes, I agree. I want to keep my marriage and my husband." She said with passion, "I love you, Olu."

He returned the look of passion, "I love you too, Lola."

Taju and Bisi were enjoying the loving exchange between the couple, when Bisi asked her husband, "Why don't you ever look at me like that?"

Everyone in the room began to laugh, lightening the mood.

Abimbola remarked to her daughter, "Yes, he looked at you too much that way, Daughter. That is why I have two beautiful grandchildren."

Mr. Adegoke rose and summoned the two young people to him. They knelt in front of him, holding hands.

"My children, God bless you. I will continue to pray for you, for God knows you have a hard road to travel. Lola, we beg your patience and pray that Janice learns to accept you."

Then looking at his son, he said, "My son, I pray for you to have endurance in this matter, and that you will deal impartially and equally with your two wives. Amen. This meeting is adjourned."

The steward, Sunday, announced that dinner was being served and the two families walked happily into the dining room.

Segun arrived in Ilesha and reached the house just as the phone was ringing. He refused to answer it; he did not know that it was his mother calling to tell him the outcome of the meeting. He rushed to throw a few things into a small bag and drove to the highway towards Lagos. It was a few hours drive, so he had plenty of time to plan how he would tell Janice about Lola. He passed through many towns and villages, stopping only to buy petrol and eat. He would not rest until he had finished this quest.

Titiloye decided to return home after dinner to her village. Emmanuel lent her his car and driver since Segun had left. She arrived home, expecting to meet her son there, but was disappointed to find his bed had not been slept in. She prepared to go to bed and rest, glad that they had come to an amicable agreement for her daughter.

Everyone went to bed in the Adegoke house except Lola and Olufemi. They had two years to catch up on and were wasting no time. Lola had many questions for her husband, especially about her new mate.

"Olufemi, you never answered the question — why didn't you tell her about me?"

Olu looked into her eyes. There was no reason now why he should not be honest with her.

"I ... I ... I ...," he stuttered, "I didn't want to lose her. If she knew I was married, she would never have agreed to marry me. American women, even African-American women, are not like us. They do not understand polygamy or African culture. They are raised in a monogamous culture."

Lola listened intently to his words.

"I know of a few American men who have many women on the side, but it is illegal to have more than one wife. Only a few religious sects practice polygamy openly." He paused to hear Lola's remark.

"Really?" she asked surprised. "I thought that it was the same everywhere. So America is very different from Nigeria."

"How did you meet her?"

Olufemi told her how he and Janice met and how it was at the tail end of his time in the U.S.A.

"I never intended to fall in love with anyone, Lola. I had been away from you for so long, and I was vulnerable."

With that remark, Lola became angry.

"But you never gave any thought to my feelings; I mean, I really suffered, Olu!"

Lola began to cry. He held her close and whispered, "I am sorry, so sorry. I never meant to hurt you."

With those tender, heartfelt words, Lola felt all the fight in her melt away, replaced with all the want and need she held inside for so long. She had publicly accepted the fact that Olu and Janice were married and she would have to share her life with another woman, unless the woman chooses not to accept her. That was the card she was holding in this game, where there were no true winners...

Chapter 13

I had just finished helping Joseph, the steward, dry the dishes and put them away.

"Is there anything else you require tonight?" he asked.

I told him no and went to join Ajoke and Taju Jr. watching television. I asked Joseph if he wanted to join us. As we were walking into the den, the doorbell rang. I wondered who it could be at this time of night, because the family would not return until tomorrow.

Joseph opened the door and there stood a strange man, a Nigerian, tall, well dressed, and attractive, who spoke to Joseph. He appeared to be familiar with the steward. Suddenly, he pushed the door open and walked past Joseph, stopping when he saw me.

"Sir, wait! Wait! You can't come inside!" the steward shouted.

I was startled by the stranger's abrupt entrance into the house and asked the man, "May I help you?"

Before he could answer, Joseph rushed into the room. "I am sorry, Madame, but he pushed his way inside."

I felt myself becoming perturbed at the nerve of this man and asked him, "Are you looking for Bisi and Taju?"

I stood there facing the stranger in my blue cotton caftan, my long, brown hair hanging loose, and my eyes flashing...

He just stood there, as if in shock, looking at me, shaking his head as if in disbelief. Ajoke came running into the room calling,

"Aunt Janice, are you coming?"

Suddenly the stranger found his voice saying, "You are Janice Adegoke, Olu's second wife?"

I did not acknowledge him, and he looked as if he could not believe it. I then smiled a welcome smile, "Oh, are you a friend of Femi's?" I asked.

The stranger answered, "No, umm, yes, I am Segun Shodeye," he introduced himself.

I was thinking *Olu never mentioned him.* I walked towards him, extending my hand to shake his, when he stepped back.

Joseph stepped towards him quickly, asking, "May I help you, sir?"

"No, no thank you. I want to speak to Mrs. Adegoke, alone."

I was curious as to who he was and what he wanted to talk to me about, so I invited him to come inside and have a seat. I was cautious though, since he refused to shake my hand. I thought that it was probably another one of their customs; after all, handshaking is an American tradition. I led him to the living room and asked Ajoke to return to Taju Jr., promising to join them shortly.

"Please sit down, Mr. Shodeye," I politely offered.

Segun said curtly, "I prefer to stand."

"As you wish," I said, sitting down on the couch. I began the conversation carefully, unsure of what he wanted.

"If you are not a friend of my husband, then you must be related to Taju."

He eyed me arrogantly and said, "No, I am not; in fact, I am Omolola's brother." He was quiet then, as if judging my reaction to his announcement.

"Omolola? I don't think I know her," I replied, while thinking ... then it came to me as I repeated the name, "Oh my God! Lola! You are the brother of the woman Femi was to marry!" I exclaimed.

Segun looked at me, and then decided to finish the job. He was very cunning with the way he started, as if thinking; *now it is time to push in the dagger.*

"What do you mean *'was'* to marry? He was already married to my sister before he went to America. They have been married for three years."

I was stunned by the words that came from his mouth. I felt like I had been hit. I rose up and stood at the back of the couch, as if trying to shield myself from further abuse. I took a deep breath and when I found my voice; my words were filled with anger.

"What do you mean 'he was married before he came to America'?"

My voice was shaking with emotion; my face became flushed, with my nostrils flaring. The tall man stepped back, gauging my reaction to his words. He watched me warily, unsure of what I would do next.

"I felt you should know the truth about everything."

"The truth," I said sarcastically, "What truth? That my husband is married to another woman, when he is married to me?!"

I felt the significance of the words that I had just uttered, and what they meant to me. My hands kneaded the leather couch, trying to regain control, as Joseph came into the room upon hearing me raise my voice.

186

He walked over to Segun, demanding, "I think you should go, sir. You have said enough for one day."

I looked at him with hatred, feeling the anger boiling inside of me. "Joseph!" I shouted. "I need to call Mr. Femi!"

Looking at Segun and pointing toward the door, I screamed, "And you, sir, need to leave. Get out! Get out!"

Upon hearing my screams, Ajoke and Taju Jr. ran into the room. I could not hold the tears back.

"Auntie, Auntie, are you all right?" Ajoke asked, grabbing my hand. I shook her hand loose and walked over to the man who had just destroyed all my happiness.

"You are evil. How dare you come here with these lies?"

Segun stepped towards me and cried, "No, Madame, they are not lies. I know now that you are not to blame for what Olu has done. He is there, right now, with my sister in Ondo. The family is having a meeting about you and her. They will decide today what will become of my sister's marriage to Olu."

I was in shock. I felt the room spinning. I refused to believe this bearer of bad tidings.

"You say what? What do you mean, 'what will become of her marriage'?" I asked through my tears. I walked around a chair and fell into it.

Segun stood in front of me, pacing the floor as he continued to explain about the family meeting. All I could think about were the lies and games that everyone had played with me. So there was no family emergency. The only emergency was what to do about

Lola! I looked at Segun, hating him.

"Why did you decide to tell me this, sir? What can you possibly gain from this? I don't even know you."

He stopped pacing and stood in front of me, his handsome features softened as he spoke in deference of his sister.

"I do not mean to hurt you, but I saw how my sister suffered everyday that Olu was away. When he wrote her that he was marrying you, I saw her completely destroyed. I just wanted you to feel some of her pain. But, now I can see you are not to blame. You see, she loves him as you do."

Joseph handed me a handkerchief. I wiped my eyes and blew my nose, my mind in a whirl of thought. My head and heart dropped in defeat as all the words sank in to my consciousness.

I was thinking, *Femi, Femi, how could you do this to me?*

The pain must have shown on my face because Segun came over to me and took my hand, kneeling down, saying, "Madame, I am so sorry, so sorry."

I snatched my hand back screaming, "Get out! Go away and go away!" burst into tears again.

"Sir, sir," Joseph began, "I beg you, please leave."

My body was racked with sobs, and I could not stop. I didn't want to think anymore; I just wanted to die! How could this be happening? Oh, God, how could this be?

Joseph showed Segun to the door. Once outside, Segun thought to himself, *Well, Lola, I have done it now. She knows...*

But, somehow, Segun did not feel the self-satisfaction he thought he would as he began his long drive back to the village.

*****

The phone rang at the Adegoke house in Ondo. Emmanuel got up and answered it.

"Hello, *tani-kilo-fe'?*"

"This is Joseph, sir. Mr. Femi should come back, for, Madame is not well."

"Joseph, what is wrong with her?" Mr. Adegoke asked.

Joseph went on to tell him what had happened.

"I tried to stop him, sir, but he pushed his way into the house and upset Miss Janice."

As Emmanuel was asking Joseph what Segun did, his wife, Abimbola, came to see what was keeping her husband.

"Emmanuel, what is it?"

He held up his hand for his wife to wait while getting the rest of the news from Joseph.

"He told Miss Janice about Mr. Femi and Miss Lola's marriage!"

Emmanuel almost dropped the phone, "What? What? He did what? Oh, no," he replied. "How did she take it?"

189

"Not too good, sir. I think someone should come quickly."

Emmanuel told Joseph to hold on.

"Bimbo, go and call Olufemi to the phone."

He explained to her what happened. She was concerned and rushed upstairs to her son's room. Olu and Lola lay entwined in each other's arms; they had just finished making passionate love and were drifting off to sleep when they heard a knock at the door.

"Tani? (Who is it?)," Olu asked.

"E'-mi (your mother)."

He jumped up and ran across the room, grabbing a wrapper to cover his nakedness. Then he opened the door and joined his mother in the hall, trying not to disturb Lola.

"Yes, mother, what is wrong?" he asked, seeing the worried look on her face.

"Come, Joseph is on the phone from Lagos; something has happened."

The fear showed on Olufemi's face, "Mom, what?"

She would not say more, but hurried her son to the phone. Olufemi took the receiver from his father and listened to Joseph retell the story.

"What? Oh my God. And Janice, where is she?" he asked the steward.

"She is lying down, sir, but I fear for her; she has not stopped crying, sir."

"Okay, Joseph, I will be there on the first flight in the morning."

Olufemi asked Joseph to call me to the phone. I was lying on the bed, thinking about my life ... wondering where I went wrong to deserve this. *Oh, Femi, where were the signs?* I thought sadly when Joseph knocked on the door and said that I had a call.

"I didn't hear the phone ring, Joseph."

"Please, Madame, you have a call," he insisted. I got up and picked up the receiver; it was Femi.

"Hello, Janice."

The very sound of his voice evoked an emotion that cannot be put into words. When I did not speak he cried, "Janice, Janice, are you there?"

Suddenly a flood of obscenities came bursting from my mouth, "You *bastard*, you dirty, low-down *bastard*! How could you? How?"

I started sobbing hysterically and dropped the receiver on the floor, and then I fell back across the bed.

Joseph picked up the phone and Femi asked him what had happened. He told him I was hysterical and could no longer talk, and to please hurry home.

As Olufemi hung up the phone, his mother was wringing her hands, "Oh my son, is she alright?"

Olufemi just stood there, shaking his head in disbelief. Emmanuel and Abimbola were upset seeing their son so distraught. Olufemi clenched his fist and shouted, "That Segun! Damn that man!"

Lola had awaken and stood by the door, hearing only the tail end of the conversation. She called to her husband, "Is everything alright, Olu?"

Olufemi rushed to her and told her that he must leave in the morning for Lagos.

"Why, Olu? What's happened?" she asked, concerned. Olufemi, pacing the floor explained,

"Lola, Janice knows about you. Segun drove to Lagos and told her."

He was visibly upset as he repeated the story. This unnerved Lola, who said angrily, "Why must everyone walk on egg shells because of her? I am tired of being the one who does not matter. After all, I am your first wife!"

Lola did not see her mother- and father-in-law standing in the doorway, listening to her outburst. The three of them turned and looked at her, surprised at her display of emotion. Instead of being a loyal, faithful, subservient wife, they saw a tiger, stopping at nothing to protect what was hers. Olu walked over to her and put his arm around her, attempting to console her.

She shook his arm off, snapping, "Save it for your other wife."

And with that, she bid everyone good night.

Olufemi arrived at the airport in the morning for his flight to Lagos. His father had to pull a few strings to get him a seat.

"Call us, Son, if you need our help. We will be coming on a later flight."

Femi thanked his family for their support and boarded the plane. He and Lola had had a heated exchange this morning. She wanted to go to Lagos with him, and he refused to take her.

"Why can't I go, Olu? I have a right."

Olu cut her off before she could go on any further. "You have only the rights in your own home, not in my sister's home."

Lola's head hurt; she did not sleep well last night. No one did.

"Olu, maybe I can help," she said, as he packed his bag. But she could not persuade him to change his mind.

"No, Lola, this is my final word. I must see Janice alone."

Realizing that he was shouting at her, he calmed down and said softly, "You can come with Bisi and Taju."

But she would not give up.

"Olu, I need to speak to her and explain," Lola said, thinking to herself. *Yes, explain what a liar you are and how you spent last night with me!* Lola finally agreed to wait, but she intended to return to Lagos as soon as possible.

*****

The plane landed at the airport, and Femi took a taxi to the house. I paced the floor of our room, trying to piece together the events of last night. I'd vowed to shed no more tears; they only make a woman weak. I sat down on the bed, exploring my options. I could leave Femi or return to America or kill Femi, kill Lola ... Oh hell ... I knew better than that. *My God,* I thought, *what have I gotten myself into?* To top the whole thing off, I had missed my period twice. I began to feel the waves of nausea wash over me as I ran into the bathroom to throw up. I kneeled on the cool tiles of the bathroom floor as the last of my breakfast came up. It didn't take a fool to figure out that I was pregnant. I wanted a family right away, and so did Femi, *but two surprises in one day were too much for me,* I thought, as the gags racked my body. I lay against the tub, resting, then got up and washed my face and mouth with cool water, trying to regain my composure.

I returned to the bed and lay down, watching the ceiling fan turn, thinking about my options. I never needed my mother so much in my life as I did right now. I needed someone to talk to. When the door opened, it was as if God had answered my prayers.

"Aduke! Aduke, where did you come from?" I cried weakly from the bed.

"Oh, Janice, my friend," she said, rushing to the bed. "How are you?" She sat down and cradled my head in her arms.

"When did you arrive, and who called you?"

She told me Bisi had called her. She had arrived Friday from London on holiday.

"Oh, thank God you are here," and I proceeded to tell her what had happened.

"Oh, that fool," she stood up, stomping her feet on the floor. "I warned him."

Stunned by her reaction, I asked, "You knew, Aduke?!" I said, my voice rising to a scream. "You knew Femi was married?"

Before she could answer, I heard Femi's voice in the hall talking to Joseph. Aduke's face became flushed and beads of sweat had appeared on her forehead and upper lip. Then Femi rushed into the room, glancing at Aduke.

"Please leave us alone," he said.

She left the room, visibly upset at my discovery that she had lied as well. Was there anyone that I could trust? I sat up weakly on the edge of the bed, too tired to stand;

the previous outburst had zapped my strength.

Femi walked over to me, so tall and handsome, with his beautiful eyes.

Steady, steady, I said to myself. I thought. *God, why?* As I put my hand to my mouth and bit my lips to hold back my tears.

"Janice," he said as he reached towards me. I drew back, as my anger rose to the surface. He grabbed my shoulders and turned me to face him. I could not bear to look at him. I felt the bitter taste of bile rise into my throat as I fought the urge to vomit. I swallowed and looked at him.

"You are a liar, Femi Adegoke!" I screamed as I shook loose of his hands, continuing to curse him.

"You are an awful human being to bring me here, knowing you had a wife already. To top it all off, you married me, knowing you had a wife!"

Saying the words brought the bitter bile into my mouth. I ran to the bathroom, kneeled in front of the toilet, and threw up again.

"Aduke, Aduke," Femi called, scared, "Janice is sick; please hurry!"

She pushed past him into the bathroom and held my shoulders until the gagging subsided. I sat on the edge of the tub while she put cold compresses on my neck and face.

Femi picked me up and lay me on the bed effortlessly. I let my head fall on his chest, "Oh Femi," I cried, "I want to go home to my mother; look what you have done to me."

Aduke cooed, "Shh, shh, Janice, everything will be okay. He was wrong to lie, but he loves you so; look at him."

I looked at him. The tears and pain showed on his face. He was crying, unashamedly, as he held me. Aduke slipped from the room, leaving us alone to grieve. He sobbed,

"My darling, Janice, I should have told you. My father warned me, and Aduke warned me of the consequences, but I did not listen. I have loved you from the moment I met you. I knew I would lose you if I had told you about Lola."

With the mention of her name, I felt needles in my skin. I stiffened, and as he felt me pull away, he held me tighter. I pushed him off.

"Femi, look at me," I insisted. As he looked, searching into my eyes, trying to read my thoughts, I continued, "Are you really married to another woman?" I needed to hear it from his lips.

"Yes," he answered, his gaze not wavering.

"Do you really love her?"

"Yes," he answered quickly.

My lips were beginning to tremble when I shouted, "Then how can you say you love me?"

I slapped him twice on his face as I fired my words at him. My nails became claws — all I wanted to do was to hurt this offensive figure in front of me; he became the object of my anger and frustration. I kicked at him, cursing him.

"You bastard, you demon, damn liar. You are a destroyer of dreams and all my

196

happiness!"

Every profane word I ever knew flew from my lips, because I wanted him to hurt as I did. I wanted him to feel the pain I felt. He tried to stop me, all six feet of him, but I became a madwoman, insane, completely out of control as I began throwing everything I could get my hands on. I grabbed the bedside table lamp and threw it. It hit Femi in the head, as Aduke ran into the room, pleading,

"Stop, Janice, stop! You will hurt yourself!"

"God!" I cried, "Please help me, help me!"

Femi stood there, no longer trying to protect himself, taking it all. His head was bloody where the lamp hit him, and his lips were cut and bleeding. His eyes were filled with tears as he shuddered in pain. I was not finished yet; so, I ran over to him and began showering him with blows from everywhere, kicking and scratching him. Then, suddenly, as if he came to his senses, he pushed me off of him to the floor.

He began moving towards me menacingly. I saw murder in his eyes and so did Aduke. She rushed over, grabbing and pulling me to safety. Joseph rushed to Femi, who had fallen to his knees. I was completely hysterical as Aduke struggled to get me outside the front door. Bisola and Taju drove up just as we got outside. Taju saw Aduke struggling to hold me, and he came over to assist her. He held both of my arms, so I could not inflict any more damage on anyone else.

I was covered with Femi's blood and wet with sweat. I was enraged with hatred. Femi was no longer the man I loved, but a bitter enemy that needed to be terminated. Bisola's scream could be heard throughout the compound.

"Taju, Taju, *egbamio* (help me); call a doctor my brother is injured!"

It all happened so fast; Taju dropped my arms and rushed into the house. Aduke and I stood near her car. Out of the corner of my eye I barely saw a woman jumping out of Bisi's car, who ran into the house. I did notice that she was Nigerian, wearing a print wrapper and slippers. She wore no headscarf; as she ran, her braids fell up and down her back. Aduke was still holding my arms when I let out a loud scream and all went dark...

Chapter 14

Taju sent his driver to the airport to pick up his in-laws. When they arrived at the house, everyone was in a state of pandemonium. Bisola quickly relayed what had happened to Femi and Janice to her parents on the way to the hospital. Upon reaching there, they put me in the maternity wing and Femi in a private room. Abimbola looked at her husband and said,

"This has gone too far, Emmanuel."

He seemed preoccupied, deep in thought. He wondered why his son used such poor judgment in handling his personal affairs. Maybe going to America was not the best thing for him; after all, look what had happened when he went to England. He should have learned from past mistakes. The car reached the hospital, and the concerned family rushed inside. They were told where their children were.

"I will go and see Janice, Emmanuel," Abimbola volunteered. "You go and see our son."

Aduke was sitting with Janice, holding her hand when her mother-in-law walked in.

"Eku se', (well done) Aduke."

"Yes, Ma," Aduke greeted the elder woman and knelt on the floor. She then gave her the chair as I looked at my mother-in-law. I didn't know what to expect from her, and I was frightened.

"My child," she said, taking my hand gently. "Janice, I know that my son has hurt you. He has been very foolish. I assure you that he loves you."

She went on to tell me about the injuries that I inflicted on Femi. I winced at the description.

"I did not know that I had hurt him so badly."

"My husband is with him now; he will be all right."

My eyes filled with pain as I thought about Femi's injuries. I closed them and thought, *oh my God, what have I done?*

"I want to ask you how you feel, now that you know about Lola."

My eyes held a look of surprise at her lack of tact and consideration for me. But since most of my anger had gone now, I felt better able to bear the insult. I just felt used and betrayed. When I did not answer, she went on to ask another question.

"Are you pregnant?"

"Yes," I replied, "about six weeks along."

"Does my son know?" she asked as one eyebrow rose.

"He should know by now!" I said, my voice raising, agitated. "Mama Femi, I don't understand the culture. You are the only wife that Baba Femi has." She nodded her head in agreement.

"Then where does Femi get these ideas about polygamy?"

She looked straight into my eyes, carefully choosing her response. "Olufemi's grandfather, my father, was a polygamist. He had three wives; my mother and two stepmothers raised me. He had a total of sixteen children. My husband's brother is also a polygamist; he has three wives and eight children. Even Taju has another wife; her name is Abbe. He was married to her before he married Bisola. Abbe was barren and lives in the village. He supports her financially and goes to see her occasionally. She chooses not to divorce him, but she is young and some day, she may change her mind. We gave Omolola the same options."

"What are they?" I interrupted.

"Whether to stay married or divorce my son."

"And what did she choose?" I asked, anxious to know.

"She chose to stay, because she also loves him and he her."

I was trying to understand what she was saying, when I remarked, "But it is not possible to love two people equally at the same time."

"Well, I won't say that," she replied. "Maybe not in the exact same way, but I believe that it is possible to be in love with two people in different ways."

My mind could never understand it. It went against everything I learned about love and romance. I grew up in a monogamous society, and even though television in America showed unfaithful relationships on soap operas and talk shows, I still could not fathom this.

"I don't understand; I don't want to understand; all I want to do is to go home. I feel so betrayed."

She looked at me and said sternly, "Janice, Olufemi is an African, a Nigerian. Our people, the Ijebu, descend from kings. Why did you ever consider marrying out of your culture?"

I looked at my mother-in-law. She was a proud and elegant woman; her coffee-brown skin smooth except for the two tribal marks on each cheek. It was almost as if someone scratched her there by mistake. Her white teeth were small with a wide gap in the middle. I had read somewhere that meant sexuality or fertility or something. Her slender, long neck held her head gracefully, and her large, round eyes almost filled her face. She walked with such grace, that I could picture her as a girl carrying baskets on her head, walking barefoot through her village. The long, slender fingers turned over my hand, holding it. She was as much Femi as he was his mother; both had the same aristocratic appearance as she sat regally in the hospital chair. Even at forty-nine, she was still a beautiful woman. A mother's love shone in her eyes, and in those same eyes, I saw her love for me. I returned her look shyly and began to answer her sincerely.

"I wanted to be a part of my ancestral heritage. I wanted my children's veins to run with the blood of kings; I wanted them to have a stronger tie with the motherland Africa."

My eyes held a mystical look as I spoke of a time, a place that I dreamed of, but wanted my children to have.

"Once I met your son, I worried about your culture, but I knew he was for me."

She nodded her head in agreement, understanding as a woman, the need to fulfill your dreams through your children with the man you choose.

"I saw Femi as my gateway to Africa."

I was gripping her hand tightly now, afraid she would let go. We both sat in silence, understanding each other for the first time.

"Yes, Janice," she responded after some time. "I do understand, but now, you must try to understand. You have the same choices that Lola had. You can stay and try to be a family, or you can return to your life in America."

"But what about our child?"

Before she could answer, Mr. Adegoke came into the room. I could see he was angry. I was ready for anything now. After all, what did I have to lose?

*****

In his room, Olu sat up in his bed; he looked a sight. His head was bandaged, and he had scratches on his face and a swollen lip.

"Do you need anything, Olu?" Lola asked sweetly, her soft brown eyes giving her husband an adoring look.

"No, Lola, I am fine."

Kemi and Jide were also in the room. Lola had called them from the hospital.

"You should have beaten her, Olu." Jide said, looking at his friend's bandages. "I would never let my wife abuse me that way."

"*O ti to*, Jide," Lola injected. "You were not there and so do not know the circumstances surrounding the fight."

"Even so, Lola, she still had no right!"

"*Jide, Jide*," Kemi broke in. "Those Americans are so violent. You never know what they will do!"

Olu told her to be quiet, that she did not know what she was saying.

Kemi looked at her friend for support, but instead, Lola remarked,

"Only I can understand her anger, and why she did what she did. After all, who is to blame for all this mess?"

Olufemi touched his sore lip, remembering yesterday. He had barely seen Lola as she rushed into the room in the house in response to Bisola's screams. She saw Olu on his knees, bleeding and holding his head, being helped up by Joseph and Bisi.

"Hurry, Lola!" Bisi cried." Come and help us."

The three of them got Olu into the car and took him to the hospital. Janice had already arrived with Aduke and Taju. Olufemi's only concern was Janice.

"What happened to her?" he asked, looking from face to face.

"We don't know," they all said, and then Lola stammered,

"I saw her in the driveway with Aduke, so she must be here as well."

Olufemi began to curse himself, "Damn, what have I done to her?"

"Oh, be quiet, Olufemi," Bisi reprimanded him. "I warned you of this in America."

Olufemi just sat there, holding his head, repeating, "I know, I know."

*****

Mr. Adegoke entered Janice's room, and Abimbola became his subservient wife again.

"Madame, go upstairs and see to your son. Go and see what this woman has done to him!"

My hand flew to my mouth, "Oh God, is he that bad?"

He went on talking to his wife, ignoring my question. "He is not even concerned about himself, only her," he continued talking, totally ignoring me.

"I give up trying to understand my children," he said, his voice holding the air of defeat.

I felt guilty and tried to console my father-in-law. "I am sorry, I am sorry."

"Why?" Aduke asked, bursting into the room. "You did nothing wrong, Janice, except to love him. You were tricked, Janice."

"Aduke," I asked her, surprised by her words. "You knew all the time?"

"No, that is not true, Janice. I found out after your engagement, the night of the dinner."

I rolled my eyes at her, "But you knew before I got married," I said angrily.

"Janice, Femi told me not to tell. I was afraid that it would destroy our friendship. I regret not telling you now. I had hoped that you would have found out, before you came to Nigeria. I knew how you felt about him, and I did not want to be the reason that you broke up."

I turned my back on her. I felt betrayed by everyone Nigerian. How could I trust anyone? My mother-in-law saw my dismay and told me to just go by what I feel in my heart. She then kissed me on my cheek and left the room with her husband. Aduke walked to the window, looking out at the street — people rushing, carrying goods on their heads, the touts and taxis, and countless children...

"I am going back to Chicago next week, Janice, so we can spend some time together while I am here." Aduke said quietly. "The doctor says he will release you tonight." She walked back to the bed looking at me, "Are you going to talk to Femi?"

I nodded my head, looking at my wedding ring. "Is she here, Aduke?" I asked slowly.

"Who, Janice?"

"You know — Lola." She shook her head yes. I felt my throat tighten; I swallowed, feeling the nausea return.

"I want to see her."

Aduke looked at me surprised.

"Why, Janice?" she asked. "You will see her soon enough."

"I know, but I want to see Femi as well. I need to see his injuries and to tell him about the baby. I think I caught a glimpse of her last night. She came back with Bisi and Taju, didn't she?"

She nodded then asked, "Do you think that you should see her now? Why not wait until Femi is out of the hospital?"

"What kind of wife would I be if I did not attend to my husband, even if I am the one who inflicted the wounds on him?"

Aduke and I were unaware we were being observed by Lola. She had been listening outside the door for some time. She thought to herself, *Oh no, she is pregnant.* She felt like fainting at the shock, but stood fast, looking at Janice, as if mesmerized. She had not prepared herself to see her in the flesh. *So different from her pictures*, she thought. *Jide was right. They do not do her justice. Her hair is like silk, and her eyes shine like amber.* Lola saw the pointed nose and fair skin, with a hint of pink on her lips and cheeks. Even in a hospital gown, she was stunning. Olu's love gave her the courage to go and see Janice. She needed to see her competition. Now that she had satisfied her curiosity, she rushed back to her husband's side. All the family had left. Olu told her he would be released tomorrow.

Lola fluffed his pillows and poured him a glass of water. She was giving him the glass, when unknown to her, Aduke and Janice had come upstairs to Olu's room soon after Lola had returned from her spying mission. They were peering into the room. Aduke was surprised at Janice's reaction to the loving scene.

So this is Lola, I thought to myself. *She is lovely, but we are exact opposites.* Lola's figure was impeccable; her tight wrapper was showing all her curves as she leaned over Olu to give him the water. Her long braids were falling gracefully down her back and shoulders. Her legs looked strong and shapely, ending with her perfect, painted toes. Her hands gently caressed the glass as she held it for him. She was lovely; her skin was flawless, her complexion was almost copper in color.

"Perfect picture of love," I whispered sarcastically to Aduke.

I did not miss the look of love that passed between them. Aduke and I almost wished that I had inflicted more damage on my husband than I did. I was about to crash in on the loving scene when Aduke grabbed me and pulled me away.

"No, Janice, don't! That is not the way; you two will meet soon enough."

207

I was frustrated with rage as I walked back upstairs to my room. Aduke left a few minutes later, and I was alone. I found out that the nurse that came in to take my temperature was an American, like me. She was from New York City. Her name was Sharon Njoku; she married a Nigerian from Anambra state and had been living in Nigeria for five years. They had one child, a daughter; name Ngozi, who was three years old. I was so happy to meet an American, especially an African American like me, because most of the embassy staff that I met was white, which I thought was odd. I felt that our missions abroad should reflect our diversified population. I felt the need to identify with one of my own kind. I was pregnant and needed a close friend, someone who I could depend on. Frankly, I just needed someone to talk to. I asked Sharon to come by on her lunch break, so that we could eat together. She picked up her teacup after finishing her plate of rice and salad.

"So, you are the second wife?"

I looked at her, amazed that she had that information.

"You know, hospitals are notorious for gossip."

I was embarrassed that she should know about my situation, so I said, "I thought that what we were doing was normal for Nigeria."

"No, not really, girl, only for Nigerians, but since you are American, it is big news."

Sharon had made her point and went on to tell me that the Adegoke/Balogun family is well known in Lagos. "Even I have heard of your brother-in-law's factory."

I was really impressed. Femi had told me his family was wealthy, and I was glad that Sharon had filled me in on the family status.

"I am going to give you some advice, Janice." Sharon started, "Men will be men, and you make your marriage what you want it to be. I don't believe in polygamy either, but it is their culture. You need to talk to someone who is like you. When you are feeling better, I want you to come to my club meeting."

A club in Nigeria! I was anxious to know more about that. I had been isolated too long from people other than my family and Femi's friends. Sharon went on to tell me about the club. It was made up of American women of color who were married to Nigerians.

"It is a support group, Janice. It gives women a forum and a place to go and talk. We also have seminars and parties, and we celebrate the holidays as well. We meet every two weeks at a different house, and everyone brings a dish. There are two American women I really want you to meet; both are living in polygamy. One of them is the third wife."

I was surprised at what I heard. I could not believe that someone would consent to share her husband, especially someone from our country.

"Okay, Sharon, it's a date," I said excited.

We exchanged phone numbers, and she left to go back to work.

Later that evening after visiting hours, I walked over to Femi's room. Lola was gone, and I startled him.

"Janice," he flinched, as if afraid I was going to clobber him some more. I knew my husband was no coward, yet I was puzzled by his behavior. What I saw shocked me.

"Femi, did I do this to you?" I looked at his swollen face and bandaged hand. He must have got hurt when I threw the lamp at him. There were scratches all over him from the broken glass.

"Oh, Femi," I cried. All the thoughts of Lola were gone. "I'm sorry for what I did to you."

You could hardly recognize him. His beautiful eyes were all red and swollen and his nose and lips were cut. I reached out to touch him, but he pulled back from me.

"Sorry, Janice?" he asked in a conciliatory tone. "Why should you be sorry? I only got what I deserved."

The first tear fell like salve on his face. I kissed every mark I had inflicted on him — his lips, eyes, and head — and I massaged them through the bandages. My tongue rolled across his swollen mouth until he caught it and returned the kiss. I opened my mouth and let him probe deeper and when he moaned, I stopped abruptly and asked, "Am I hurting you, darling?"

His good hand grabbed the back of my long hair and pulled my head back to his. Our lips met, and we kissed hungrily, oblivious of his pain. I climbed up to lay over him as he winced in pain. I had kicked him in the ribs, and his back was sore. Even with one hand, he was able to touch me and evoke moans of pleasure. He moved me to his uninjured side, and we lay like that, just looking at each other until I whispered in his ear, my tongue flicking his ear hotly,

"Are you too hurt to make love to me?"

He drew in his breath because I knew this was his sensitive spot. His hand grabbed my buttocks, pulling me back on top of him. I felt him ready to love me. I remembered where we were and said, "Femi, someone could come in here and see us."

"So what?" he whispered. "We are husband and wife."

"Yes," I said coyly, "but first, let me tell you something." I leaned on one arm, my light-brown eyes sparkling with mischief and love. The smile that was on my face was like the sun shining, filled with so much warmth.

"I am going to have a baby!" He drew in his breath with surprise, his dark eyes smoldering with desire and so much love. He smiled and hugged me, his strong, white teeth flashing. He thought, *something kept me from fighting her back yesterday. To think, if I had hit her, I could have caused her to miscarry.*

"Oh, Janice, Janice, when? How?" I told him in about seven months.

"So that's why you were so sick. Thank God I did not hit you."

And with those words, he could no longer contain himself. We made the most exquisite love that we could in the narrow hospital bed, in spite of his injuries. We came together several times, reaching heights of passion untouched before. We fell asleep in each other's arms. Nurse Sharon walked into the room to check on her patient and saw the two lovers sleeping, still entwined in each other's arms. She softly backed out of the room so as not to disturb them and closed the door.

"This can wait," she chuckled to herself.

*****

Lola walked into the kitchen of her flat. She washed and put the dishes away. She had finished preparing dinner to take to the hospital when the phone rang. It was Bisi, calling to tell her that Olufemi was being released and would be at her house and that her parents would also be there. She paused and asked Lola if she was prepared to meet Janice.

"Yes, I am Bisi. I have already seen her."

"Where?" Bisola asked, surprised. Lola went on to tell Bisi how she stood outside her hospital room and observed her.

"She is beautiful, Bisi, and I heard she is pregnant!" Lola said sadly. Bisi was shocked at this news and had sympathy for her sister-in-law.

"I overheard her talking to Aduke," Lola said with envy. "That is how I found out about the baby."

Lola was tired of this situation and in spite of the baby; she just wanted to get on with her life.

"Bisi, I have been on hold for two years. I want to begin again. I will be moving to the house at Surulere on Saturday."

"Good, good, (sister *mi*), my sister I am glad that I will be seeing more of you now."

"It should be me that is pregnant, not her," Lola said sadly.

"Take heart, Lola; your time will come soon enough. My brother is man enough for the two of you."

After they hung up, Bisi rushed to tell Taju the news about Janice. They both nodded in sympathy for Lola, for in Africa, the wife who has the first child is revered...

Chapter 15

The air was filled with tension at the Balogun house. Bisi and Taju were arguing about Olufemi and Janice.

"Darling, why are we fighting?" Taju asked his angry wife.

"Oh, I don't know; I guess I am just tired of this whole affair," Bisi said, frustrated.

"Well, you know that this situation could have been avoided if your brother had been honest," Taju said thoughtfully, looking at his wife.

"That's what bothers me, Taju. He has always been honest before. I wonder what happened to him to make him change. I know that our tradition says that you can have more than one wife, but he could have taken two Nigerian women instead of complicating things by marrying a foreigner. These days, people cannot really afford to have more than one wife."

Taju agreed with his wife and told her to stop worrying, that everything would work out. Lola and Janice were strong women. "Well, I do not believe in happily ever after," Bisi said, her lips pouting. Taju walked over to his wife and with a rare show of emotion, he held her gently, saying,

"You should, dear; after all, look at us."

She looked at him through the corner of her eyes, remembering all the times that he tried to bring other women into the home; but instead of being spiteful, she just smiled and enjoyed the moment.

Later that day, the driver arrived with Olufemi and Janice. Olu's wounds looked 100 percent better as Joseph took his bag, then he and Janice walked into the cool house.

"I will be glad when we move into our home, Femi."

He nodded in agreement. Bisola and Taju welcomed us home and soon Ajoke and Taju Jr. joined us. When my mother- and father-in-law arrived, they were welcomed in the traditional African way by everyone.

"Where are your brother and his wife?" Abimbola enquired.

"Which one, Mama?" Bisola joked.

With a twinkle in her serious eyes, Abimbola told her daughter "Janice is the one I want to talk to."

"Oh, they are waiting in the den." They walked into the den to join us, and Femi and Taju prostrated before their parents. I got up and curtsied as a show of respect. The air was heavy with anticipation. My father-in-law was still reserved with me for hurting his son, while my mother-in-law was more open with me after our talk at the hospital. Everyone began to converse in Yoruba, and Femi held my hand and translated. I was grateful, but I still felt like an outsider. At that time, I recalled Sharon's words, and they gave me the strength to go on. *"Don't let them win, Janice. Show them what we are made of."*

I tossed my long hair back off my shoulder and held my head high. One thing that I inherited from the Bordeaux family was strength of character. My mother was a very independent woman, and I was a lot like her. When my father died, she endured the hardship of having to raise a child alone. I have to admire her courage and perseverance. I loved Femi and was ready to face anything, but I was ill prepared for our next visitor.

When she walked into the room, everyone turned to face her. A hush fell over the room. She was wearing a multicolored lace wrapper and *buba*. Her head tie was red, complementing the colors of the outfit. Her sandals matched the head tie, and she wore two gold chains and four bangles on each arm that made a tinkling noise as she walked confidently into the room. This was Lola, the woman I saw in Femi's hospital room yesterday. An older woman followed her. I tensed and dropped Femi's hand, but he reached for mine. I placed it in my lap, out of his reach, for at that moment, I did not want to touch him. As her eyes focused on me, her nostrils flared and the corner of her mouth quivered as she attempted to remain composed. This is Omolola, the woman I am to share my life with! Titiloye arrived last night to support her daughter in her most trying hour. Lola had asked her mother not to come today, but it was to no avail. So together, Titiloye and her daughter boarded a taxi to Ikoyi. Neither had much to say; it was as if it all has been said.

"Lola, you must welcome the American into our family," her mother told her in no uncertain terms. "She is the *Iyawo* (the junior wife), and you are the *Iyale*, (the senior wife). She is not from our culture, and you must teach her our ways."

Lola knew her mother was right, but cringed at the prospect. It seemed so unfair that all the burden of acceptance rested with her. Now was the moment, when all the future would hang in the balance.

Lola looked at me, who, she thought, was so beautiful and confident. My long hair hung down my back; my light-brown eyes were filled with fire, ringed with dark-brown lashes which gazed at her; my eyebrows arched in surprise; and my long, slender

215

fingers that she saw push Olu's hand aside were painted pink. To her, I was a goddess, and I made her feel nervous.

"*E'kabo, e'kabo!* (Welcome!)"

Abimbola stood up and rushed to greet the two women; they bowed to each other and she hugged Lola, and I felt a twinge of jealousy. Femi just sat there as if in shock, looking nervously at me. Mr. Adegoke said something to Femi in Yoruba, and then Femi jumped up to greet the two women. I sat there amazed; surveying the scene, wishing the floor would open up and swallow me and the couch I sat on. I thought to myself, *well, this day had to come sometime.* Better now than later when I was all out of shape with our baby growing inside of me. I felt underdressed, really at a disadvantage compared to Lola, who was stunning in her full traditional attire.

The excitement caused the queasiness in my stomach to return. In a few moments, my mother-in-law called me to meet Mrs. Shodeye and Omolola. I stood up and walked slowly to the group. Everyone's eyes were on me as I drew from my mother's strength and joined the group. Standing face to face with Lola, I took a deep breath as we were introduced to each other. I held my hand out to shake hers; she slowly reached for it, never taking her eyes off mine. The bile began to rise in my throat, bringing tears to my eyes. I blushed and swallowed, vowing to remain composed through this trying ordeal as we shook hands. We pulled away quickly as I turned to greet her mother. Titiloye was thoroughly taken in by my appearance. She was speaking in broken English to me, but I understood her welcoming me.

"So we meet at last, Janice. I am Lola's mother. You have already met my son Segun. I must apologize for his impudence."

"Thank you," I said politely, remembering that he was the one who destroyed my whole world. Through the interchange, Femi was very quiet. He kept his eyes locked on the both of us and smiled, then he went back to sit down. It seemed like everyone took a deep breath because they were afraid of my reaction.

Well, I fooled them all, but now I was going to be sick, so I excused myself and ran to the bathroom to throw up. Femi got ready to rush after me, when Titiloye spoke,

"No, Olufemi let Lola go."

"Is that advisable, Titiloye? I mean, after all, they just met," Emmanuel said.

Titiloye stood up and addressed the room, "Better to know how the *oyinbo* will react to my daughter with all of us here, than later, while they are living together."

Olu spoke softly, "We will not live in the same house."

"I know that, my son-in-law," Titiloye continued, "but there will be occasions when you must all be together socially."

Sensing her brother's confusion, Bisola volunteered to go.

"I'll go, or mama can go."

"No," Emmanuel said. "I agree with Titiloye; let Lola go to her."

Lola looked at Olu, took a deep breath, and hurried into the bathroom. I was on my knees at the toilet. She took a towel and ran cold water on it, then placed it gently on the back of my neck. I felt the cool towel on my skin and began to feel better. I had no idea who was there except that the perfume was unfamiliar. She helped me to my feet and as I rinsed my mouth out, I glanced in the mirror, and saw it was Lola. I put my hand to my mouth to still my trembling lips.

The morning sickness had drained all my strength. I could not speak. I just rushed to the bed and threw my face on a pillow, sobbing. Lola rushed to my side, bringing the towel with her. She looked at me crying and took the towel and wiped my face. I sat up, and she removed the wide head tie. Her braids fell loosely around her face that was now as wet as mine. We embraced each other, both crying by then at the sheer helplessness of our situation. I was alone with no family, the man I loved had betrayed me, so it was ironic that the woman he kept from me was now holding me, and we were crying together. I wiped her tears with the towel, and she mine. We looked at each other, trying to see through to our hearts. It was as if we had crossed the sands of time. Here we were, just two women sharing a common bond, both betrayed, both deeply in love with the same man. I wanted to hate her, but I could not; she wanted to hate me, but she could not. Neither of us spoke; we just held hands, looking at each other, begging for acceptance. Six months ago I would never believe that I would be caught dead in this situation; no, not I, conservative Janice Marie Bordeaux from New Orleans! That I would be in Nigeria, in my bedroom with my husband's other wife, holding hands. No one would ever believe this!

I cleared my throat, "Can this work? Does it ever work?"

When she spoke, she reminded me of Aduke; her lilting accent complimented my Southern one. "Sometimes it does; it all depends on the people involved."

"Lola, do you really love Femi enough to go through with this arrangement?"

Oh, Lola thinks to herself, *she calls him Femi.*

"Yes, I love Olu with all my heart. I could never give him up, and after all, it is part of our Nigerian culture. Many men have more than one wife."

So, I thought to myself, *she calls him Olu.*

"I am not a Nigerian. I was not raised in your culture; in America, it is against the law to have more than one wife."

"You can learn, Janice. May I call you Janice?" she asked, unsure how to address me.

"Yes, please do, and may I call you Lola?"

"Yes," she answered lightly as a twinkle came to her eyes. "My full name is Omolola Afolake."

I felt that the barrier had been removed, and at least, we felt comfortable enough to talk to each other. Femi entered the room as if afraid of what he would find.

"Thank God!" he exclaimed. "Are you alright?"

"Yes," we answered in unison. Then I said sarcastically,

"Did you think that we would kill each other in a fit of jealous rage over you, Femi?"

"Yes!" Lola jumped in, "I can see you have very little faith in your wives, Olu!"

He stood back, feeling defeated.

"I am just glad that you two have come to an understanding," he replied concerned.

I looked at Lola; she took my hand, seeing my diamond ring shining in the light of the room.

"Oh, Janice, it is so beautiful!"

She looked at my long nails painted pink and chuckled, "You have what I have always wanted; you are carrying Olu's child."

She dropped my hand and touched her flat stomach. Femi came over to the bed and looked at us both, each in a different way. He took our hands and put them both to his lips. I was tempted to pull mine away, but held fast, waiting for him to speak.

"I want you both to believe that I never meant to hurt either of you; it is strange how I love the two of you. True, Janice, our culture may not seem fair, but you are trying so hard to give it a chance. I respect you, for you are courageous woman. I commend you for at least giving it a try."

"You need to hold that thought, Femi. It still may not work; we are just beginning."

Lola shifted uneasy at my words.

"I know, Jan," he continued, "but at least you are willing to try."

Then he turned his eyes to Lola, "Lola, you know me; I never meant to hurt you, but now that you have met Janice, can you understand a little of how I feel?"

Lola pulled her hand away and responded nicely, "Oh, yes, I understand, Olu." But deep in her heart, she knew that no woman could ever truly understand this.

"Let's go and join the others, so that we may begin our lives together," Femi said softly to us.

Lola and I gave each other a knowing look as the three of us returned to the den and joined the family. It was the beginning of an experience I will never forget. On the surface, all is not what it appears. So for the rest of the day, the family toasted the happiness of the three of them and prayed for the success of the marriage. It was after 8 p.m. when everyone started to leave. Lola and her mother were the last to go. They walked out to the courtyard, preparing to enter the car. Taju told his driver to take them home. Titiloye got inside, satisfied that all was well. Lola would be moving into the house at Surulere that weekend. Her daughter would have a car and a driver at her disposal. She would also have a cook and steward. She felt her daughter was finally getting what she deserved, after waiting for her husband for two years. Lola stood outside the car, as if waiting for Olu to ask her to stay. When all he said was "Good night, Lola," she lowered her eyes with disappointment.

"When will I see you, Olu?"

I stood by the door waiting for him to say something.

"I will come by your office tomorrow, and we will have lunch. By then, I will have worked out a schedule." My heart sank at this news and judging by the look on Lola's face, she was unhappy as well. Titiloye stuck her head out of the car window saying,

"Just be fair, my son-in-law; just be fair."

Femi nodded and kissed Lola on the cheek, knowing that I was standing there in the doorway. She held him close; she wanted him so. He could feel her yearning, but pushed her back as he helped her enter the car. He would have to learn to control his own desires as well.

"I love you, darling," Lola said with sincerity, *"Odaro."*

I was exhausted; all I wanted to do was to sleep. I did not want to think of the choices that I made today. Femi reached over for me and for the first time since we were married, I rolled over to my side of the bed. I guess this was not going to be as easy as he thought.

The next day as Femi was preparing to go to work, he came over to me where I was laying in bed, afraid to stir lest the morning sickness overtake me. I was tired and had a restless night.

"Janice, are you awake?" he called softly.

"Yes, Femi?"

"Good. I want to tell you the schedule so that there will be no surprises. I will be with Lola one week and with you the next; that way, each of you will see me at regular intervals."

I listened intently, unable to believe my ears. I am now on a schedule as to when and how I sleep with my husband! He continued, tying his tie, "On social occasions, we all will attend the function. That goes for family gatherings as well."

I propped myself up on one arm, amazed at how easy it appeared for him to just tell me when I was and was not going to see him. It's almost like trying to set up your sexual life on a schedule. Oh, well, there goes spontaneity! This was going to be real hard. The waves of nausea washed over me.

"Femi, why didn't you tell me you were married before we got involved? It would have saved us both a lot of grief. Lola is a nice person. I don't see how you could have treated her so badly."

Femi turned to me, his eyes blazing with anger. He walked over to the bed; his fists were balled tightly at his side.

"I have had enough, woman. You are my wife, and I will do anything to make you happy! Lola was my wife before you; I love her. You, Janice, somehow bewitched me; your beauty was unparalleled. Also I was lonely, just plain lonely."

The anger drained from his face and was replaced with a lost look.

"I was alone and celibate for two years, so don't blame me for being human. You could have asked me, Janice, if I was married."

I lay there, stunned by his admission and frustrated. I sat up and said, "Femi, I did ask! You told me that you never married her, remember?"

He looked away, remembering his words guiltily. "Well, that is past; we must look towards the future."

"What future," I said angrily. "I have to share you with Lola. I had never planned on that, and now I am pregnant. Oh, this is all too complicated for me, Femi. I am just a simple woman, and I wanted a simple life, like being married to one man and having children — not married to a man with a wife!"

He turned back to the mirror and continued dressing. When he finished, he brushed his hair and walked back to the bed where I lay.

"Janice, I can't change what I have done; I can only say, I am sorry you had to go through this. I love you, and I will be totally faithful to you within our marriage."

"Oh, you mean when you are *with* me," I said with sarcasm.

The waves of nausea increased, as I got more upset.

"Yes, as long as I am with you; but when I am with Lola, I will do the same for her."

Then he sat on the bed, reaching for me. I pulled back angrily.

"You have been sleeping with her already, haven't you?"

"Yes, I have," he replied arrogantly.

The tears stung my eyes as I reached out to hit him. This time, he grabbed my hands. I was powerless against him. Femi was a strong man; his hands covered my own as he tried to protect himself.

"Let me go! Let me go!" I hissed through my teeth. "Let me go, or I will throw up on you!"

I pulled my hands free, rushing to the bathroom, crying. I stayed there waiting for him to leave. Soon I heard the bedroom door shut as I lay on the cool tiles on the floor, wondering what I would do next. Crying, feeling sorry for myself, thinking, *Oh why God?,* I prayed, "What have I done to deserve this?"

Chapter 16

Olufemi sat in Taju's office and asked his brother-in-law how a man could be so unjust to two beautiful and loving women.

"Ah, ah, little brother, are you having a conscience now, at this late date?"

"I feel that I have been so wrong, Brother Taju. I mean, if you could have seen the look on Janice's face this morning. I have never seen her so angry. If she had a gun, she would have shot me."

Taju sat back in his chair and pondered the thought, "No, Brother; she is not that type. She is hurting right now and with good reason. Remember, she is pregnant, and women are sensitive at that time. You must be patient, Olufemi; in time, she will come around. Janice loves you very much; I have seen the way she looks at you. Any other *oyinbo* (foreign woman) would have left you and gone back to America, but not Janice. I think you underestimate her character, Olufemi. Just give her time."

"You may be right, Taju. I am meeting Lola for lunch today, to let her know about our living arrangements."

"Olufemi, to some men, you would be the envy of Lagos. I mean, two gorgeous women at your beck and call, but I know how difficult it can be. That is why Abbe stays in the village."

"I almost forgot about your other wife, Taju. I'm glad that you understand what I am going through."

Taju continued talking to Olufemi, talking about his own living arrangements and

225

the problems that he had with it.

"You know, Bisi absolutely refused to even live in the same city as Abbe. She gave me pure hell, every time I went to see her. I never intended to have two wives, but Abbe could not give me children and I wanted a son. So she agreed that I could take another wife."

"Didn't they both live together for a while in the same house?" Olufemi asked.

"Yes, they did, while I was building the factory and money was tight. We lived in Festac Village. Those two women fought every day. I got to the point that I did not want to come home."

"What did you do, Brother Taju?"

"I spoke to my father and asked him how he kept peace between his six wives. He told me he never keeps them in the same house together. Always give them separate, but equal, accommodation. I remember as a child," he went on, "that I never lived with my sibling's mothers. My mother had her own house."

"I don't intend for Lola and Janice to live in the same house. I want then both to live in Lagos, but Lola will be in Surulere, in my father's house, and Janice in Ikeja."

"I think that is a wise decision, Olufemi. Keep them apart. Abbe chose to leave and go the village. It was either that or a divorce, and you know how our people frown upon that. Abbe was using all types of *juju* on your sister. She was behaving very wickedly. You know that Bisi lost two babies before I sent Abbe away."

"Really, Brother Taju? Bisi never told me."

"She even tried to hurt me, so I decided she should go and live in the village with

226

her parents."

"Do you still sleep with her, Taju?"

"Not often, Olu. She comes to Lagos twice a year, and I go to the village to see her about once a month. There is a lot of bitterness between Abbe and Bisi, so I never stay long. Your sister accepts the fact that I am still married to her, so she lets me go to her. I love your sister. Abbe's wickedness turned me away from her. She knows how I feel, but I still do perform my duty to her and her family. They are all well taken care of."

Olufemi told Taju that Lola was not happy to be living separately. "I know that she is especially not happy with Janice being pregnant."

"You are a strong, young man, Olufemi," Taju joked with him. "It won't be long before Lola is also expecting."

"I hope you are right, Taju, though my feelings for Lola are different than what I feel for Janice. But Lola is African; she keeps me in touch with my culture."

"And what is Janice to you, Olufemi?"

Olu scratched his chin, smiling at the thought of his wife, Janice.

"She is sophisticated, educated, and indescribably beautiful. She knows how to love me, not just physically, but completely. Janice makes me feel whole. I cannot lose her."

"Then you must take care, my brother, that you are fair to them both ..."

The morning went slowly. Before afternoon, Olu had another visitor. It was Jide, his friend.

"Kini-kan, Jide; long time."

"How is everything?"

"I am healing, my friend," Olu said.

"Kemi and I are inviting you and Lola to dinner at my place."

"I am just going to meet her for lunch, Jide. Will you join us?"

"No, I am rushing to meet Kemi at work. Remember Sunday, okay, Odaro?"

*****

Alhaji Mohammed Yaro called Lola into his office to take dictation. When they finished, he asked her how things were going. They had not talked much since she returned to work, nor had they mentioned the incident when he made advances to her and she returned the earrings.

"Lola, how is your husband, Olu? Is everything alright?"

He was probing for a sign — any sign. He still had a crush on her. Even though he had three wives, none of them were like her. His first two wives were from his village in Kano state. They were married young and were not educated. He tried to get them into school, but they had no interest, beyond serving him. His last wife did finish high school. She taught the younger children at home. He wanted a woman to travel with him on his business trips, and hold a decent conversation with him, not be preoccupied with children and religion. To him, Lola represented this. She was intelligent, sophisticated, and beautiful. Today, Lola had taken particular care regarding her appearance. He looked at her wearing a two-piece linen suit and matching heels. Her hair was uncovered. The braids wrapped around her head like a crown. She began to feel uncomfortable under his gaze.

"Sir, is there anything else? I would like to go to lunch ... My husband is picking me up at noon."

"Lola, you did not answer my question. How did things work out? I hear he has an American wife."

Lola thought to herself, *News sure travels fast around here.*

"Yes, it is true. I have a mate."

So, he did it anyway; he kept her. "How do you feel being the senior wife?"

"Better than being number four, sir," and with that, she ended the conversation and walked into her office.

Lola was completing the letter when Olu walked in. He looked so good in his suit and tie. His face glistened with sweat because the afternoon in Lagos was hot and humid.

"Hello, darling."

Lola rushed to greet her husband and threw her arms around his neck.

"I missed you," she said, kissing his lips. He embraced her, pulling her body close to his, feeling himself becoming aroused.

"The bandage is coming off tomorrow," he told her as she gently touched his head. Lola was so gorgeous today; her perfume filled his nostrils as he kissed her neck and pushed her away.

"Come on, I have reservations at the Bar Beach Club."

Lola buzzed her boss on the intercom to let him know she was leaving for lunch.

The driver drove them through the heavy afternoon traffic to the club on Victoria Island. A waiter showed the handsome couple to their table. Lola tried to feel as sophisticated as she looked, but inside, she was shaking. She took the menu and ordered the pepper soup and moyin-moyin. Olufemi had the red snapper and rice.

"I hear the fish is very good here," he said, smiling at his wife, trying to make her more comfortable. He knew that she was not used to going to high-class restaurants, preferring to cook at home for him. Before he left for America, he used to urge her to accompany him to cocktail parties and business lunches, but Lola always found an excuse not to go. He tried to bring her into his social world many times and had failed.

There was a mixture of people in the club restaurant, from politicians to expatriates. Olufemi ordered their drinks. When they arrived, he sipped his slowly, amused by Lola's discomfort. A business associate of his came by the table. He was openly admiring Lola. Olufemi introduced the man to his wife, and then excused himself while they discussed some business. Lola looked around the restaurant; she was fascinated. She knew that this was the kind of lifestyle that her husband had before he went to America. She basked in the admiring looks that many of the men were giving her. *This was not a place that married men brought their wives in the afternoon*, she thought. She was proud that Olu brought her. The gentleman left and they were alone again. Olu cleared his throat; his dark eyebrows knitted together as a serious mood took over.

"Lola, I've written a schedule for you and Janice, which I think will work."

Lola was quiet, hanging on every word. He repeated the same information to her that he had shared earlier with Janice.

"Olu, if this is what you want, then I cannot go against it. You are the man of the family, and I agreed to this dual marriage, so I will do my best to make it work."

She lowered her eyes, fingering her napkin. Their food arrived before more could be said. Lola's appetite was gone, but she forced the food anyway.

"I saw Jide today, Lola," Olu said through a mouthful of food. "He and Kemi want us to come over for dinner on Sunday."

Lola knew why they got the invitation, and she shared it with her husband. "They want to discuses their wedding plans. They are planning for next month."

The couple remained quiet as they finished their lunch. There was no further mention of the arrangement or of Janice. Olufemi had written the schedule down and handed a copy to her. She slipped it into her purse.

"When are you moving into the house, Lola?"

"I am moving this weekend."

"Good. If you need any money or anything, just go to the bank."

With that, Lola's mood changed. *Maybe Mama was right*, she thought. *It was time that I took my place as senior wife. I need to provide a good home for my husband.*

"I miss your cooking, Lola," Olu grinned, his eyes twinkling with mischief.

"I'll make something special for you on Monday for dinner. It will be my week, Olu."

"Great, darling. Come on, let's get back to work."

Olu paid the check and left a generous tip. He waved at a few people that he knew as they walked to the car. He took Lola back to her job and walked her to her office. Her boss was still out to lunch, so she closed the door and held her husband in a passionate embrace.

"Oh, Olu," Lola cried, stretching her arms around his neck. She pulled his large, tall frame down to her level, her breast straining against his chest. He put his hands on her buttocks, pulling her into his body as he kissed her with desire. The air-conditioned room became very heated as they drank the nectar from each other's lips. His breathing became heavy as his hands tried to enter her clothing. Lola moaned as he pushed her back to the desk, lifting her off the floor. She wanted him as much as he wanted her. His mouth moved to her neck, then lower to her chest, biting through the fabric. He moaned, frustrated.

"Lola, I want you." He looked into her brown eyes, appealing to her.

"Later, Olu, later," Lola said as she pushed him away and rearranged her clothes. "Later, darling. Saturday, we will be together."

Then with a final kiss goodbye, a frustrated Olu left her office.

"Damn," Lola stomped her foot in anger! She held her stomach, willing the pain of separation to go away. Alhaji Yaro walked in and saw the look of pure desire in Lola's eyes.

"Lola, are you alright?"

The look of love and desire on her face did not escape him. He looked suspiciously at her; unable to mask his own desire and the frustration he felt when he saw her. He walked over to her desk; she got up and moved away from him to the window.

232

He stood behind her, smelling her cologne and touched her shoulder.

"Lola is everything alright?" he said, surprised that she let him get this close. Her tall, handsome boss turned her to face him when she did not answer. Lola was fully aroused. Olu had left her that way. Her full lips were still swollen from his kisses, and her face was flushed. Alhaji could not help but notice how her nipples were hard and showing through her light linen suit. He took out his handkerchief and gently wiped off the lipstick that had smeared around her mouth. She had her eyes closed, behaving as if she were in a trance. He could not resist the urge to take full advantage of the situation, so he embraced her and felt his body come alive. In a few seconds, he went from being her boss to her lover, in his mind. Lola sensed this and snapped back to reality, saying coyly,

"Oh, sir, I am so sad and lonely. My Olu has given me a schedule, and I must follow it. It's going to be hard being away from him."

Alhaji Yaro gazed lovingly at his secretary before speaking, sensing that this was his chance.

"Lola, let me fill in the time that he is away," he said passionately. "You know how I feel about you!"

He reached out to grab her again, but she pulled away, facing him.

"Alhaji, I appreciate your offer, but I love Olu and always will. I am afraid that I cannot give myself to anyone else so long as I am married to him." Alhaji was furious that she turned him down again and said spitefully,

"Well, I hope he has enough left for you, after being with *her* for a week!"

She came back to life, fully regaining her senses after that mean remark and spit

233

out words filled with fire of her own.

"Why! Is it because you don't have anything left after being with your three wives?"

Alhaji's face bore a devious look as the countered with, "Who told you I sleep with all of them?"

With that remark, the confused look on Lola's face was enough for him as he walked past her into his office. She sat at her desk, mystified, thinking, *I wonder what he meant by that?*

*****

I woke up late and had brunch. Breakfast was out of the question, as I still had trouble keeping it down. The day passed by slowly, even though I was busy getting the house ready for us to move into. As Joseph cleared the table, he began to tell me about a friend of his looking for work as a steward.

"Madame, I have a good friend who is looking for work. He wants to be a steward. I know you and Mr. Olu will be moving soon and will need help, especially with the baby coming."

I looked at him and agreed.

"Okay, Joseph, bring your friend around tomorrow. I will be at the new house so I can interview him there. We are moving on Saturday."

Bisi walked into the dining room, asking if I was ready to go. We were going shopping to buy more things for the house. Our things shipped from America fit right in place. The house looked even better than Bisi's. I sensed her envy when she entered and saw what a decorating job I had done.

"You have been busy, Janice. Your taste in decor is exquisite, but then, your apartment in Chicago was nice too."

I took a deep breath and thanked her for the compliment, glad that we had jumped over that hurdle. I did not need any more enemies. Bisi helped me put the last knickknacks in place. Even I knew that I'd outdone myself. It was a comfortable, but elegant house, with four bedrooms and a bath for each one. The house boasted four-room boys' quarters, three-car garage, and a swimming pool. It also had a sunken living room and a stonewall fireplace. Taju had built this house for his first wife, Abbe. Bisi was glad that after I finished decorating, that it bore no resemblance to the one her mate lived in. She cried *ooh* and *ah* at the oriental motif, mixed with traditional decorations. She also fingered the jade carvings and foo lions on my antique teakwood chest. Femi had said, "Spare no expense." He wanted me to be comfortable. He even installed a barbecue grill and satellite dish. It was more of a house that I ever dreamed of having. *If only Melinda could see me now*, I thought as a sad feeling came over me. I missed her so much.

I had been so busy with the house that I had forgotten to call Sharon and find out when the next club meeting would be. It was time that I branched out away from the family and found my own friends. Bisi was all right, but I sensed an unspoken loyalty to Lola rather than to me; however, I appreciated her acceptance and friendliness.

Some men came to install the telephone. I thought, *At last, a link to the outside world!* Having a phone is a real luxury in Nigeria. I looked around the living room. The furniture was now all in place. Joseph's friend came, and I interviewed him with Bisi, and we agreed to hire him. His name was Peter and he was married; his wife said that she

235

would help when the baby came. I sat down on a comfortable chair, patting my stomach and decided to call Sharon now. She told me the meeting was to be Sunday at her house. She gave me directions on how to get to her housing estate. I assured her that I would definitely be there with a large pot of Louisiana gumbo.

That evening when Femi came home from work, we drove to the house to take a few boxes. He was astounded at what I had done to the house. We decided to move in immediately. Since I knew that "the schedule" would start Saturday night, I wanted us to spend our first night together in our home. I was trying to prepare my mind for it. That night we dedicated our new home with a lovely gourmet dinner and toasted our happiness with champagne, and then we made love in our new king-size bed. We did not talk after making love, but slept deeply. When I awoke in the morning, Femi was already gone to work. Later in the day, he called and told me he would be late for dinner. I told him that was okay and went for a swim in the pool. Peter, the new steward, brought me a drink by the pool after my swim, and I lay back on the chaise, wrapped in a towel, enjoying the cool tropical breeze. I thought about Saturday, the beginning of my first week away from Femi, and I decided I needed to talk to my mother. I did not hear the doorbell ring as Peter walked outside and announced that I had a visitor. To my surprise, it was Aduke.

"Girl, I thought that you had already left for the states."

"I stayed over an extra week with my cousin. You are not still mad at me, Janice, are you?" She asked, her lips pouting cutely.

"No, girl, you know I cannot stay mad at you for long. I am all over that. I have a new crisis looming now."

Aduke loved my home; she showered me with complements on my decorating skills. She looked cool and comfortable in her floral sundress and sandals. Her hair was in braids, and she tossed them over her shoulder as she told me her plans.

"I am going back to school in a few weeks, and I will miss you, Janice." She got up and came over to hug me, tears falling on her cheeks.

"Will you be alright here without me?"

I nodded and smiled sadly.

"How are things, Janice? I heard about the arrangement, girl. How are you going to do this?" I looked at her, trying to remain composed, lest the nausea overtake me.

"Aduke, I don't know how I am going to get through next week ... I guess I just have to take it one day at a time."

She left after a tearful good-bye, promising to come back in December when school breaks for the holidays.

*****

"Jide, Jide, be careful with that box," Kemi exclaimed as he almost dropped a box of Lola's fragile things. Lola was moving into the house in Surulere with the help of her friends. It was early Saturday morning, and she wanted everything to be perfect for her first night in their new home.

"What are you going to cook, Lola?" Kemi asked, her arms loaded with linen.

"My husband's favorite meal, amala with egusi soup."

"Umm, you will spoil that man," Kemi said, joking with her friend.

It had been such a long time since Kemi had seen her friend so happy and relaxed. Jide walked in with a box of cooking pots, and Lola directed him to the kitchen. After all the heavy moving was completed, the three friends took a tour of the house, checking to see that everything was where Lola wanted it to be. It was decorated with African motif. Overstuffed couches and chairs, pictures and statues, and lots of tropical flowers and plants were spread out everywhere.

"Comfortable," Kemi remarked, "very comfortable," as she sat down in one of the chairs.

"This house is good, Lola, but you should see the one in Ikeja," Jide said. "It even has a swimming pool!"

"I can't swim, so I don't need one," said Lola.

"Her house is newer and bigger," Kemi went on...

"Oh, stop it, you two. I am not competing with her," Lola said angrily. "I am happy to have Olu and nothing — nothing — is going to change that. Let her have her pool and her fancy house; it's good for her. I won't let negative thoughts spoil my evening."

"Well, I never ..." Kemi said. *"Odabo."* With that, the two friends left in a huff, and Lola rushed to finish dinner. Olu would be here in a few hours, so she decided to bathe and be ready for him.

*****

At home with me, Femi packed a small bag while I sat in the living room, waiting for him to come out. He came slowly, not looking at me, and said,

"I am going, Janice. What will you do all week?"

"Don't worry, Femi," I said, my voice tinged with sarcasm. "I'll keep busy. I am going to Sharon's house tomorrow."

"Good, I know you don't know many people; I'm glad that you have met Sharon. She seems to be a nice lady."

He reached over the back of the chair that I was sitting in and kissed my head. I refused to turn around, choking back the tears. As he walked towards the door, I suddenly jumped up, running to him, crying desperately,

"Femi, please don't go!"

We held each other, my hands holding onto his muscular arms, our lips together.

"Femi," I whispered through the tears into his chest, "don't go."

He sighed, "I must go, Janice. You'll get used to it."

"No! No, I won't! I won't, I know I won't!"

"Janice, please, please, don't make this any harder than it already is."

He pulled away from me and walked out the door of our new home. I stood there ... numb and helpless ... tears falling with the knowledge that Lola would share his bed tonight, Lola would fix his dinner, Lola would touch him, Lola would kiss him. I balled up my fist and pounded the closed door, sliding to the floor, sobbing until I was exhausted. Then I dragged myself into the bedroom to our king-size bed, so large, so lonely ... "Mama, Mama, I need to talk to you." I picked up the phone and dialed her number.

"Hello, Mama, how are you? This is Jan."

"Baby, Janice, baby, how are you? How is Femi?"

"I am fine, Mama. What about Mindy?" I asked. "How is she?"

"She called me last night, dear, and asked if I heard from you. The pictures you sent are beautiful, baby. I've been showing them to everyone."

"Mama, I have something to tell you. I'm pregnant ..."

There was a pause on the line as my mother digested the news that she was to be a grandmother.

"Are you alright, baby? You don't sound too excited."

She could sense something wrong with me even 10,000 miles away.

"I'm okay, Mom, just tired, and I have morning sickness. I want you to come and visit, Mama."

"Okay, baby. I have two weeks vacation coming up over the holiday. I can take it then."

"Please, Mom, can't you come before then?"

"Janice, you sound so stressed out. What's wrong baby? I know you, Janice."

"I'm alright, Mom."

"Where is Femi? Let me talk to him."

"He's on a business trip for a week," I lied. I was unsure how my mother would take it if I told her the truth. She would probably tell me to get on the next plane to New

Orleans.

"Mom, I love you."

"I love you too, Janice," she replied, unconvinced that I was all right.

"Call me often, dear, and I'll tell Melinda to write and give her your new number."

"Okay." I hung up reluctantly and lay in bed, crying, until I could cry no more. Finally I fell asleep, wondering if they were already making love...

Chapter 17

Lola took one last look at the house. She was pleased that everything was perfect. When she heard the doorbell ring, her heart began to beat faster. She excitedly whispered to herself, "It's him!" Then she opened the door and greeted him.

"E'kabo, Olu." Lola knelt before her husband, welcoming him in the traditional African way. *"E'kabo,"* she repeated again happily. "Welcome to our new home."

Olu was taken aback; he smiled and lifted her from the floor.

"E'-ku-se' (Well done), Lola."

Still shaken by Janice's tears, his mood remained reserved even though he appreciated the welcome Lola gave him. Lola sensed this and went out of her way to change it. He was quiet, contemplative, and having doubts. *I hope this will work,* he thought to himself. Then he took Lola's hand and kissed her delicate knuckles and palms. She blushed and said,

"Come and see the house."

He took his bag and carried it into the parlor. His father's house appeared the same except for a few things that he recognized from their old home.

"Looks great, Lola," he complemented her.

"Come upstairs to the bedroom," she said, taking his hand. They walked up the stairs holding hands.

"I have prepared dinner, Olu. Why don't you put your things away and freshen up while I set the table."

She rushed downstairs so she could start serving her husband the dinner she had prepared. She hugged herself happily in the kitchen, then quickly — but momentarily — detoured to the living room to pop in a cassette by Sunny Ade, one of his favorite musicians. After they finished dinner, Olu said with pleasure,

"I am so full, Lola. The food was delicious — your cooking has not changed. It is just like before."

She smiled at her husband and started to clear the table.

"Lola, you don't have a steward?" Olu asked, surprised.

"I thought that Mom and Dad had a man come in and clean for them when they were in Lagos?"

"No, they didn't tell me," she replied.

"Anyway, I would prefer a woman. My mama has a lady who is going to start tomorrow."

"Good. What's her name, Lola?"

"Her name is Grace. She will be living in the quarters with her husband, who will be the driver and gardener."

"Seems like you have taken care of everything. Before I went to the U.S., you were so dependent on me. I guess living alone and having to fend for yourself has changed you."

"Not really. I am still your wife, Olu, and I am ready to serve you," she said sincerely, looking at Olu, her eyes declaring it. They were like an open book to her heart.

She loved this man with a passion that bordered on obsession.

"Olufemi, I love you and always will, even though you hurt me deeply. I know it was no fault of mine, and I will do everything to make you love me as you did before."

Both Olu and Lola took great pains not to mention Janice, even though she weighed heavily on their minds.

"Come, Olu, let us go up and sleep. Maybe tomorrow we can plan some things to do together."

"Yes, Omolola Afolake, my queen," he replied tenderly. His gentle tease sent shivers up and down her spine. She walked ahead of him up the stairs, intentionally swaying her waist, making her round buttocks roll inside her loosely tied wrapper. On the step near the top, Lola deliberately stopped, causing Olu to bump into her. She felt his hardness against her buttocks and without turning around, reached for his hand to put on her breast, making sure she brushed his maleness. Olu then moaned with pleasure as he pushed himself closer to her and began rubbing gently against her body. They moved apart only to enter the bedroom and once inside, he placed his hand on her breast, kneading gently and the other wrapped around her waist. Facing each other, he felt the hardness of her nipple in his hand and this was making him more aroused with passion. All thoughts of Janice and the world outside the house were fading from their consciousness as they slowly undressed each other. Olu lifted her up off the floor and walked over to the bed, gently laying her on the top of the bedspread, while whispering into her ear,

"Mo-fe-besun."

She moaned, "*Olo-lu-femi*, I love you, my dearest. I have missed you so much, darling."

Lola decided that this was the time to express her longing for a baby.

"Olu, I want to have your son ..."

"I know, Lola, my dear. Maybe we will make one tonight."

"Yes, my darling," she cried joyfully. "Yes ..." she sighed as she wrapped her shapely brown legs around him. She moaned with ecstasy as he entered her moist body, raising her hips to meet his, and soon they moved in unison, each not missing the other's beat. Lola wrapped her legs around his neck as he drove deeper into her depths, seeking the end of the tunnel. She responded to his every movement, always ready to please her man. She found herself experiencing the renewed passion of a woman who had gone for too long without a man in her bed. They climaxed together, filling the room with cries of love and newfound passion. Lola lay beside her husband, fondling him, and soon they were making love again and their lovemaking continued through the night.

"Oh my darling, my darling," she whispered, as they immersed themselves in each other's emotions. Olu tried things with Lola that brought out a new side to their lovemaking. It was wonderful and exciting, and Lola could not get enough, especially when he kissed her. Soon they reached passionate heights never before attained in their three years of marriage.

*****

I woke up late Sunday morning. I didn't get much sleep due to the visions I kept having of Lola and Femi making love. The thoughts made me so sick that I stayed in bed.

Peter, my steward, knocked lightly at the door.

"Are you well, Madame?"

"I'm fine, Peter. I'll be down shortly."

Then I got up, showered, dressed, and went down for breakfast. Peter had made me toast and fixed some melon. After eating, I decided not to mope around — I would get busy doing something. Bisi had called and asked me would I like to accompany her to the market. She knew that this week was not going to be easy for me. She also told me that I had gotten a letter from home. I maneuvered the car through the Lagos traffic with ease now. I was beginning to be a real *Lagotian*. I could speak a bit of Yoruba and broken English. I had even learned to bargain with the traders in the market. I reached Bisi's home and Joseph welcomed me and told me Bisi was in the parlor.

"Hi, Bisi," I said cheerfully.

"Welcome, my sister," she greeted me in turn, trying to appear happy. "You look well today. How is your new home?"

"It's wonderful, but lonely."

"I can understand that," she replied.

I wanted to ask Bisi about her mate, Abbe. I had always been afraid to mention her, but since I was in the same situation now as she was, I decided to venture in.

"Bisi, how do you do it?"

"Do what, Janice?" she asked, with obvious interest.

"How do you share Taju with Abbe?"

She got quiet for a moment, deep in thought. When she finally spoke, it was with an air of burden and resignation. She began,

"Let me be honest with you, Janice. I never liked it; in fact, it is the hardest thing for a woman to do."

"Why should it be so hard? It is the African way, isn't it?" I replied with an irresistible tinge of sarcasm. Continuing my desperately needed opportunity to strike back at someone, I kept my barrage going. "And you are African, so why is it so hard? I mean, isn't it a part of your culture?"

"No, Janice," Bisola replied angrily. "It is a part of African *Male* Culture!"

"Then why did you marry Taju, knowing that he had another wife?"

She explained to me that her parents gave her no choice. That Taju's first wife, Abbe, could not have children, so Taju's father searched for another wife for his son.

"It was actually after our marriage that I fell I love with Taju. I have had dealings with Abbe and she with me. We even had to live in the same house, together, for a while," she said in anguish.

"It did not work, Janice ... Oh, the fights we had ..."

She looked away from me and continued her story with sadness and regret. "After the children were born, Abbe tried to take a major role in caring for them, but I did not trust her with my children. Eventually she knew that she had lost and moved away to the village."

I took a few moments to digest this information, and then said, "Bisi, Lola is no Abbe."

247

"Yes, you are right, Janice. Lola is a lot like you."

"That is what I fear, Bisi. I know that I can never compete with her; after all, she is Nigerian, like Femi."

"That's true, Janice, but why compete? Can't you be satisfied just being my brother's wife?"

Instantly and passionately I snapped, "No, I cannot! I can only be satisfied if I am his *only* wife!"

"Then my, dear," she said frankly but sincerely, "you have a real problem, because Lola will never leave Olufemi."

I turned my head away so she could not see my tears. The truth hit hard.

"Bisi, it hurts so badly," I said, almost as if pleading for understanding. My body trembled as I began sobbing. She rushed over to me and held me like a mother holds a child, with the compassion and empathy I needed.

"Janice, you were given such a bad deal. I pray that everything will work it self-out; you just have to give it time. You are overly emotional now because you are pregnant."

"You may be right," I said, blowing my nose on the handkerchief she handed me.

"Come on, Bisi; let's go to the market now. I have a meeting to go to later."

"I don't feel like shopping now, Janice. You go on, and we'll get together another time."

She had also obviously been deeply affected by our exchange.

"Okay, Bisi, thank you for being so understanding."

After I left, Bisola walked over to the bar and poured a glass of bourbon, frowning from the sting of the whiskey as it went down. Then suddenly, the elegant woman threw the glass into the fireplace, shouting with anger, "Damn! Damn, damn!"

Taju was in the village this week on business, and she knew he was with Abbe. "Yes, Janice," she said through her tears. "You just get used to it," she said, with a mocking tone. "What a *bloody lie!*"

*****

I didn't have trouble finding Sharon's house with the directions that she gave me. Once I located her housing estate, it became easy to find the house. After parking my car, I walked to the bungalow lined with palm trees and rang the bell. Her steward answered and showed me to the lush tropical garden filled with women.

"Janice, Janice, welcome," Sharon called as she walked towards me. She was delighted to see me and made a show of it by grabbing my hands and hugging me.

"You look great for a pregnant woman, Janice."

I thanked her as she led me over to the others I was to meet.

By the time Sharon took me around the garden, I had met so many American women that I was overwhelmed. I even met one from Chicago. We sat together and talked about the city and its changes since she had been home three years ago. Her name was Rhonda. Her husband worked for SCOA; she was a teacher at the Lebanese School in Lagos. I also met Linda, who was the second wife to a powerful politician in Lagos. She and I made a date to get together for lunch at her house. Sharon later gave me a tour of her house. It was a traditional colonial bungalow, a legacy left over from the British colonists. I could see that it was a home filled with love. She made every curtain herself and many of the other decorations. She introduced me to her cute and active three-year-old daughter, Ngozi. Looking at her made me anxious to see what Femi and I would produce.

We returned to the garden just as the chairwoman called the meeting to order. The women each had a report to make about some event that occurred recently in their lives. It was more like group therapy than a meeting. After all the speakers were finished, the women paired off into groups. As I mingled from one group to another, I was fascinated to discover that there were so many foreigners married to Nigerians living in Africa. I had the opportunity to speak with several ladies who were living in circumstances similar to my own, some by choice.

Linda told me that lots of women come here and end up going back home because they cannot adjust to the culture. *I can see why*, I thought bitterly.

They decided that the next meeting would be at Linda's house in two weeks, and by then everyone was ready to eat. We all brought a specialty from our hometowns. As promised, I made a big pot of gumbo. All the women raved about it as we ate under the shade of the palm trees. We all shared a common bond — we were women of color, married to Nigerians living in Africa.

After the meeting was over and everyone was leaving, I thanked Sharon again for making it possible for me to be a part of the club. Already I had made a few friends, and we had exchanged telephone numbers. I said good-bye to all the women, promising to come to the next meeting and bring some shrimp jambalaya. They said that they couldn't wait. Then Sharon pulled me aside.

"Janice, where is Femi? I overheard you talking to Linda about him."

I was embarrassed that my secret was out; I did not want everyone to know that my husband was with his other wife, but she could see through me, so I told her the truth.

"He is with Lola this week."

"You mean he really went through with the arrangement?" she asked in surprise.

"Yes, Sharon. I feel so betrayed, but what can I do?"

"Girl, you really need to talk to Linda."

"I am. We're getting together at her house on Wednesday."

"That's good, Janice. Call me when you get home. I don't like the idea of you being at the house all by yourself. Your husband should be ashamed of himself, leaving you all alone in Nigeria," she said with disgust.

"I have my steward, Peter, with me so I'll be all right."

"Well, call me anyway. I worry about you, Janice," Sharon said, hugging me.

The drive home was uneventful for a Sunday evening. As I walked out to the pool, I saw my reflection in the water. The moon shone bright on this lovely tropical night.

"Janice Marie Bordeaux-Adegoke," I said, looking at the reflection in the pool, "What have you got yourself into, girl?"

The call to the Muslim prayer could be heard faintly in the distance, and a dog was barking nearby. Peter came out, bringing me my favorite drink. I sat back, sipping the drink and began wondering what the two of them were doing now. I pondered ... maybe it would be better if Lola and I live together; at least I wouldn't be left all alone, in Africa, so far away from my home ...

*****

Lola was in the kitchen preparing breakfast for Olu when he rushed down and hugged his wife. "Good morning, darling," she cheerfully greeted him, handing a plate of eggs and fish. "Did you sleep well?"

"Yes, I did, my dear," he said, not telling her that he was worried about Janice through much of the night. Quickly diverting the conversation, he asked, "Is Jide picking you up for work today?"

"No, I asked him not to come. You can drop me at the office, if you have time, Olu."

"Okay, Lola, it's on my way anyhow."

Finishing breakfast, they both rushed to the car to enter the hectic rush hour traffic. After promising to meet for lunch, they kissed quickly, and then Lola jumped out of the car and walked to her office. Alhaji Yaro, her boss, had been watching the loving exchange from the window.

"Are you living with him now, Lola? Whatever happened to his American wife?"

"*Sannu* (Hello), sir." Lola spoke with controlled indignation, hoping to embarrass him.

"And to answer your questions, he is with me this week."

252

"So that is how it is," he said, rubbing his chin deviously.

"Well, I do my wives in a similar fashion, except I spend extra time with my favorite one."

"That is not fair, Alhaji. With my husband," she rebutted, "there are no favorites."

"In time, Lola, in time there will be, especially if there are children."

"I plan to have a house full of them, sir," she replied.

Alhaji looked at his beautiful secretary, rubbing his chin, smiling smugly, inquiring, "And what about her? I hear she is pregnant."

"Yes, she is, sir; she is just a few months pregnant," Lola said, beginning to get depressed with this conversation.

"Haba, kai, Lola," he said with the pretense of astonishment. "You mean, the junior wife will give birth before you?" Alhaji Yaro genuinely surprised, but not as alarmed as he wanted to appear, pressed on for the advantage.

"Well, yes sir," she somewhat timidly answered. "Why do you say it like that?"

He raised his eyebrows, knowing that he had touched a sensitive spot. He cleared his throat when he saw the pain in her eyes. "Lola, I didn't mean anything by it."

She turned away from him so he could not see the tears that threatened to overflow.

"I ... I want to have a child, but I have not spent enough time with my husband."

"Nawa, my second wife, gave birth before Fatima, my first wife. Those times were difficult — they fought all the time. When Fatima gave birth to my son Amir, she was happy and everything was all right again. So don't worry, Lola," Alhaji said, trying to console her. "You will give Olu a son, and everything will be fine."

But Lola was not so sure now.

*****

The days went by slowly; I tried to keep busy with this and that. I finally went to the market with Bisola, but even shopping could not take my mind off the situation. I had read three novels and since my morning sickness was over, I was even more restless. Tuesday came and went, and then on Wednesday, I went to Victoria Island to visit Linda.

Linda Hassan was married to a northern politician from Katsina state. He was very wealthy and kept Linda in a style that a queen would envy. I drove up the long driveway of the estate to the doorway. When I rang the bell, I was met by a butler, who showed me to the receiving room down a long hall with marble floors. Linda came down and met me. She saw I was impressed and promised to give me tour of the mansion later.

"Let's go to my apartment."

As we walked through the house, I was fascinated by the opulent display of wealth.

"Oh, Linda, this is a palace!"

She only laughed and continued towards her wing of the mansion.

"My husband is fond of beautiful things, as you can see."

I looked at her and wondered what she meant by that remark. She was an elegant and stunningly beautiful woman. About 30, she was tall and slender like a fashion model,

254

with long black hair and large hazel-green eyes. She was from Sacramento, California, and lived a life comparable to that of a Hollywood movie star. Linda had two children: a seven-year-old son name Rabiu and a four-year-old daughter named Amina. We entered the wing of the house that she lived in. Just before reaching there, we passed a woman, who appeared to be Egyptian or Fulani. The two women were cordial in the hall, but I was surprised when Linda did not introduce us. Overcome by curiosity, I asked,

"Who is she?"

"That is my mate, Yasmin."

My eyes showed a look of pure horror and pity at the casual way she said it.

"You mean, you two live in the same house?"

"Yes," Linda replied. "Come in and sit down so we can talk."

Her rooms were like pictures from a decorating magazine. It was as if you were in Paris instead of Lagos. The decor was exquisite. I looked around the room with awe, realizing that although I was a good decorator, I could have taken lessons from whoever designed these rooms.

"Janice, please have a seat."

I sat gingerly on the brocade love seat and Linda sat across from me on the sofa. She kicked off her shoes and curled her feet under her and began softly.

"We have lived like this for eight years. Our husband is a very rich man. Like I told you, he loves beautiful things. Yasmin is about five years older than I am and has five children. Her youngest is eight. They are all in boarding school in Switzerland. I keep mine at home, though my husband wants me to send them away to school. I cannot

255

bear to be separated from them."

She looked away from me, but not before I saw the tears in her eyes.

"They are my life."

I nodded my head with complete understanding.

"Linda, why do you do it? You obviously could have any man you want, so why do you choose to live in polygamy?"

She answered with no regrets, in a matter-of-fact tone of voice, "I love my husband. I can't bear to live without him. No man can give me what he has given me in more ways than one."

She paused, looking around the room and at the large diamond on her finger. "He is the father of my children. They love him very much."

"I can understand that," I said nodding.

"Janice, I know that you are very much in love with your husband; the pain of separation shows on your face. This is your first week away from him. It will pass, and you will go on as usual."

"What about your family, Linda? Your parents? How did they react to your decision to live this way?"

"Let me tell you, girl, they were not happy about it at all. My parents came here to visit and stayed about three months. They saw everything, even the disagreements. My mate, Yasmin, is from Egypt; she was very friendly and welcomed them as her own parents. I trusted her for a while, until I saw that it was just to impress Ali. At first, we got along. Then right after I had Amir, we started to disagree and little accidents began to occur. Ali became very angry with the both of us and refused to come to either of us. I calmed down and weighed my options. I love him, and I must have him. He will never leave her or let his children go. So I stay. You see, Janice, it is not easy, but it is possible to live with another woman."

"How do you share him, I mean, when do you have sex?" I asked boldly.

"He comes to me every other week," she replied, not meeting my eyes and blushing.

"I see him when he is in town every other week. Last month, I traveled with him to Rome. So I can enjoy time with him alone."

"How do the children feel, I mean, to see dad every other week?"

"Oh, no, Janice, they see their father every day. There is no time frame for him to be with the children. In a way, we are a large family with two mothers," Linda laughed. I was surprised that she appeared to have adjusted so well. I wondered if I could ever accept Lola.

"The feelings you have, Janice, are real. Right now, you need to think about your baby. Do you want to raise him or her by yourself or with its natural father?"

I thought to myself, *I want a traditional American family, one mother and one father, not two mothers.*

"Why did you marry an African, Janice?" Linda asked, confused. "I mean, Africans are like that. It is a part of their *unwritten* culture."

I went on to tell her my story of how I met Femi in America, that he never told me

257

about Lola, and how I found out when I got to Nigeria.

"It was her brother, Segun, who told me about her; I was so distraught, and I didn't know what to do — you see Linda, I had just learned that I was going to have a baby as well."

"So, liar or not," she said with her eyebrow raised, "it's hard to leave them, isn't it?"

"Yes, it is," I said, feeling the trapdoor close on my options.

"So, what will you do Janice? You don't seem ready to accept Lola, and you know for sure he won't leave her."

I was quiet, not ready to make a decision yet.

"It helps to talk to you, Linda, and to know that I am not alone in this."

Linda rose and walked gracefully to the balcony, where her view of the ocean was spectacular. The cool breeze blew the sheer curtains back as she said, "You kind of learn to live with it and create your own happiness."

"I guess you are right, Linda; I guess you are right," was all I could say, as the two of us watched the sun set over the ocean.

Chapter 18

Lola stretched, long and lazily, as Olu turned over towards her in the bed, yawning.

"Oh, darling, don't get up yet; let us sleep in today," she said seductively. "We can stay in bed all morning and make love all day."

"Umm," Olu growled, "the prospect sounds good. Come over here to me, my little tiger."

Lola moved closer to him, snuggling into his chest. His long, strong arms wrapped around her luscious body as he began to nibble on her ear lobe. It sent shivers of joy down her spine. Lola was amazed that her husband now tried many new exciting things on her each time they made love.

Olu took his wife and kissed her long, with great passion. She was not used to this, but enjoyed every minute of it. She decided to try to be more aggressive. Bisola told her that American women are very aggressive in bed, and that was one of the things that Olu liked about Janice. Lola lay on top of her husband, initiating every move. Olu was surprised at this advance and lay back, enjoying her gentle probing. She looked him deep in the eyes and smiled teasingly as she moved her lips slowly down his chest. He sighed and grabbed her firm buttocks into his large hands and began kneading them in a circular motion. Lola, seeing that her husband was ready, moved to get on top of him. Slowly she put him inside, teasing him all the way. He let out a deep breath as she took total control of all moves. Lola was magnificent. All Olu could do was to lay back and savor the moment. He had never seen his wife so involved in pleasing him. At first, her movements were slow and gentle until she became totally aroused. His hands reached to touch her nipples as she reared her head back from the feeling. She never took her eyes off his and she kept moistening her lips with her tongue, as the feeling became more intense. When she felt he was ready, she squeezed her buttocks hard and he exploded with such force that the bed vibrated with the heat of their passion. Lola held tight until he was no more, and then lay silently across his chest, his body still inside her. She kissed his lips sweetly and whispered,

"It is always good like this, Olu. Why can't you stay? I want you to stay with me always," she said with passion.

The request brought him back to reality. Lola had never made love to him like that before. He hated to let her down, but an agreement was an agreement.

"Lola," he said, exasperated, "we have been all through this. I am tired of talking about the same thing every day."

He was perturbed and jumped off the bed and went into the shower. She lay there, feeling abandoned. She had tried all week to convince Olu that she was all the woman he needed, and that he didn't have to go back to Janice. He stood in the shower, frowning, and talking to himself out of frustration, "Why does she have to keep asking me? I have already made my decision. I told her that I love her; why isn't that enough?" Then he had pushed her off with such force and walked into the bathroom to shower.

Lola was devastated. She had tried everything she knew to convince Olu that she was the only woman he needed. She sat on the ruffled bed, her tears adding to the moistness of the pillow. *I will not give up,* she thought to herself. Then she wiped her eyes and went to the bathroom down the hall, not wanting to disturb her husband.

He finished his shower and walked barefoot into the bedroom, wrapped in a towel. His skin glistened with droplets of water that accentuated the solid mass of muscles on his back. He stood before the mirror, noticing that Lola had already made the bed. He knew that she was already downstairs, getting his breakfast for him. Grace, the maid, was in the kitchen with her, helping.

*****

"Eku se', Grace."

"Yes, Madame," she replied to her mistress.

"I don't know what I would do without you, Grace."

"Madame, if you don't mind me saying so, I believe that your husband is wrong."

"Why do you say that, Grace? I know you are a friend of my mother, but I don't think you should say things like that about my husband."

"No, Madame, I believe that he doesn't know his own mind. I think that woman done put a spell on him to make him love her!"

"I don't think so, Grace. He was lonely in America by himself and just wanted someone to love him."

Grace injected, "I talk to your mama, and she say you not happy with him like this. Maybe you talk to my preacher ... maybe he can help you."

"Thank you, Grace," Lola said carefully, knowing full well what she meant. "I'll let you know if I cannot handle things."

"Yes, Madame," the housemaid said, then Lola went into the parlor, closed her eyes, and thought to herself, *If my womanly charms are not enough to hold Olu, then I don't deserve to have him.*

Right after Olu and Lola ate breakfast, she went off to the market. It was Saturday, the day Olufemi would return to his other wife. She needed some time to prepare for that. At the market, she ran into Kemi.

"How are you, my sister? You look down my friend," Kemi remarked, concerned by Lola's mood. "Tell me what is wrong."

Lola began sadly, "Today is Olu's last day with me; he returns to Janice tonight."

"Oh, I see ... Cheer up, Lola. My wedding is in two weeks — you are my matron of honor, and Olu is Jide's best man. So be happy."

"Oh my God," Lola exclaimed. "It falls on the day that he is with her!"

"Kilo-se'; what will you do, Lola?"

Lola thought for a moment and knew that there was no other alternative. "Kemi, Janice has to come to your wedding, too. It is part of the agreement."

"Kilo-se. Are you crazy, Lola? I will not have that woman at my wedding!" Kemi said adamantly.

"Then Olu will never agree to be in the wedding, Kemi," Lola said sadly. "Janice is a part of the family, Kemi, and you should welcome her as I did."

"But, did you really welcome her, Lola," her friend asked suspiciously, "or are you just biding time, hoping that she will go back to America?"

262

"Kemi, why are you so cruel to me? You know that this is not easy. I am not doing anything more than what is expected of me. I'm doing what I must to try to make this work."

"Sure, sure my friend," Kemi said angrily. "Well, I refuse to let her ruin my wedding."

"She won't, Kemi. You'll see. All will go as planned," Lola stated confidently.

*****

Olu sat at the bar and poured himself a glass of orange juice. He had stopped by his sister's house before going home to Janice.

"How did the week with Lola go, Olufemi?" Bisi inquired.

"It went better than I expected."

"Have you spoken to Janice since you left her?" Taju asked, appearing very concerned.

"No, I haven't," Olu, replied calmly. "I am going home this evening."

"You don't seem in a hurry to see her, Brother. Are you beginning to have doubts about this arrangement?"

Bisi's inquiry was laced with spite and sarcasm, stemming from the fact that Taju had just returned from Ekiti. Taju looked at his wife, knowing he was the real target of her subdued anger.

"Don't mind your sister, Olu," Taju said sincerely. "You see, this is how she treats me when I come home. So, don't expect Janice to come running into your arms."

"No, she may throw a pot at your head," Bisola broke in. "I'm so tired of you men treating women as though they have no say about anything."

"Enough of this," Taju said tartly. "We will not continue this conversation any longer."

Seeing the foul mood that his sister and brother-in-law were in, he hurried to finish his drink, knowing that his presence was no longer wanted. He bid Bisola and Taju good-bye and drove home. Femi had a lot on his mind. As he wondered how Janice would treat him, he felt the small scar on his forehead where she had hit him during their fight. And he could still feel the hot kiss and tears of Lola as she begged him not to go. *I guess I will have to see how Janice feels when I get there,* he told himself.

He drove into the driveway and walked to the porch. Putting his key into the lock and opening the door, he called, "Janice, Janice, I'm home." At that, Peter the steward rushed in from the kitchen,

"Welcome, Mr. Femi," he said warmly and took his bag.

"Where is Madame?" he asked Peter.

"Sir, Madame went out this morning with some friends to spend the day. She will be returning in the evening for dinner."

Femi was taken aback, expecting to find his wife at home waiting for him. He began to think he had underestimated her reaction. Disappointed, he went out to his club for a drink.

*****

Sharon and I sat in the shade of a palm tree in her lush tropical garden and sipped our drinks. "Did you enjoy your visit with Linda?" she asked.

"Yes, I did. She seems content to be a second wife. Her husband is very rich, and he gives her everything but himself," I said sadly.

"But is it so bad, Janice? I mean, how do you feel?" Sharon asked, concerned about my change of mood. "It has been a week, and you have had time to adjust to a life without Femi. Think about it, girl. Soon you will have a child to worry about."

"I have thought about it, Sharon, and that is my biggest concern. I mean, what will I tell my child?"

Sharon sipped her drink, shaking her head as I continued. "And what about my mother? She would never agree for me to live this way."

"Listen, Janice, if you are not happy and can find no peace of mind in your marriage, and then maybe you should go home. A lot of women do, you know."

"I would feel like I was such a failure, Sharon, if I give up. My feelings for my husband have changed since I found out that he lied to me. I am so confused; I don't really know what to do."

"Then don't do anything, Janice," Sharon responded lightly. "Just go along for the ride and try to make the best of things until the baby is born. All this confusion is not good for your health, you know."

"I know Sharon, and thank you for caring."

Sharon's husband Uche called to us in the garden, "The mosquitoes are coming out now, dear. You and Janice need to come inside." As we walked back into the house I told Sharon,

"I'd better be going now, Sharon. Thanks for spending the day with me. Femi should be home now, and I need to be there."

"Okay, Janice. I'll see you soon." Sharon walked me to the car and gave me a big hug. "Take care, little sister. I know that you will be fine. Call me tomorrow — maybe we can have lunch."

Sharon stayed and watched me drive away. She seemed to have so much confidence in me that it encouraged me. I thought of how happy and how lucky she was to have her husband Uche and not have to share him.

When I walked into the house, Femi was not there. So I decided to go and take a shower before dinner. Peter was setting the table for me and the roast was warming in the oven, so dinner would be served when I finished. I got out of the shower and stood before the mirror naked, looking at my belly. I ran my fingers over it and felt a fluttering inside like butterfly wings.

"Oh my God!" I said, breaking the silence of the bedroom. I felt it again, when just at that moment, Femi walked into the bedroom. I could see that he had been drinking.

"Janice," he spat, his speech slurring, "Where have you been? Don't you miss me?"

I looked at him. Uncomfortable with my nakedness, I reached for my robe on the bed, attempting to cover myself. He snatched it from me. I saw the pain in his eyes as he said,

"So, now you don't want me to see your body? Who are you hiding from, Janice?"

"Femi, you're drunk. You need to go to bed and sleep it off."

"No, no. I need my wife."

I blushed from head to toe as he walked over to me, his breath smelling strongly of the whiskey that he had consumed. It made my stomach begin to turn. He grabbed my shoulders and tried to hug me, but instead he stumbled into me. I leaned back on the dresser trying not to fall, with the edge pressing into my buttocks.

"Stop it Femi ... not now; you're hurting me!" I screamed, as I pushed him off yelling, "You smell of whisky!"

"Where were you, woman?" he demanded.

"I was at Sharon's house," I answered reluctantly, "as if it matters to you."

"So, you would rather be with her than your husband?"

I smiled a half smile and said sarcastically, "What husband? Don't you mean Lola's man?"

The slap stung even before it hit my face. I reared back; the tears came into my eyes as I looked at my husband with horror. I could see that he was sorry — even in his drunkenness — before the words could be said. I was overcome with pain and rage and immediately ran into the bathroom to put a cold towel on my face. He just stood there, unsteady, staring at his hand in disbelief. I cried and cried until I was weak. My face bore the red mark of his fingers. I knew it would be black-and-blue tomorrow. Femi was so drunk that when I came out of the bathroom, he was lying on the bed, fully dressed, and knocked out cold. I knew he would not remember what he had done, but my face would be clear evidence and a constant reminder to him. I put my robe on, went to the kitchen, and asked Peter to put the food away, and to make up the guestroom. He looked at my face and sadly said,

"Yes, Madame."

My jaw had begun to swell. Femi was drunk, and I knew that he did not drink often. The situation was becoming too much for him as well. I slept fitfully in the guestroom, knowing that he was down the hall. I wanted to forgive him, but he had hurt me so badly and after just coming back from a week with her. I was finally able to get a few hours sleep.

The next morning I was stirred to wakefulness by a cool feeling over my body and the sensation of water dropping on my face. I wiped my face, chasing the wet sensation. As I reached half consciously to pull the sheet over my body — my nightgown must have risen during my turbulent sleep — I looked up to see Femi's naked body leaning over me, staring pitifully. The water had dropped from his still wet hair. At first, I thought the glaring redness in his eyes were left by his drinking; however, a closer examination showed that the remnant of tears were still in his eyes. The towel he must have worn into the room lay on the floor near the bed. His naked body made it very apparent that he desperately desired me. I saw his eyes were focused on the ugly bruise on my cheek.

"I did this to you? How could I be so stupid?" he asked, looking defeated and berated. I pulled away quickly with the agility of a cat as he reached for me and began to speak again,

"Janice, I'm sorry."

Fully awake now and breathing heavily, my nostrils flaring and adrenaline flowing into my limbs, I didn't believe in his sincerity and answered, "Did you come to finish the job?"

"No, Janice, I am truly sorry. I was drunk and angry not to find you at home. The other guys at the club goaded me on. When I told them that you were gone when I returned, they suggested that you were with someone else. I was already hurt that you weren't here. I was drinking, and I remembered how you were about me leaving. When Peter told me what happened last night, I hated myself. I am so ashamed of myself. How could I have done this to you?"

"So you come to me naked, Femi. Haven't you had enough sex with Lola?"

My words stung him, because he was not prepared for me to mention her and the week of lovemaking that he had with her.

"Janice, please don't do this to me; don't make me relive this again. It is not fair to the agreement. We are not to discuss the other woman with each other remember. I love you."

I felt the anger leaving me, replaced with the desire that I had stored away for a week. All I saw before me was the raw sensuality of this man. I had wounded his Neanderthal pride. Rejection, no man can face that. What I felt at that moment was raw primeval femininity as I looked at his nude body. I felt my hands move slowly over the ripples in his chest. I missed it; his strong-arms, his soft and demanding lips. I kissed the hand that had bruised my cheek; he took that as a sign of forgiveness and we began on the long road to re-discovery. At first, his moves were tentative; slowly he kissed me and the pain of the past week slowly melted away and was replaced by the irresistible desire to fill my need. It was almost like the first time we made love. The waiting, the longing to be together as one, was satisfied with the raising up of my hips to meet his. His lips kissed every inch of me, and I answered with the same. My hands rubbed his back, neck, and shoulders and drank the sweet nectar of his lips. *Now* was all that mattered, right now, this room, this bed, this second, this time. We would worry about *yesterday tomorrow*.

*****

Lola awoke, her arms reaching out for Olu. She sighed and held the pillow, vowing not to cry. *No need to cry*, she thought to herself. *Olufemi is with her now and I must go on with my life. But what life? I have no life without him*, she acknowledged with sorrow. I am an African woman, proud and strong; yet I feel that I am nothing without my man. She paced the floor until she was tired, then decided to go and see her friend Kemi after church. She walked into the kitchen, where Grace was preparing a breakfast of yam and eggs.

"Madame, your breakfast," Grace said pleasantly.

"Thank you, Grace."

"Did Madame sleep well?"

"Yes, Grace, but I missed Mr. Olu when I woke."

You poor dear, Grace thought to herself. *It is not right that an oyinbo should come and take our men from our women.*

"Grace," Lola said inquisitively through a mouthful of yam.

"Yes, Madame?"

"How long have you been married?"

"Twenty-five years, Madame; my *pikin* all grown now. Your mama asks me to take good care of you." Lola felt safe and secure knowing that.

"Will you be needing us after church, Madame?"

"No, I will drive the car myself, so you and your husband can have the rest of the day off."

"Thank you, Madame."

Grace and her husband went to church. After the service was over, she spoke to her preacher about Lola and Olufemi's case, despite Lola's discouraging of this. Lola knew that the type of church Grace attended practiced the native medicine. She did not believe in their way since she was raised in the African Methodist Church. Her mother had told her stories about the old religion that only pagans practiced, and it was blasphemy. She always told her daughter to stay away from them.

Titiloye knew what she was doing when she sent Grace to Lola. She knew that Grace would help her daughter find a solution to her problem, and keep her safe from Janice. Grace spoke to her preacher in private. He gave her an envelope and asked her to say the prayers in it every night and in time, the *oyinbo* who is hurting her mistress would leave Nigeria.

Grace then rejoined her husband, satisfied that she had strong medicine to fight the *oyinbo's* power. Her one goal was to see Mistress Lola smile and be happy again. Her husband asked her what the preacher said to her. She shrugged as if it was nothing important. "I needed to get some powerful prayer for the family," was all she would say.

271

Her husband eyed her and warned, "I know you are up to something, woman."

"Oh, shut up, old man. You know nothing," Grace responded angrily.

He was worried because he had seen his wife like this before. "What thing you go do now, woman? Don't do nothing to mess up my job."

"You de craze, old man. I'm just trying to help my mistress."

Grace's husband knew from past experience what could happen when she meddled in other peoples' affairs. He had been fired before because of her, and he needed this job. He liked Miss Lola, and was not ready to return to work on the farm back in the village.

*****

Segun drove the taxi down the road towards the village store. He arrived to find his mother, Titiloye, working behind the counter. A smile lit her face as she saw him.

"E'kabo, Segun. How are you, my son?"

"I am fine, Mother. Have you heard from Lola?"

"Yes, I spoke to her yesterday."

"I heard you sent Grace to work for her. How is she working out?" Segun said as he took a mango and began to peel the skin off the ripe fruit.

His mother responded rather cautiously, "Why do you ask, Segun?"

"I heard some rumors around the village about the last family she worked for."

"What is it you have heard, Son?"

"Well, Mama, it may be nothing ... but that she had to leave because someone got sick in the family. They blamed Grace because she did all the cooking."

"Segun, I have known Grace and her husband for many years. She is a good woman and will protect your sister."

"Protect her from whom, Mama?" Segun asked, wondering what or who Lola needed protection from. When his mother didn't answer, he repeated, "Why does Lola need protection, Mama? She is living away from the American woman."

"We don't know much about the *oyinbo,* and we don't know if she would try to hurt your sister."

"No one could hurt her more than her husband, Olu, did!" he shouted angrily.

"Well, the fact remains, Son that the *oyinbo* is pregnant, and she may want Lola out of Olu's life. Grace will protect her."

"It seems to me, Mama," he argued, seeking to understand the logic, "that Lola would be the one to want to hurt the woman, since the *oyinbo* is pregnant and Lola is not."

"Why do you say that, Son?" Titiloye was dismayed by his words. "Lola wouldn't hurt a fly."

"I am only saying, Mama, Lola has reason to want her out, because the American will have a stronger hold on Olu when the baby is born."

"Why do you say so, Segun?"

"Think about it, Mama. Since Lola is not pregnant, she is no competition for the woman," he said cockily, munching on the mango.

"Just the fact that she had Olu should be enough," his mother replied, still trying to convince him.

"Then if you felt this way, Mama, why send Grace? Look at Taju's first wife, Abbe. Remember how after Bisi had her son, Abbe was sent to the village because she was barren!"

"My son, your sister is not barren. She is just slow in conceiving."

"That may be true; Mama," Segun said thoughtfully, "and it will be even slower now that Olu spends a week away from her with the American woman."

Titiloye was upset by her son's truthful observations.

"God knows, Son, I have prayed and prayed for my children's happiness. A mother never suspects anything like this would befall her children. I pray, and you, Segun, must pray for your sister's happiness."

"I do, Mama. I wish Lola all the happiness she deserves. I would give my life for her, if it would help."

"Thank you, Segun. Again, thank you. I'll not have my daughter banished to the village because of the *oyinbo*. Lola will have a child and soon."

Segun, however, could not help but add, "Not before the American woman, Mama."

Chapter 19

Emmanuel and Abimbola went to their processing plant to see if the manager had any problems. The crops had just been harvested and sent for processing. They met with the manager and took his report. They were preparing for a business trip to China to purchase some products and spare parts. It had been a few weeks since they had seen their children and decided to travel to Lagos and drop in on Olufemi while he was with Lola to see if everything was going well. As they drove into the familiar driveway, Kemi was leaving the house. She greeted them in the traditional way and reminded them her wedding was taking place in two days and that she looked forward to seeing them there. She had just finished ironing out the final details with Lola.

"Welcome, Ma, welcome Sir," she curtsied to them with respect. "I will see you at the wedding then?"

"Yes, dear, we wouldn't miss it. Your family and ours go back a long way."

Lola welcomed her in-laws into the house. *"E'kabo* (Welcome)." She offered them some refreshments.

"Where is Olufemi?" Emmanuel asked.

"He is at the office, sir, but he will be home soon."

"How are you, Lola?"

"I am fine, sir. I was off work today, so I stayed home."

"How are things going between you and our son?"

"It is all right, sir. We are very happy."

Emmanuel sensed something in the way she said it. Abimbola looked at her daughter-in-law, feeling sorry for the situation her son had created. He had really hurt her. It showed in the underlying sadness of her eyes. Grace served refreshments and the three of them caught up on current events. They shared lunch while waiting for Olufemi to return. Lola appeared uneasy in the presence of her in-laws. Olufemi came in a few minutes after lunch was finished.

"E'kabo," Olufemi said, as he prostrated to his parents. "How are you, sir?" he said as he shook his father's hand.

They had been talking about Kemi and Jide's wedding and Olu joined in the conversation. Lola suddenly became the attentive wife as she hung on every word that Olu spoke. This fact did not go unnoticed by Abimbola. She had an uncanny way of reading a person.

"Olu," said his mother, "you say you are the best man in the wedding, but tomorrow you start your week with Janice. How will you handle this situation?"

"I am taking Janice to the wedding."

"Olufemi," his father said, afraid for Janice, "do you think that wise?"

"Don't worry, Emmanuel; she probably will not go," his wife said, reassuring her husband.

"Janice will be there," Olufemi stated with confidence. "All the Adegoke family will be there to support her as well," he said, directing his gaze to Lola, who was looking at the floor.

Satisfied that the matter was settled, Olufemi took a deep breath and squeezed

Lola's hand, asking," What's for dinner dear?"

*****

I was sitting by the pool when I heard the doorbell ring; Peter answered and informed me that I had a visitor. I went to the living room and there stood an older Nigerian woman, holding a large package. She greeted me in Yoruba, and I asked, "May I help you?"

"My name is Grace; I was sent by my mistress, Lola."

"Lola?" I asked, eyeing the woman with suspicion.

"My mistress say I should bring this cloth for you to wear to the wedding tomorrow. Mr. Olu and my mistress are in the wedding."

Peter looked at me and shifted uncomfortable. I looked at him and asked, "Do you know about this, Peter?"

"Yes, Madame," he replied, "but Mr. Femi will be here soon and I trust he'll inform you, Madame."

I slowly walked over to the woman, who stared intently at me, and smiled. "Thank your mistress for me," and carefully I took the package from her.

She looked around the elegant room with awe at the beauty of the decor. She was clearly taken aback by the fact that my house was larger and more elegant than Lola's. Grace was also caught off guard by my reaction to her. She did not think that I would welcome her; my sophistication and beauty also stunned her. She thanked me, and then Peter showed her to the door.

I took the package to the bedroom and laid it on the bed just as Femi came home. I turned to face him with anger instead of welcoming him home after his week away.

"Thanks for telling me about this wedding," I said, pointing at the package.

"I'm sorry, Janice. I was surprised to see Grace in the driveway, and I had wanted to tell you first."

He looked at his wife. She had dark shadows under her eyes and appeared tired. He could see the small bulge in her stomach where his child lay. I was conscious of his look, and I blushed. *He still had a way of getting to me.*

"Janice, Kemi and Jide are my best friends. I am his best man and Lola is the matron of honor. This is my week with you, dear, and remember what we agreed about social occasions."

"Yes, I remember," I said, reluctantly looking at the package on the bed.

"Well, dear," he said trying to sound diplomatic, "this is one of them. Everyone will be there — my whole family.

"No, not everyone," I said. "I refuse to be a part of this, Femi! It's bad enough that this had to happen, but I don't think I want to be surrounded by her friends and family."

"Janice, you must," he insisted. "You agreed."

I sat down on the bed, covering my face with my hands, "No, no, I won't!"

Femi rushed to my side, trying to sooth me. God, how I missed him. I looked into his eyes pleading. "Femi, why?"

He begged," Janice, please, just try; please, do it for me."

I was very apprehensive about this whole affair. The wounds began to reopen and the animosity I felt came flowing back again. I was trying; for two months I tried to adjust to being away from him. I tried to adjust to him being with her, making love to her, returning to me used. Femi was well able to satisfy two women easily, as he possessed a very large sexual appetite, and Lola and I were different. Especially since I was pregnant and my body was constantly changing. I'd always wanted the birth of my first child to be a special occasion, but now, I felt it was soiled and tainted by lies and deceit.

"Look at the outfit, Janice."

He opened the package and took the silver and blue *Ashoke* from the paper. They had even included slippers, a purse, and head tie with it.

"Come on, Janice, try it on."

I sat there dumbfounded, wondering if I should just go and cooperate with him. I had never been to a traditional African wedding before. It would be a new experience to see how Lola and Femi were married.

"Okay, Femi," I said giving in to my better judgment. He gave me the dress, and I tried it on. The colors highlighted my hair and eyes, and when I put on the head tie, he caught his breathe in pure admiration.

"Janice, you look like the majestic Queen Amina."

I shrugged. My image in the mirror was indeed exotic. I was stunning; my tan skin and light-brown hair flowing down my back was a perfect complement to the royal material. Every woman loves beautiful clothes.

"How much does an outfit like this cost?"

"Around $1000," he said lightly.

"Wow, are you kidding, Femi?" I said, fingering the cloth.

"No, *Ashoke* is hand-woven cloth, and it takes a long time to make just one yard of it."

"We will need a gift, won't we, Femi?"

"That has all been taken care of."

I knew Jide and Femi had been friends from childhood. I guess I could stand it if his family would be there too. So I agreed to go.

*****

Lola adjusted Kemi's head tie, as her mother placed the lace veil over her face. The guests had arrived and everyone was in place for the service.

"Where is Olufemi, Lola?"

"He's coming with Janice."

"Oh, Lola, my poor friend. You have to endure so much for love."

"It's alright, Kemi. This is your day. I will be fine. Come, let's go and get you married."

When Janice and Femi entered the open-air hall, everyone's eyes turned to look at the strikingly handsome couple as they made their way down the aisle. Yes, Janice was beautiful. The African outfit suited her well. Jide walked over to them and welcomed the couple. Then he turned to me and said, "You are welcome here, Madame."

"Why, thank you, Jide," I said courteously.

Femi took my hand and led me to my in-laws. I was glad to be surrounded by people I knew. I said hello to everyone and sat down next to Bisi and Taju. Femi went to take his place at the table next to Jide. When the bride came out, Lola accompanied her. Kemi was wearing the same blue and silver *Ashoke* that Femi and I had on. The couple exchanged their vows in the traditional African way. The exchange of dowry was completed as the crowd shouted a cheer of praise when the ceremony was over. A band in the other room began to play the latest Fuji music. The guests were all Nigerian, and I appeared to be the only foreigner there. Most of the guests came over to where I sat with Bisi and admiringly remarked over how well the outfit suited me.

Lola finally made her way over to where I was sitting; our eyes met with a challenge. I said, "Hello, Lola; it was a beautiful wedding."

"Yes, it was," she said casually. "Thank you for coming."

She then went on to speak to the other family members. I was totally taken by surprise when Femi came over to us and said," Come on, my wives. We must join the bride and groom in the first dance."

Lola looked at him with dismay and me with bewilderment as Femi led the two of us, holding our hands, to the dance floor. Kemi gave me a dirty look as she stood dancing next to Lola. I felt the crowd appreciate the show of family unity, yet I was uneasy. I was outnumbered and out danced by Lola. She avoided my eyes, and I hers. When the drummer began to beat a rhythm that only the African can understand, Lola and Femi were caught up with the spirit and began to laugh and dance together, leaving me out. She danced seductively with him, as I stood nearby dancing, feeling abandoned. I kept moving to save myself from the embarrassment of being left alone when I felt a hand on my shoulder, encouraging me to continue dancing. I turned to see Bisi and Taju behind me. Taju began to spray me with money, so I was distracted long enough not to see Lola and Femi getting down to the Fuji music. When I stopped to pick up some of the money that had fallen to the floor, I saw the two of them dancing, moving away from me, swaying to a beat as only they could, caught up in the rhythm of the moment. It was their language, their culture, and their music. I felt totally and miserably left out. Bisi stayed with me and pleaded,

"Janice, don't say anything."

I looked at her and said, "Do you see them? I knew that it would never work."

"Janice, it is only one dance."

"No, Bisi, it is more than that."

I rushed towards the door in a flurry of silver and blue. My mother-in-law saw me leaving through the crowd and rushed over to stop me.

"Janice, where are you going?"

She saw the tears in my eyes as I pointed at the offending scene behind me. "Look at your son; he doesn't even miss me!"

She said with sympathy, "I see everything, Janice. I am sorry. Please don't go; try to understand."

"Understand what?" I screamed. Some people looked at me. "I understand that your son is a liar and a cheat. I am tired of all the bull. Here, give him this!" I pulled off my ring.

Abimbola was mortified at my action and said angrily, "I will not take your ring, Janice. You are behaving very foolishly. Please talk to him."

I began to laugh hysterically, pointing at Lola and Olufemi dancing, "You mean to them! No thank you, I'm not talking to anyone who cannot understand me."

With that, I pulled away and rushed into the street, dragging my wrapper with me.

"Taxi, taxi!" I cried.

"Janice!" She cried, following me outside into the traffic, "Wait! It is not safe for you to go alone."

I didn't care anymore; I just wanted to get away from the sight of Femi and Lola dancing together. Lola was so happy to be dancing with her man. She totally forgot I was there. Olu was also having fun dancing with Kemi and Jide It was just like old times. Suddenly Jide asked his friend, "Where is your other wife?"

Olufemi stopped dancing, looking around, "She is probably in the toilet. She will be okay; my family is here, and they will keep her entertained."

Lola kept quiet and danced closer to Olu, for she had seen Janice run from the hall. So they continued to dance until the wee hours of the morning. Olu was oblivious to my absence.

*****

The doorbell rang at the Njoku home. Sharon was surprised to find me weeping, standing on the porch.

"Janice, come inside. What has happened to you?"

I was tired, and my feet were swollen. Her husband, Uche, came to ask if I was all right.

"She will be," his wife answered and shooed him out of the room. After removing my shoes, I felt better. Sharon brought me a drink, and I began to tell her what happened at the wedding.

"Janice, why didn't you call me? I would have advised you not to go. What you did was very dangerous."

"What do you mean?"

She began dryly. "It is not safe for you to be with Lola when she is with her friends. This is Nigeria, girl, and they practice *juju*. You were probably surrounded by many enemies, Janice!"

"Oh," I said. "I know about all that; after all, I am from New Orleans."

"Yes, girl, but if Lola wants to hurt you, she can, especially in her territory. Your husband should have known better, Janice. You are very new to Africa; it is his responsibility to protect you, especially with you being pregnant. The other woman is probably very jealous. I am just glad that you two don't live together."

"I see what you mean, Sharon. Can I stay here tonight?"

"Why sure, girl. You know you are welcome."

"Thanks. I 'm not ready to go home to Femi, even though it is my week to be with him. He insisted that I come to the wedding, and now look what has happened. I wish I had followed my first instinct not to go. Sharon, I am going back to America. I just can't take anymore."

"Are you sure that is what you want, Janice?"

"Yes, I'm positive. I'm tired of this game. I don't want to be here anymore. I would rather go back home, where at least I am a part of the culture, and I speak the language."

"I wish your husband were more like my Uche. I know being the wife of a polygamist is difficult and definitely not for a weak woman. You are the most courageous woman I know, and I admire you for sticking it out this long. Come on, let me get you something to sleep in and show you to the guestroom."

Sharon led Janice down the hall to the guestroom then left and returned with a nightgown and a robe.

"I hope that you will be comfortable."

"I will be fine, Sharon, and thank you for being so understanding."

We bid each other good night. I lay in bed, wondering if Femi even knew that I left or if he even cared.

*****

Abimbola looked all of her forty-seven years as she went to join her husband; "Emmanuel, Janice has gone."

"Gone?" he asked. *"Kilo se'?"*

"Well, see for yourself."

He turned and saw Lola and his son with the others dancing and spraying each other.

"The two of them act as though Janice were never here."

"All right, my wife; this is our son's problem, not ours."

"Emmanuel, I need to tell them Janice is gone," Abimbola said, concerned.

"No, no, Bimbo; let our son handle his own mess."

"I am tired, my husband; let's go home." Abimbola walked over to Titiloye's table, where she sat talking to Kemi's mother and her son Segun.

"E'kabo, Bimbo; leaving so soon?"

"Yes, I am tired, and we need our rest. We are traveling to China in a few days on business."

"Your son and Lola look fine on the dance floor. What happened to his other wife?" Titiloye asked.

As if she really cared, Abimbola thought with sarcasm.

"She must have left with Taju and Bisi; after all, she is pregnant and probably was tired after the excitement of the wedding," Abimbola lied, wishing it were true.

"When is the baby due, Bimbo?"

"In about four months," she replied.

"Oh, how wonderful," Kemi's mother said, to Titiloye's chagrin. "You must be very proud."

Titiloye squirmed uncomfortably in her chair, thinking that neither of her children had given her that honor yet.

"Yes, that will make three grandchildren," Emmanuel beamed proudly.

"Well, we must be leaving, *odaro* (good-night*)* ladies," he said graciously, and then he and his wife hurried to leave.

"Your daughter is very lucky, Titiloye, to have Olufemi," Kemi's mother remarked.

"Yes, my friend, and Jide is blessed to have your Kemi."

"I agree," and the two women toasted their children's happiness.

Chapter 20

It was five in the morning when all the guests finally left. Olufemi was tired but happy. He never even missed Janice, assuming that she must have gone home with his family. Lola came over and embraced him.

"Ah, ah, Lola," he teased, pulling away. "It is not your week."

"Who will know, my love?" she replied sexily. "She is not even here."

"I had better go and call home to make sure she is all right."

"Don't, darling," Lola begged. "She is probably asleep already. Come home with me and call from there. I need a ride anyway."

The couple bid Jide and Kemi good-bye and many happy returns. They got into his car and Lola reached over to kiss her husband, who returned it greedily.

"Oh, woman, I want you so."

"You mean you miss me already, darling?"

"Yes, I do," Olu said huskily, gazing deeply into her eyes.

They reached the house and walked straight up to the bedroom. He forgot all about the phone call he wanted to make to Janice as Lola undressed him. Her wrapper fell open, revealing her slip, and she lay on the bed.

"Let me call Janice, Lola."

She was pulling him onto her, "But, darling, she is probably sleeping," she purred. "After all, it's five in the morning!"

Olu kissed her neck passionately, and then his mouth slid to her breast, as she struggled to remove the rest of her clothing. Their expensive outfits quickly became a pile of cloth on the floor.

He could hardly contain his desire long enough to enter her. They made love, deep, passionate love, she rising to meet his every thrust, their hot fire burning with love.

They were both totally consumed with each other's wants and needs. Lola moaned with each movement and answered him until their rhythm was in unison. He drove her to the peak of her desire, and then they came together. The two lovers drifted off into a deep and satisfying sleep, wrapped in each other's arms. Olu never gave the phone call to Janice another thought.

*****

I turned over in the unfamiliar bed and lay on my back. The baby was restless this morning. I felt the moves more often now. It was a wonderful feeling to know that life is growing inside of you. I looked around the spacious room and wondered what Femi's reaction would be when he found out I was not at home.

I got up and dressed in the clothes that Sharon had left for me. Wearing my silver slippers, I went out to the kitchen. She was gone to work, but Uche was still at home.

"Hi, Janice. Did you sleep well?" he asked very sincerely.

"Yes, I did. Is Sharon already gone?"

"Yes, she is. Can I drop you at home?" he asked.

"Thank you, Uche; would you?"

I gathered my things, and we drove to my house. Traffic was light, so we got there quickly. I thanked him and entered my home.

"Peter, Peter," I called to the steward.

He came rushing from the quarters. "Yes, Madame?" puzzled to see me coming in the door.

"Is Mr. Femi still in bed?"

He looked at the floor, avoiding my gaze, and softly said, "No, Madame."

"Hum," I said under my breath as I walked into the bedroom, hoping my feelings were wrong. But they were not. Neither of us slept at home last night. I was furious — I cursed, "Damn, damn, that man and that bitch! This is my week."

I calmed myself down, remembering Sharon's warning about the baby and thought about what to do next.

I decided that the time had come for me to give Lola a piece of my mind. I showered, changed my clothes, got into the car, and drove to the house on Bode Thomas Street in Surulere. I walked to the door and rang the bell. The woman who had visited me, Grace, answered and was shocked to see me there. Unshaken by her, I asked, "Is my husband here?"

She took a protective stance and replied, "You are not welcome here, *oyinbo*, so you should leave!"

My resolve was strong. I stared at the rude servant. I balled up my fist, held it to her face and said firmly, "Who are you but a servant; move out of my way."

I pushed her aside and went into the parlor. She ran behind me, but it took me only a few seconds to find the master bedroom. I opened the door and walked inside. There they were naked, and they looked as if they had just finished making love. I stood there, determined, staring at them with disgust. Lola had a smug look on her face, but Femi was horrified. I advanced further into the room shouting, "YOU BASTARD!" I ignored Lola, who was trying to cover herself with the sheet.

"You dirty, low-down bastard!"

He just stood there naked, and then started to walk towards me trying to calm me down.

"Janice, please calm down. I can explain ... think of the baby. You should not be here!"

I drew in my breath. *"NEITHER SHOULD YOU!"* I spat at him. "You are a lying bastard; this is my week. Did you forget?" I hissed through my teeth, seething with rage. It was then that the realization of what they had done dawned on the two of them as I went on still screaming, "You didn't even notice that I left last night. You didn't even know that I did not go home because you never came home, did you?"

Grace was at the door, ready to protect her mistress.

"Madame Lola, are you alright? I tried to stop her!"

I turned to face the older woman, shaking my fist at her, yelling, "I told you to stay out of my way," as I slammed the bedroom door in her face.

"You need to control your help, Lola, you scheming, conniving, underhanded bitch! You probably planned the whole thing, coaxing him into not coming home, even

291

though you knew this was my week!"

Lola jumped off the bed and pulled a wrapper to cover herself as Olufemi grabbed the sheet. We squared off to fight.

"Come on, bitch, you knew that this was my week," I said. "Come on ... you want some of this?"

She then murmured *o-lo-shi* in Yoruba and charged at me. She hit me in my eye and reached for my ponytail. I was ready for her: I kicked her in her groin and gouged at her eyes. Femi grabbed Lola, trying to stop her from hitting me, but she hit him, too. I was five months pregnant, but I was fighting as if my life depended on it. I had the most to lose, but kept on hitting anyone who was near me.

Femi succeeded in separating us as we continued kicking and screaming. Her wrapper came loose, and then her breast broke free, swinging, so she was caught off guard as I hit her hard in her face. Femi saw Lola raise her foot to kick me in my stomach when he grabbed her foot and threw her on the floor. She lay there, stunned, amazed that Femi would do that to her. Then she screamed, "Olu!"

As I jumped on her, holding her arms and hitting her with all my strength, I grabbed a handful of her braids and pulled them when I felt Femi grab me from behind, lifting me off her. I shook free as he went to help her off the floor. I was satisfied that I had inflicted enough damage to her when I felt a sudden twinge, then a sharp pain as I doubled over, holding my stomach. I screamed, "Femi! The baby!" and I blacked out.

When I finally woke up, Sharon was standing over me.

"Sharon, where am I; what happened?"

292

"Shhhhh, Janice. It was touch-and-go for a while. You almost lost the baby."

My body felt sore everywhere as I tried to remember the events that had occurred at Lola's house. Sharon went on to tell me that Femi told her what had happened.

"Janice, are you crazy? Don't you realize that you jeopardized your baby's life? You cannot go around fighting everyone. I should have stayed at my house with you. What possessed you to go there?" she asked me in a scolding tone of voice. I thought for a long moment, my face taking on a serious expression.

"Sharon, maybe I had to see them together like that to get a reality check; it made me realize the hopelessness of the whole situation and has enabled me to take the next step."

She looked at me with sympathy. "And what is that?" she asked, holding my hand.

"To give up and go home ..."

I spent the next two weeks in the hospital, refusing to see Femi. The rest of my family and friends came to see me, and the room was filled with get-well cards and flowers. Linda came to visit. We talked and she reassured me it would work out, but I didn't want to hear anymore. I'd made up my mind and asked everyone to stop trying to change it. I had Sharon book a flight to New Orleans. I decided that it would be best for me to stay with my mother until the baby was born. I called my mother and told her part of the story, leaving out the part about Lola — she was confused and upset that I wanted to have the baby without Femi, but she was happy I was coming home. I refused to see or talk to Femi. I really did not want to see him or Lola again. The vision of them naked in bed together made me angry every time I thought about it.

My father- and mother-in-law returned to Nigeria from China and came to visit me.

"Janice, you cannot leave. What about the baby? I can understand your anger. I tried to stop you from leaving the party, but you ran out."

I walked over to my mother-in-law and embraced her.

"Mother, I love Femi, but I am not cut out to be a second wife. I am hurt and frustrated. I am no match for the culture."

My father-in-law broke in, "What are you saying, Janice? Did we not welcome you into our lives? We never wanted our son to marry outside of his culture, but we accepted you into the family. We understand it is difficult for you, but you cannot take our grandchild out of the country."

Abimbola knew that her husband had gone too far. He had never been a sensitive man when it came to women's issues. She knew that he had just alienated me with his words and rushed over to me, trying to give me comfort.

"Janice, Emmanuel means that it would not be fair of you to deny Olufemi the chance to see his child. If you leave, how will he see the child?"

I sat down in my chair; the baby was kicking and making me uncomfortable. I explained to them that I could not take the pressure that I was living under and that it was affecting the baby. They tried to talk me out of leaving until they realized it was pointless, and then they begged me to at least see their son, telling me that he was miserable. I refused, vowing never to see him again.

"Janice, please, what about the baby — my grandchild?" Abimbola asked again, her eyes filling with tears. I told her I would let them know when the child was born, and that they could travel to America to see the child.

Emmanuel was furious; he could no longer hold back his true feelings. He told me how he had never wanted Femi to marry me from the beginning. I told him that I did not care anymore, that they seemed more concerned about their grandchild than my happiness with their son.

"I'm leaving and that's final."

Abimbola was very hurt at this, but had no alternative but to accept it.

*****

Sharon took me home to pack when I was released from the hospital. I would be staying with her until I left Nigeria. My decision to leave was based on a personal choice. I choose not to share my husband in polygamy. I chose not to live with a man who cannot make up his mind of who and when to love, and that when given the opportunity to have us both chose, he chose to break his own rules. I had my child to consider. It was not healthy for me to be upset all the time. The doctor warned me that the next time, I might not be so lucky and could lose my baby.

I figured that, possibly after the baby was born, I would try to forgive Femi enough to let him see the child, but at this time, I didn't want to see him at all. I finished packing my things to take them to Sharon's. Peter carried my bags out to the car. Bisola drove up as I was walking towards Sharon's car.

"Janice, I am glad you are still here. How are you, dear?"

I hugged my sister-in-law as Sharon looked on. "Bisi, I am going to miss you."

"Janice, my parents informed me that you're leaving. My father is very angry with you. I am so sorry, Janice, that my brother is such a jerk. You are a nice person and deserve better than what you got. I know ... I still have to deal with a similar situation, but I am Nigerian."

"Bisi, I don't understand the culture enough to want to live this way. I am sorry that I hurt your parents."

"Are you sure you won't even say good-bye to Olufemi?"

"Yes, I'm sure," I said firmly.

"He is with who he wants to be with, and I wish them both happiness. They deserve each other."

"Will it help you to know that he is not with Lola?"

I thought for a moment, and told her, "No, Bisi, it won't."

"Janice, don't close the door forever on my brother. I know he loves you."

"Yes, Bisi, but he loves Lola too," I reminded her.

She couldn't think of anything to say that would change my mind. "Janice, he loves you more than he loves Lola, I can assure you of that. He told me so. He just did not want to let Lola go off alone after waiting so long for him to return. Once he found out you were pregnant, he told me you are his life. He was going to leave Lola," she shouted.

"Bisi, your brother is not ready to leave Lola. He has had a taste of both worlds and wants to keep it that way. I cannot live like this, Bisi. I need my husband at home with me at night, not with another woman."

Bisola shook her head in defeat, tears rolling down her face. "I wish I were as strong as you, Janice," she said sobbing. "I accepted my plight."

We hugged and I kissed her good-bye, both of us crying as I got into Sharon's car.

"*Odabo*, my sister," Bisi cried, waving as we drove away.

*****

Lola looked in the mirror at her swollen face. "It hurts," she said to Grace, touching the tender bruises gently.

"That woman is so wicked," Grace volunteered angrily.

Lola had not seen Olu since the fight. After Janice passed out, he had rushed her to the hospital. She was determined not to be the cause of any misfortune that had befallen Janice.

"They cannot blame me if she loses the baby," she said, although secretly, she hoped she would lose it.

Titiloye joined the two women in the room. "Daughter, are you alright?"

"Yes, Mother, I am. Just bruised."

"The *oyinbo* is in the hospital. Abimbola told me, so I rushed back to Lagos. What did you do, Lola?"

"Oh, Mama, I did not hit her. She hit me first!"

"Lola, what has gotten into you?" her mother asked. "You know that Olu should

297

not have been here; it was not your turn."

"I know, Mama, but he came anyway."

"Where is he now, Daughter?"

"I don't know; he won't speak to me, Mama," Lola replied, upset. "All he says is that she is leaving."

"Leaving?" Titiloye cried happily. "But Olu is staying, is he not?" she asked her daughter.

"Yes, Mama," she replied sadly.

"Then you have won, my child."

But Lola did not feel like a victor at all.

*****

Femi sat in his office trying to piece together his life to this point. Janice was really leaving him, going back to America, carrying their child. She wouldn't even speak to him. She had forbidden him to come to see her. They had not really talked for so long; he missed the conversations they use to share. Living apart for two weeks, he began to notice the differences between Janice and Lola, and he remembered why he fell in love with Janice in the first place.

"Janice, oh my Janice," he cried to himself as he sat, holding his head, feeling all the pain of abandonment. Femi turned and looked out the window to the streets of Lagos — people scurrying everywhere, everyone with a destination, and everyone with a goal. Taju buzzed Femi on the intercom,

"Olufemi, I'd like to see you. Can you come into my office please?"

Femi got up and walked into his brother-in-law's office. Taju looked at the younger man. Thin and haggard, he looked as if he had not slept for weeks. His once happy eyes were now red-rimmed and puffy from lack of sleep or from tears.

"How are you, Olufemi?"

"I'm okay," he lied.

"I received a call from Lola. She is worried about you, Olu."

"Ha!" Olufemi laughed. "Worried? Lola?" he asked sarcastically.

"She should not be worried since she's getting what she wanted. Janice is leaving me."

Taju looked with concern at Olu. "I know, but you could have handled this whole affair differently brother-in-law ... I mean, I always kept Abbe in her place. You never did that with Lola or Janice; and also you broke your own agreement, being caught with Lola by Janice. Janice is an *oyinbo*; you needed to give her more attention and more time to adjust to this. You made a grave mistake when you underestimated her feelings."

Olufemi, shook his head in denial and charged at this brother-in-law, "No, you are wrong, Taju. I gave Janice more than Lola. She never would have married me if I had told her the truth about Lola. I love Janice, Taju. I don't want to live without her. I prayed continuously while she was in the hospital. I never left her side. She is carrying our child."

"Then you need to tell her that, brother; you need to make her understand and believe that she is more important to you than your marriage to Lola and polygamy. Lola is a good woman, but she is Nigerian and used to our culture. Janice is American, and though she tried to accept our ways, she really only went through the motions to please you. When I first met her, I knew she was special. I knew she could give a lot of happiness, but that she was fragile and too delicate for our way of life. My brother, you were wrong to deceive her in the first place; you insulted her intelligence."

All Olufemi could do is agree with his brother-in-law, who was so right.

*****

Lola sat in her garden, thinking over what had gone wrong. Grace walked in bringing her a cool papaya drink.

"Mistress Lola, you look sad today. Is there anything I can do for you?"

Lola replied, somewhat distracted, "No, Grace. I am just thinking about the woman."

Grace responded bitterly, "Well, I do not think she is worth the effort, and it is good that she is going away soon, to leave you with your husband."

"Grace, we have been alone, but Olu has changed. He is no longer happy, and he seems to blame me for all of this."

"No, *pikin*, you are not to blame; it is the foreign woman. She gives him ideas, big ideas — one is that the only way he can have her is to let you go, so she got pregnant."

Lola turned toward the old woman whose words spat venom. "No, Grace," Lola said sadly, "you have it all wrong. Janice was pregnant before she even knew about me, so she didn't scheme to get Olu. It is him who was wrong, Grace. He should have been honest with her. No, Grace, I place all the blame on him. So far, I have not become pregnant and I want his child so much, but I guess it's not my time yet. Maybe she was meant to have him."

A man's voice sounded behind hers, "No, my sister, you are meant to be with Olu."

"Segun!!"

Lola jumped up excitedly and ran to greet her big brother.

"Segun, you have come to see me at last. I asked about you from Mama. How are you?"

"I have been working hard," he said, as he sat down in a chair. "So I decided to come to spend a few days with you and Olu. Where is he, Lola?"

"He is at the office."

Segun had heard about the fight from their mother. She was concerned about Lola, so she sent Segun to protect her from Janice. Olu did not seem to be able to do it, and Grace was of little help.

"Grace?"

"Yes, Madame."

"Show Segun to the guestroom so he can freshen up."

Segun eyed the servant woman suspiciously, remembering the gossip he had heard about her in the village. He wondered how much she had to do with Janice returning to America.

"Segun, please hurry and join me for lunch. Grace has prepared *amala* with okra soup and coconut pudding for dessert."

"Umm, sounds delicious. I can taste it now, Sister."

"Good," Lola said happily. "I will see you in a bit."

Lola and Segun finished the last of their desert, and then they went to the parlor to talk.

"Lola, how do you feel after the fight, and now that Janice is leaving?" Segun asked carefully, probing his sister.

"If you want to hear about the fight, yes, she hurt me, but I knew I had it coming. I actually am the cause of it. You see, Brother, it was I who persuaded Olu to break the agreement. He should have gone home to Janice, but I kept him with me. I just didn't expect her to come here and catch us. Segun ..." she said sadly, her voice so low that he had to strain to hear her. "Segun, she almost lost the baby. If she had, I would be blamed for it, and Olu would hate me."

Segun leaned back in his chair, his handsome face grim as he thought about what fate would have befallen his little sister if she had caused the loss of the child. Lola broke into his thoughts.

"Janice is leaving, and yes, she is going back to America."

"So, she is giving up, Lola?" Segun asked his sister, remembering the beautiful woman with light-brown hair.

"I don't think that she is giving up; I think that she is tired of playing a game she has no chance of winning."

*****

Sharon and Janice were just finishing their coffee when the doorbell rang. It was Linda. "Hello, Linda," Sharon and Janice said in unison.

"Hi, ladies," she happily greeted them in return.

"Come and join us for a cup of coffee," Sharon offered.

The three American women sat in the comfortable kitchen and drank their coffee.

"I just came by to see you, Janice, before you leave. When are you going?"

"My plane leaves tomorrow," I answered.

"Are you going to New Orleans or Chicago?" Linda asked.

"I decided to go home to New Orleans, to stay with my mother until the baby is born. I need to get away from this stressful environment."

"Have you seen Femi since you got released from the hospital?"

"No," I said, not meeting her eyes. Sharon kept quiet, listening, not interrupting Linda and her questions. I was wondering where Linda was going with her line of questions, when all of a sudden, she pleaded,

"Janice, don't go like this. Don't let her think that she has won! Don't let him believe that they can use us this way," she pleaded passionately, brushing the tears away from her green eyes. Sharon motioned for Linda to calm down.

"Come on, girls, I cannot begin to understand what the two of you are going through, but I think Janice has been very brave, Linda. She has done what I could not do."

"Yes, you and many other women," Linda replied.

"Linda," I began slowly, "I tried to be what he wanted me to be; I tried to assimilate as much as the culture would allow me. I tried to behave amicably when in public with her, but they made a fool of me and our agreement."

"Oh, boy, do I know about agreements," the elegant woman said as she blew her nose delicately on her handkerchief. Linda stood up and paced the room before she continued speaking, "My husband has found another wife. This one is from India. Her name is Leti, and she is only 19 years old. She is the daughter of one of his business associates. So to seal a deal, he consented to marry her."

Both Sharon and I were shocked at this news.

"Oh, Linda," Sharon started in anguish, "you and Yasmin must share him again?"

I stood up angry, "You see? You see? It may not stop with me; even Femi might do that. I cannot live in constant fear that my husband may marry again and again. I cannot give up all that I am as a woman just to have a husband. Linda, no offense, but you and Yasmin should have joined forces to prevent this from happening!"

"We tried, Janice. We tried for the sake of our children because we love him. I love him," Linda wept. I held her and together we cried for all our loves and weaknesses.

Sharon came over with a box of tissue, and we all blew our noses. I hugged them both.

"I am going to miss the two of you. This may not be good-bye, ladies. I will see you both when you come home to the states to visit."

"Okay, let's make that a date," Linda laughed.

Chapter 21

After Linda left, Sharon and I decided to go to the market so I could buy a few gifts to take home. "Oh, Lagos," I said with passion while at a booth selling carved wooden statues and malachite eggs, "I will miss the friendly people." I smiled at the Yoruba trader, dressed in her colorful red and gold *Ankara* with a small baby tied on her back. I felt my own baby move and knew that soon, that picture would be me.

Sharon saw me daydreaming and took my arm, "Come on, Janice; let me get you out of the sun." We walked over to Tafabalewa Square, where I stood, awed at the humanity surrounding me.

Africa, you have not welcomed me. Mother, you shunned your long-lost child. "You know, Sharon, Femi calls me Oluyinka, Omowale."

"What does that mean, Janice?" she asked curiously.

"It means, 'Thank God, my baby has come home!' That I, Janice Bordeaux Adegoke, descended of the African slaves, have come home to Africa."

"Oh, Janice, that is so beautiful," she said looking intently at me. "Why won't you talk to him?"

"Umm, I may before I leave tomorrow. Come on, let's go to the racecourse." We hailed a taxi to the racecourse and continued the day shopping and sightseeing. Later, we ended up on the beach. "Oh, Nigeria," I called to the ocean, "you are a beautiful country; I will miss you." We went back to her house and Sharon begged me to lie down and rest for a while. I must have drifted off to sleep, and then I heard the door open to my dimly lit room.

I awoke startled. "Who is there?"

"It's me, Janice, Femi ..." My heart started to beat faster as I felt my breath, which caught in my throat. I got ready to speak.

"Please, Janice," he begged, "please don't send me away."

"Alright, Femi, come and sit down; we need to talk."

He looked at me with his wonderfully expressive eyes, all filled with longing and love. I turned on the light and studied his fine features — his full sensuous lips, his long eyelashes, his brown skin, and dark, dreamy eyes. He must have come from the office because he was so impeccably dressed in his suit, but he looked thin. I thought, *this is the man I married.* The gold and diamond band shone brightly on his large, strong hands and his white shirt showed through his jacket sleeves as he sat across from, me wringing his hands.

"Why won't you talk to me," he began softly. "Janice, you are my life ... every day, I was at the hospital at your bedside, praying for you and our child."

"Femi, I don't want to talk to you ... I have nothing to say."

He came over to me and sat down on the bed. Then, suddenly, he got on his knees in front of me and laid his head on my stomach. At that moment, the baby moved. He smiled, tears coming to his eyes. His eyes revealed the love he felt for our child and me; I did not return the look.

I sighed, "Femi ..."

"Janice, no," then he began to cry, "Oh please, please, please, Janice, don't leave me ... I love you so much. I want to try again; please give me another chance."

His hands were on my arms, kneading gently, shaking me, pleading with me. I held his head in my lap as the shudders shook his frame. I rubbed his wavy black hair that smelled of his cologne. *Oh God, how I miss him.* He cried like a baby as I held him and kissed him on his head. But, I knew that I had to be strong. *I cannot go on like this,* I thought.

"It's not good for our child, Femi. I am going home, but I will always be your wife ... I need time to sort things out, Femi. Remember, I never bargained for sharing you with another woman when I came to Nigeria. I'm tired of being taken for granted."

"Oh, Janice," he said passionately, *"Olou-fe-mi-o."*

I pulled his wet face to mine, "Yes, my darling, I know, I know ..."

Femi stayed a few more minutes, and then I told him it was best that he leave. He looked at me with passionate desire and whispered, "If that is what you want, Janice. I will not do anything to hurt you anymore. Where will you go?"

"I am going to my mother in New Orleans until after the baby is born." I looked at him, "Femi, you have Lola. She will take care of you."

My voice shook with emotion because I knew that this was our good-bye, for at least a while.

He stopped at the doorway, not wanting to leave the room.

"Janice!"

He rushed to me and embraced me with all the love and desire he had in his large, strong body. Before I could stop him, his lips covered mine. We kissed passionately. I felt my heart fly from my body and join his once again. He let go and rushed out of the

307

room.

"God, my dear, merciful God," I prayed standing there, my arms crossed over my body, shaking, "Please, give me the strength to keep from following him ..."

When Femi left me, I felt an emptiness that no one should ever have to feel. My body ached with the agony of the loss of my innocence. I felt drained of all emotions.

"God," I asked, "I *am* doing the right thing, aren't I?"

*****

Olu walked into the living room, looking for Lola. He found her in the garden, where she and Segun were sitting, talking.

"*E'kabo*, Olu, (Welcome) my husband." Lola rose from her seat and curtsied for her husband.

"Segun, hello," Olufemi said cordially, as he greeted at his brother-in-law. They were still not on good terms since their fight.

"Hello, I am fine, Brother Olu, but, if I may say so, you do not look too good."

"Well, I don't feel so good either," Olu said, his eyes downcast.

"Where are you coming from, my husband? I called your office and they said that you had gone for the day."

"I was with Janice, Lola. The time for honesty has come. She is leaving tomorrow," he said, his voice breaking. "I tried, but I could not stop her."

Segun saw the pain in Olu's eyes and felt pity for the first time since this all happened.

"I am sorry, Olu," Segun said sincerely.

"Are you really, Segun?" Olufemi asked suspiciously. "How can you be sorry when you are the one that told Janice I was married to Lola?"

"I know I was wrong, Olu. I can see how many people I have hurt by my thoughtlessness. I should have left it up to you to tell her." Then he said, "But you should never have tried to deceive her."

"Stop it, you two; just stop it," Lola broke in. "When is she leaving, Olu; on what flight?"

"Tomorrow on KLM flight 520," her husband said with great effort. The mood in the Adegoke house was sad and held little hope for any change. "Segun, will you excuse us, please." Olufemi led his wife into the parlor.

Lola gathered her strength and said, "Olu, what do you want? Do you want her or me?"

"Lola, how can you ask me a question like that at a time like this? Your competition is leaving and taking my unborn child with her."

The mention of the child stung Lola. "I know, Olu," she said, "but Janice was not happy here."

"Lola, you don't even know her. You never tried to know her. You never reached out the hand of friendship; instead, you schemed to break the agreement."

"It had to have happened anyway, Olu. She is not one of us."

Olu looked at his beautiful African wife, hearing the selfishness in her voice.

"Janice is more African than you think, Lola. You have no excuse. I wrote you and told you about my decision to marry Janice. It is our culture, Lola, for you to accept another woman. Janice tried damn hard to deal with something she knew nothing about. You knew about her long before she knew about you. You could have tried harder to accept her, Lola!" Femi screamed, lashing out at her for she was the only one other than him that was to blame for Janice leaving.

Lola sat down as if she had been slapped. This, she saw, was the man she married, the real Olufemi Adegoke. Only then did she seem to realize that he truly loved this woman. Lola had to wonder what kind of life she and her husband would have after Janice left unless she reconciled with her. She was facing a very difficult dilemma.

I must make an attempt, she thought. *I must try; I must!*

*****

At the airport, Sharon and I said our good-byes and promised to write each other.

"Where will I find another friend like you, Sharon?" I said, hugging her.

"I am as close as the telephone, Janice," she assured me.

We checked my bags and went to the departure lounge for a drink. We were ordering when I saw her, so elegant walking, with an air of sophistication. Her traditional attire was exquisite. She had a matching head tie and high heel shoes. As she walked through the lounge, I watched the men stare at this Nigerian woman. Lola Adegoke made her way over to where Sharon and I sat. She removed her sunglasses and looked directly into my eyes. I was too worn-out to make a public display, but wondered what we possibly could have to say to each other.

"Sharon, let me introduce you to Lola, Femi's other wife ..."

Sharon looked at me, surprised that I could be so calm. She excused herself, but stood nearby. I brushed back a loose strand of hair as I motioned to a vacant chair in the lounge. Lola fidgeted with her sunglasses as if trying to find words to say to me. Finally, she spoke.

"Janice, I'm sorry ..."

The silence was deafening until I asked why, looking her dead in the eyes. She looked away from me, unable to face the truth that she saw in them.

"I am sorry," she began again, "because I did not welcome you very well into the family."

"Did Femi send you here, Lola?"

"No, Janice, he does not even know that I came. Janice, we have never really talked before, and we should have. Maybe if we had, some of the bad feelings we had could have been avoided. I could have helped you understand our culture and made the transition easier for you, but all I cared for," she went on passionately, "was myself and getting revenge for Olu's indiscretions."

I looked at my glass and as the baby began to kick, I squirmed around, to find another sitting position that was comfortable. Lola noticed my discomfort.

"Are you alright?" she inquired, genuinely concerned.

"Yes," I replied, "the baby is active today."

"Oh," she giggled, her straight white teeth showing, the smile reaching her

311

almond-shaped eyes in her lovely face. Then she became serious again.

"Janice, you have it all. You have the baby, and you have the love of our husband. There is no woman alive who would not be jealous of you, especially in our situation. It is not going to be easy for me with you gone," she said directly to me. "Janice, Olu really loves you, even more than me. The child means everything to him. Through him, I've learned to respect you."

I raised my eyebrows, not really sure whether or not to believe her.

"You respect me, Lola; come on," I said unconvinced.

"Yes, Janice, you came here to Nigeria, unaware that I was in the picture, whereas I knew about you. I had ample time to prepare for you, ample time to accept the fact that my husband had decided to have another wife. It is part of our culture. Some of our men have many wives. There can be no excuse on my part."

I looked into her eyes as if seeing her for the first time. She continued with passion,

"We were so different, and yet so alike." She extended her copper-brown hand to touch my tan one and held it.

"Do not go, Janice," she pleaded. "We can work this out. Olu is devastated, and I don't know if I can bring him around alone," she said, pleading to me for help.

I gently patted her hand.

"Yes, you can, Lola; yes, you can. You are a very strong woman — you possess something that I don't. You speak his language in more ways than one. Sure, I can distract him for a while, but in time, he would crave his own kind, his own women. He was faithful to you all those years until he met me. Believe me, Lola, it was not easy for him to cheat on you," I said, remembering how reluctant Femi was to get involved at first.

"So there is nothing that I can say to you, Janice, to make you change your mind about leaving?"

"No, Lola, it's better this way. I was never raised to be a second wife. I don't think that I have what it takes to share a man."

"But what about the baby, Janice?"

I never got a chance to answer because the announcer called the boarding of KLM Flight 520 to Amsterdam over the speaker.

"That's my flight, Lola. I've got to go now."

Sharon walked over to me and gave me a big hug, "See you, girl, and take care now."

"I will, I promise."

As I picked up my handbag, I turned to look at Lola. We stood there face-to-face, woman-to-woman, both faces filled with emotion, both eyes filled with tears.

"Janice!"

"Lola!"

We embraced and said good-bye — only we understood this language.

I whispered to her, "Take care of him. Tell him I forgive him, and you be happy, girl."

I pulled away abruptly and walked towards the plane, leaving her standing there crying and holding her mouth in surprise. I stepped onto the tarmac, looking into the blue sky, the palm trees blowing in the sea breeze, and the sun shining brightly. I touched my stomach ... the baby was restless. *Come on, my child; let's go home.* I boarded the plane for Amsterdam, then onto America ... *Good-bye, Nigeria, odaro...*

Glossary

Adupe'	(ah-du-pay)	Thank you
Amala	(ah-mah-lah)	Fufu made of yam flour
Ankara	(an-cara)	Cotton clothe
Ashoke	(ah-sho-kae)	Hand-woven cloth
Ba-Ba	(baw-baw)	Father
Bawoni	(baw-whoa-ni)	How's life?
Danfo	(dan-foh)	Locally made bus
De Craz	(day-craze)	You're crazy!
E'karo	(eh-karo)	Good morning
E'kasan'	(eh-kas-son)	Good afternoon
E'ku-se'	(eh-coo-Shay)	Well done
E'mi	(eh-me)	Me
E'pele'	(eh-pele)	Sorry
Egbami-o	(ebah-me-o)	Help me!
Eko	(eh-coe)	Another name for Lagos
Eku-jo-meta	(eh-ku-joe-meh-ta)	I do miss you so (for a long time)
Fufu	(fou-fou)	Like thick-mashed potatoes
Haba	(ha-bah)	Why? (Hausa)
Iyale	(e-yah-lai)	Senior wife
Iyawo	(e-yah-woa)	Junior wife
Kai	(ki-e)	Stop it! (Hausa)
Kente clothe	(kint-ay)	Ghanaian handwoven cloth
Kilo-de'	(kilo-day)	What happened?
Kini-nkan	(kining-kan)	Hello, what's happening?
Lafiya	(lah-fe-yah)	I'm fine
Mama	(mah-mah)	Mother
Mo-fe-besun	(mo-fay-bay-sum)	I want to make love to you
Moyin, Moyin	(moy-moy)	Steamed bean cake
Nko	(un-coe)	How about?
Odabo	(oh-dabo)	Good-bye

Odaro	(oh-daro)	Good night
Oju-yin-niyi	(oh-ju-yee-knee)	It's been so long
Olo-lu-fe-mi	(o-lolu-fay-me)	My lover!
Olo-shi	(oh-low-she)	Curse word
Oyinbo	(oh-ing-bow)	Foreigner
Pikin	(pea-king)	Small child
Se'dada-ni	(shay-dada-knee)	Hope you're fine
Sannu	(son-new)	Hello (Hausa)
Spray		To give praise with money
Sunny Ade		A popular Nigerian musician
Wambi	(wham-bee)	Come here
Waayo	(why-oh)	Help? (Hausa)
JuJu	(jew-jew)	Black magic

PLACES

Ondo state	(on-dough)	A state in southern Nigeria
Katsina state	(cat-see-na)	A state in northern Nigeria
Kano state	(can-oh)	A state in northern Nigeria
Ilesha	(eh-ley-sha)	A city in Ondo state of Nigeria
Ekiti	(e-key-ti)	A city in Ondo state of Nigeria
Lagos	(lay-goes)	The former capital of Nigeria

www.ingramcontent.com/pod-product-compliance
Lightning Source LLC
Chambersburg PA
CBHW070547130626
46556CB00001B/49